BEAST

Twisted Fairytale

PEPPER PACE

BEAST

BEAST

PEPPER PACE
A novel

ISBN-13:978-1480022119

ISBN-10:148002211X

CHAPTER 1

Ashleigh prayed that her face stayed as impassive as Miss Celie's face in The Color Purple after Mister smacked her for daydreaming about her sister in Africa. She felt like Celie...like if she had a straight razor in her hand right now DeAngelo would be one second from lying on the floor dead. Not that DeAngelo had ever put his hands on her in that way. But what he'd just done was oh so much worse. Her heart couldn't even beat right; it felt like a huge invisible fist had a grip of her. Maybe she would just die and that would solve everything.

"I'm so sorry, baby. I know that you hate me right now." He watched her, probably waiting for her to default to the Ashleigh that he knew so well; the one that would melt when he flashed that perfect smile, or who clung to his arm in pride because he was so fine that sometimes just looking at him caused her entire body to ache —
because he was *her* man, Ashleigh Marie Dalton; the girl that people described as pretty-- if only she would lose those extra few pounds.

But right now she couldn't even look at him, because when she did all she could think is how stupid she was. *My boyfriend of three years has just gotten married...to someone other than me. Oh my god, this cannot be happening.*

But in truth, she knew that she had never been his girlfriend. They called people like her fluffy girls. And the only thing a fluffy girl did was pay some good-looking guy for his time. Her face burned even more as the depths of her ignorance finally sunk in. She had pretended very well, well enough to convince herself that he was with her because he truly loved her and that the other women meant nothing because no matter how pretty, or sexy, or thin, it was she that he always returned to.

"I don't even...feel anything," she lied. "I'm just tired. Just...go home to your wife," *so that I can have my mental breakdown in private.*

"Ashleigh, I love you, I still do-"

Her stomach caved at those words and anger finally sprang to the surface as she felt an almost uncontrollable urge to scratch his eyes out. "You love me? Yeah I know what you loved; and it was my money. But guess what, I'm not your fluffy girl anymore! Just slink your ass back into that hole you crawled out of!"

He shook his head in denial. "That's not what you are to me-"

"Yeah? We've been together three years! You met Shaunda six months ago!" Despite her resolve her eyes welled with tears. "Why...why did you marry *her*?"

DeAngelo paused and his expression was so pained that she wondered if maybe for the first time ever, she was going to get a true answer out of this cheating man.

"I love you Ashleigh, but Shaunda...she loves me enough to keep me." Ashleigh frowned in confusion. How could he say that? How much money had she poured into their relationship? How many times had she paid for outings, trips, dinner, gifts and trinkets for him? Hell, she had even put the down payment on his leased car, and he was actually driving one that was better than hers!

He looked away. "It's like what you just said; we've been together three years…and I've been with her six months. You knew about it and you…turned a blind eye. Shaunda, didn't. She fought for me, for us."

"Yeah…just get out." She whispered in defeat.

He looked embarrassed but he at least turned to leave. "It wasn't ever about the money," he added without looking at her.

"And yet I don't see you offering to give any of it back." DeAngelo shut the door after himself, without another word.

~***~

How stupid was it for your body to burn for a man that had hurt you so badly that you spent the first three days of his treachery in tears and then the next three missing the feel of his toned dark body against yours? Ashleigh had always liked tall, dark men. Maybe because she was short, fat and light. DeAngelo was the type of handsome that made you look twice. He was slightly over six feet tall with a lean athletic build and hair cut so short that it was barely there. By contrast, his silky black goatee drew your eye to his lush full lips. But it was the smile that did it. When his dimples appeared her body melted.

Ashleigh actually felt pretty when she was with him. Big girls could be sexy and wear lingerie to please their men, and dress fashionably and get their hair and nails done so that even though they were closer to the word fat than to plump or athletically built, they could still be sexy. She might be fat, but with DeAngelo she knew she was no slouch in the look departments.

Ashleigh had a honey complexion that matched her short and coiffed honey blond hair (compliments of Nadia's Hair and Nail salon and Dark and Lovely dye number 378). She even had light brown eyes with gold flecks in them compliments of Bausch & Lomb. Unfortunately she also had over one hundred extra pounds on her 5'6" frame. Her clothing sizes were no longer in the teens but now read size 20 or 22...

'You would be so pretty if you dropped some weight,' everyone always said—everyone except DeAngelo. That was one of the things that haunted her at 2 am in the morning. It wasn't the number of times the newlyweds had sex. She was more affected by the number of times he might have flashed *her* that smile that said, *everything is going to be alright, baby.* Or how many times he caressed his new wife's side when he thought she was sleeping. Those are the things that made tears spring to her eyes when she was at work writing a report or in the middle of laughing with her two best friends.

And then one day Kendra said, "I don't know why you wasted so much time with that loser in the first place." Lance had flashed Kendra a warning look which she chose to completely ignore. Her friend's well intentioned words left her feeling as if someone had socked her dead in her stomach.

"I know you loved him. But you could do so much better, Ash. I have been waiting for you to get rid of him. Girl, I can hook you up with someone worthy of you." Kendra gave Lance a crooked grin. "And that goes for you, too. You both need to drop these men that step out on you and treat you like shit!"

Ashleigh's back bristled. "DeAngelo stepped out on me, but he never treated me like anything but a queen." She didn't say those words with any sense of pride, just a need to clarify. She didn't feel lucky that she had considered him a good man just because he put her on a pedestal when he wasn't slutting around.

Lance could say nothing. His boyfriends cheated on him and though it may have been his *desire* to be treated like a queen, the reality is that the men he chose were usually the Divas.

"We're going to go out Friday and I'm going to hook you two up with a couple of brothers that are rated USDA Prime!" Lance looked interested because even though he was a scrawny white guy, he had a preference for big black guys. Ashleigh just tried not to slouch in on herself. Dating was the last thing she had on her mind. It had only been a month…wow, maybe it was time.

They made plans to meet after work at a favorite martini bar. Ashleigh didn't much care for hard liquor but she didn't mind the cosmopolitans or apple martinis. Kendra and Lance were a bit more daring and had specific ways that they had to have their martinis; vodka not gin, stirred, shaken onion vs. olive and on and on and on…

She loved her two friends even if she was sometimes a bit jealous of Kendra for being so perfect. Kendra was the type of person that you wished you could hate but she was an honestly good person that cared about her friends sometimes more than she cared about herself. Each of them were in their thirties, made good money, drove nice cars and worked for the same company as analysts. They had been the best of friends since applying for the same job over seven years ago. For whatever reason they kept in contact and when one heard about a great position they would tell the others until they were each working 'gravy' jobs with each other.

They went out for lunch at least once a week; one person always picked the location and the bill for the group. When it was Kendra's turn to treat you knew to expect lunch at some trendy place where executives were often seen on business lunches. Lance always found someplace exotic like a Mediterranean, Korean or Thai restaurant, and for the last few years Ashleigh took them to pubs and sports bars where the food was plentiful…and cheap. Of course they made fun of her because they knew her money was tied up in her relationship with DeAngelo. But they always kept their comments good-natured because as much as they disliked DeAngelo they knew that Ashleigh was truly happy with him.

Kendra had gotten married two years ago but it was to be expected. She was simply too gorgeous and had her pick of men. Because of this and her great personality, Kendra had a network of friends and acquaintances though none meant more to her than Lance and Ashleigh. Therefore, when Kendra offered to 'hook you up' you knew you weren't getting chopped liver.

Ashleigh hadn't been on a date in years…and maybe 50 pounds ago! At least she would have three days to get her look together. After work she went home with her take-out order from PF Chang's and an individual sized cheesecake from Montfort Heights Bakery. Everyone loved their donuts but she went for the cheesecake.

She kicked off her pumps at the door and put everything on her dining room table. She was proud of her two bedroom condo. She had always hoped that it would be her and DeAngelo's…she grimaced and was preparing to strip out of her suit and put on a t-shirt and sweatpants when the phone rang. For a brief second her heart leaped in anticipation--and then dread. He had called her once, but it was to return some clothes of hers that she'd left at his apartment.

She was fully aware that he he lingered, hoping that she would invite him in; into her home, into her bed, back into her life, but he'd honestly hurt her too bad for her to forgive him. And she'd taken her belongings and closed the door after a brief thank you. She had been strong that day. She didn't know if she would be as strong the next time.

"Hello?" She said breathlessly as she'd had to hurry into her pants and then to the phone.

"Ash? Are you exercising?"

It was Lance. "Hell no!"

"Well why are you breathing so hard?"

"Um…so I can live." He laughed. "Pretty In Pink is coming on at eight-"

She squealed. "Pretty In Pink!"

"Yep, I'm coming over with a pizza-"

"I already got PF Chang's! But not enough for you," she added. "So you better eat before you come over…and maybe pick up some ice cream to go with this cheesecake."

"Mmm. Cheesecake. I'll be there in an hour."

"Is Kendra coming?"

"You know she's not going to watch a John Hughes movie. I don't think she watched a John Hughes movie when she was sixteen!"

True. And it was cool with just her and Lance because he was like her little sister... well if she had a white sister with a penis.

Everyone always made fun of her for being a grown woman that would drop everything to watch Sixteen Candles or The Breakfast Club and her personal favorite Some Kind of Wonderful. She always wished that she was the star of a John Hughes movie because then she would always have a happy ending. There would be some achingly handsome guy holding a boom box above his head right outside her window, or the school jock would dump the cheerleader girlfriend for her. But in reality the cheerleader always got the man.

Several hours later, the two friends were listening to the music playing at the ending credits and contemplating the nature of life through the eyes of a sixteen year old. Lance always took the most comfortable seat; the chaise while she flopped down on the couch. He had brought pizza anyways and her stomach was making strange sounds since she couldn't help herself when she grabbed a few slices even though she was bursting from the PF Chang's.

"God," he groaned. "I can't believe she didn't choose Ducky."

"I know. Why couldn't she see that they were so perfect together?! Blaine was such an asshole."

"Yeah, he threw her to the wolves and then had the nerves to show up at the prom with that bad wig trying to look pitiful."

Ashleigh chuckled. "Yeah…that wasn't a convincing wig. And Andie just caves in and takes him back." She got up and carried their trash into the kitchen. Lance helped her.

"Well you know why that is." He said.

"Why? He had a big penis?"

Lance paused. "No. Blaine doesn't have the big penis, Ducky does. But Andie will never know that because she was too wrapped up in the fact that Blaine has money and popularity, something she secretly wants but can never have."

"Shallow bitch."

"Aren't we all? I read a list stating the top five reasons why a person that has never married is single. Number five said it's because you're just not good enough."

"Ouch. That's harsh."

"But true." He leaned against the counter still holding an empty diet coke can. "Think about this, we're single because we aren't looking for partners that are our equals. We're looking for somebody *better* than us; more money, better looking, yada yada yada."

She nodded conceding to that one. "And number four?"

He scratched his neatly trimmed chin hair. "I think number four is you're selfish, number three is you're a slut, number two—"

Ashleigh held up her hand to halt him. "A slut? How does that factor in to not being married?"

"Because you are giving the goodies away instead of holding it for ransom." They both had to burst out laughing at that one.

"Okay and what is number two?"

"Two is you're shallow; which we both determined was accurate and the number one reason for not being married...is because you're a bitch."

"Really?" Ashleigh crinkled her nose. "I don't know if that's true."

"Oh...Ashleigh," he nodded his head with a grin. "You've been a bitch before. We all have. Remember when the heating and cooling guy couldn't get the thermostat to work in the office and-"

She blushed. "Yeah yeah, I remember!" She sighed. "You know what? I think that list is actually pretty true." She looked at him and her eyes shined a little too brightly with something that looked like unshed tears. She tried to offer a smile, albeit a shaky one. "But I still would have chosen Ducky over Blaine!"

Lance smiled softly and hugged her.

~***~

Ashleigh wore a cream pantsuit that cost almost as much as her car payment, but she looked great in it. Big women that wanted to also be stylish knew the secrets for hiding the added pounds. It was all in the cut of the jacket that cinched her waist, hid her belly and showcased her cleavage where her low-cut blouse showcased her 'crowning glory.' She wore heels that matched the earth tones of the blouse and big loopy earrings.

As she hurried into the restaurant, already a few minutes late, she knew she looked good but felt far from confident. Pretty face/fat body. It was just a matter of preference whether someone would like her or not. It made her feel ill that she found herself praying for some complete stranger that she'd never before met to like her.

Lance spotted her first as she entered the dimly lit club and he waved her over to where they were waiting just inside the main entrance. Her eyes didn't know what to take in first. Certainly she'd seen her friends dressed for a night out on the town, but Lance and Kendra both looked really hot and sophisticated, not to mention Kendra's husband Jeffery. He was an athlete turned business owner. He had several properties that he rented out for commercial use. He and Kendra both had deep mocha complexions with exotic looks like they'd come over from the Caribbean. Lance was extremely good-looking and never had trouble getting men...just keeping them.

But her eyes were riveted to the two men that watched her approach. Her eyes met those of a man so gorgeous that he almost made DeAngelo look like dog food. Kendra knew just what she liked. He had to have been over six feet with muscles that were evident even beneath his expensive yet casual jacket. He was dark; so dark that she could only think of midnight and when he smiled he had a dimple just like...

She smiled back. Her friends greeted her enthusiastically and she apologized for being late all while never removing her eyes from the sight of Mr. Wonderful.

Kendra smiled broadly. "Let me do the introductions again." She gripped Ashleigh's arm in a strangely possessive manner.

"Ashleigh, meet Ivan." But Kendra was not looking at Mr. Wonderful. Ashleigh's eyes landed on the person that Kendra was gesturing to. Well…he wasn't tall. This new man; Mr. Not-so-wonderful was…different.

Ashleigh plastered on a smile and held out her hand. Ivan was probably a bit over 5'10" and was almost as light-skinned as she was. He wasn't bad looking with a neatly shaved face and reddish brown hair that had a nice curly texture — either due to mother nature or a visit to a hair salon. Ivan had light brown eyes and a few freckles on his face; a black man with freckles and big Bugs Bunny Teeth.

"Nice to meet you, Ivan." He took her hand and shook it while giving her a pleasant smile.

"I heard a lot about you, Ashleigh. I'm happy to finally meet you," he said.

All Ashleigh could think is that they looked like the number 10 standing together. He was thin. Could he even do the things in bed that — ?

She put that thought out of her mind. "It's nice to meet you too."

"Ivan is a doctor of pediatrics at General Hospital," Kendra said while giving her a meaningful look. Kendra smiled awkwardly before glancing at the other man and then introduced him quickly as a new Rookie recruit for the Bengals.

Ashleigh almost collapsed. Lance gave her a discreetly apologetic look before Mr. Wonderful placed his hand on the small of Lance's back and led him into the club. She almost groaned in disappointment before giving Ivan another smile.

Later, in the restroom, Kendra began talking even though Ashleigh hadn't said a negative word. "I chose Ivan for you because you both have so much in common. You both like sappy romance movies and he likes his women...large."

Ashleigh hid her discomfort.

"And, girl, he's a DOCTOR. He's never been married and he's a really good guy."

Ashleigh bit her lip. "But...don't you have another friend that looks like Rick? I mean...I think he's really attractive."

Kendra hesitated. "But Rick's gay."

"I get that. But I'm talking about another friend."

Ashleigh thought she caught the shadow of a grimace on her friend's pretty face. "Ashleigh...when I hook you up with a friend..." Kendra seemed to search her mind, "I have to make sure that the attraction is a two-way street-"

"Oh." Ashleigh said in realization and her cheeks flamed.

"No no no! You know I think you're beautiful. I mean, you have a gorgeous face and Ivan is really taken with you. But, you know...I have to make sure the guy is into big girls because I would never want to put you out there like that."

Ashleigh smiled and nodded. "It's fine."

Kendra closed her eyes and when she opened them she placed her hand on her friend's shoulders. "Ashleigh, I'm sorry. I didn't mean that to sound the way it did. Match making isn't easy. It is a two-way street. But if you're not attracted to Ivan…"

"Ivan is perfectly okay. It's just—"

"You're more attracted to Rick."

"Guys like Rick." Ashleigh swiped at the wetness that had crept beneath her eyes as she chuckled to herself. "I know that guys that look like Rick want girls that look like you—and bitch, if you say that I have a pretty face one more time I actually will cut you!" Kendra looked down in embarrassment and then they both laughed.

"Ivan is perfectly alright. I enjoy talking to him-"

Kendra was already shaking her head. "But he's not right for you. Ashleigh, my friend, you are through with settling. Do you hear me?"

Ashleigh nodded. *I am not good enough. I am a selfish, shallow, slut, bitch.*

CHAPTER 2

In the sub-basement of the Federal Building where Ashleigh, Kendra and Lance worked, is a tunnel system used to transport prisoners from the Federal Courthouse that sat directly across the street, to the Justice Center. She wasn't exactly sure why the sub-basement went beneath the street and why the transportation of prisoners had anything to do with their building but for these questions there were no answers. All Ashleigh knew is that the gym was also located in the sub-basement.

Federal employees got to use it for a small fee. It wasn't the money, or even how good the facility was—which actually was just so-so compared to the expensive gyms. But it was all about the quiet. She'd been to big gyms before where really toned people worked out damn near every day. They would pound away on the treadmill at a sprint for nearly an hour and then look at you with a friendly smile and say shit like, 'Hi, how's it going?' And you just wanted to say, 'bitch, shut up,' while you're panting after ten minutes of brisk walking.

It just wasn't for her. Good intentions failed at the sight of so much perfection. She needed a small place where it didn't seem that people were there for the purpose of making a hook-up. She could deal with a handful of perfect people, but not fifty of them.

After returning home from her disastrous blind date with the very sweet but boring Ivan, Ashleigh had done a very critical self-assessment of herself. Ivan found her attractive because he liked big women, DeAngelo had been into her because he wanted her money but Ashleigh wanted someone to want her for just being Ashleigh Marie Dalton; whether she was big or small. But the key fact is that she wanted someone that she was physically attracted to. Oh she could sit there and think about how she had no room to be judgmental, but if toned, in-shape guys wanted the toned in-shape women, then she'd just have to be that person…or she would have to settle for being with someone that she didn't find physically attractive. And that was all there was to it.

So she tossed out the cakes and chips knowing that keeping them in the house would be too much temptation. She bought boneless, skinless chicken breast patties to put into the boiler, turkey lunchmeat and salad packs. And when Monday rolled by she bought her gym membership. Ashleigh had never even been to the sub-basement and was a bit intimidated by the underground facility as she was given a tour.

"Now, I just want you to understand that when the red light flashes it means that the floor is going on lockdown while they transport prisoners. You'll have five minutes to move around before the doors and elevators lock."

"When you say lock…you mean locked in the basement with prisoners?"

"Well the prisoners never come into this section and you wouldn't have access to their section. It's just a precaution to make sure that you are completely secure in the area that you're located in."

"But you said the elevators lock…"

"Oh that. You'll have time to move from floor to floor before that happens, so don't worry."

Ashleigh was worried. She had a slight case of claustrophobia and the idea of being in a basement was disturbing enough, but the high ceilings and openness helped. Yet the whole trapped-in-the-elevator thing was a little different.

"Has anybody ever been trapped in the elevator before?"

"Oh yeah, but it's no big deal. Lockdown never lasts longer than ten minutes. And there is a call button inside of each elevator and stairwell."

"Oh! Can you show me the stairwell?" That would be much better for her. It would only be two flights of stairs; the basement, then the sub-basement, much better than to risk being trapped in an elevator. The woman led Ashleigh from one corridor to another, explaining how to follow the ever changing diagrams until they finally reached the stairwell. She gave her a dubious look.

"Oh don't worry, you'll find your way around here in no time."

"Now, I'm not going to accidentally walk into a restricted area, will I?"

"Oh no. You'd have to have card access for that."

Ashleigh sighed in relief. Tomorrow she would come to the gym before work and she'd do it each day until coming to the gym became like any other routine. For the first time in a month, Ashleigh felt like she was actually doing something to put back the shattered pieces of her life.

~***~

Christopher Henry Jameson stared at the monitor screens. Most didn't actually stare at them the way he did. Most talked on their cell phones to their girl friends or they played on their handheld gaming systems. Some even snuck magazines and books in even though to get caught would be a boot to the rear end.

But Christopher actually enjoyed watching the monitors. The people entering and exiting the buildings had lives that he caught a glimpse of and in his mind he would recreate them into an image that he would find more acceptable than the ones they probably led.

"Beast. Beast?"

He finally tore his eyes from the screen. "What?" He saw that it was his Commander and he straightened and cleared his throat. His voice sounded even more rough than usual. He didn't spend much time talking and wasn't much of a people person. It tended to cause many to take it that he was a bad ass when actually he was just a loner. With his looks it had been a choice not all his own, but being alone was something he'd gotten used to regardless of whether or not he would have wanted it differently.

"Go take a break. I'll take over."

Bruce was his commander, but also someone that he thought of as a friend. Though to Christopher, a friend was just someone who didn't take pot shots at you. Bruce treated him fairly and therefore Christopher thought of him as a friend.

He got up out of the rolling secretary chair and headed for the commissary where he went straight to the refrigerator for his bag lunch. It wasn't quite the bag lunch that would come to mind for the average person. His was an actual grocery bag half filled with food. Of course Christopher Henry Jameson—also known as Beast wasn't the average man.

He stood 6'5" and weighed three hundred and two pounds. He didn't like the extra three pounds. He rather liked being in the two hundred weight range even if it was by just one or two pounds. Regardless there wasn't an ounce of fat on his perfect body. Beast was muscles on top of muscles, yet not hulking like some of the others that worked in the Marine Corps division assigned to The Department of Home Land Security or better known as DHS. Too big made you slow. He'd seen guys bigger than him hospitalized during the CRUCIBLE training.

Crucible had been a breeze for him. He'd long ago pushed his body to its limits. He never needed much sleep, and he had learned a long time ago to keep his mouth shut and to see without being seen. Even now, as he watched the monitors for the Federal Building and the Federal Courthouse, he saw the same people arrive each morning; how they dressed, who they hung around with and not one of them had ever seen him.

He took his bagged lunch over to the crowded table and was greeted by several others that worked with him in the sub basement. Once upon a time when he was a kid no one would have welcomed him to their lunch table. But it didn't matter to these guys if he was ugly. He had proven himself to them and they judged him rightfully on that and not on his looks.

"Yo Beast," he was greeted in a friendly manner. He assumed people called him this because of his face and not because of his build—most of them were built the same way if not bigger. But they didn't mean it in a bad way and so he didn't mind.

"What you bring us for lunch?" TK asked. He was a black male that wore sunglasses every single day, even in the subbasement.

Christopher grinned and opened his bag, spreading the food out before him. Half a loaf of bread, a big bowl of spaghetti, another big bowl filled with salad, a container of ranch dressing, a carton of Kraft Parmesan cheese, a gallon sized jug of Lipton Citrus Iced Tea—half empty and a Twinkie.

TK reached for the Twinkie and Christopher's hand shot out, gripping the other man's wrist tightly but not painfully.

"Not the Twinkie." The black man dropped the snack cake and only then did Christopher release his grip.

TK scowled. "You gonna heat that spaghetti up?"

"Nope." He opened the lid and forked cold congealed spaghetti into his mouth. TK made gagging sounds. Everyone ate a lot, but not everyone ate the way Beast did. But not everyone worked out the way he did, either.

As a member of the Federal Protection Services; or FPS for the Department of Homeland Security, surveillance was more or less downtime. It was alternated by field assignment. Most thought DHS was just about terrorism but they worked a lot of drug enforcement, gangs, and even international assignments. That was when his scary looks really paid off. But here; monitoring the protectees, it didn't do well to show himself.

After lunch he, Porter and TK headed over to the courthouse via the underground tunnels. They transferred prisoners to the transport and then ran a sweep. It was night when he finally climbed into his Dodge Ram and headed home. He pulled his cap low over his face which helped. Pulling up his collar also helped but people still stared due to his size alone. But he didn't have to think about that since he didn't have to do anything but go straight home.

Maggie greeted him with several low purrs. He dumped his things into the closet and reached down and tickled her behind her ears. She arched her back and her tail stiffened and pointed straight into the air as she purred loudly.

He chuckled and put cat food into her bowl and got her fresh water. Then he turned on the stereo and checked his messages while John Mayer played softly in the background.

"Sonny, you come down visit granny Sunday. Uncle Goo and Aunt Verna goin' be there for spring break. They gonna bring Millie in from the special school and no tellin' when the next time we'll get a chance to see the poor dear. Call me back. Love you, son."

He smiled and called his Mom right back. "Hi Mom. You need me to bring anything? You want me to drive?" She exclaimed that she didn't want to put him out and for him to get down to Corbin early enough to visit. He promised he would and chatted for a while before hanging up. "See you and Daddy Sunday. Love you."

"Love you, son."

Christopher started dinner; meatloaf, mashed Yukon gold potatoes, and steamed green beans. He made it as much for dinner tonight as in anticipation of several meatloaf sandwiches for lunch the next day. While dinner cooked he went into the spare bedroom and changed into athletic shorts and an old shirt. He hit the treadmill as he watched the news from the flat panel television that was mounted on the wall. After his workout he showered and by then dinner was ready.

Christopher sat down at the table and ate his meal. His eyes drifted to the empty chair opposite him as he chewed.

~***~

Christopher headed for the subbasement gym. No one ever came in at 5:00 am; no one. Most of the FOB employees didn't begin straggling in until about 6:30 and he would be finished long before then. He liked the little gym because it was small. He would go in, slip in a mixed tape or CD; usually something with guitars and more than likely some vintage rock. He was only 25 but liked Zeppelin, The Who, and Ozzy just as much as he liked the The Dave Matthews Band and Jason Mraz for their singing ability. Good music was good music no matter when it had been made.

He cut on the lights and slipped in Neil Young's; Cortez the Killer. As the mellow guitar rift drifted from the speakers Christopher stretched. It wouldn't take much for him to lose the extra three or four pounds without sacrificing his daily Twinkie.

Wearing workout pants and a hoodie which he kept over his head when in this portion of the subbasement, Christopher hit the treadmill. He loved to run. More than that, he liked the control he had when he exercised. There was nothing much else the loner could do as a teen but workout. He didn't have any friends and he had learned that while it didn't matter that beneath his shy shield he would have been a good friend to have, but most never tried to find out. You couldn't really change what people thought even if you smiled your crooked smile or said thank you softly or even if you kept your head down and didn't meet anyone's eyes. But what you could do is run. And then when his body began to transform he lifted weights.

His parent's didn't have much. There were four kids to feed on one income. But they lived in Corbin Kentucky where you didn't need to try to scrape up the funds to play school sports when you could run through the mountains for free. And Dad had found him an entire weight set from his weekly visit to the Salvation Army. And then Christopher had found a way to spend his free time. It was a catch 22, though because as he got bigger he just became even scarier.

Christopher hated thinking back on those days and put it out of his mind as he allowed the music to carry him away while his feet pounded along the treadmill.

...He came dancing across the water...

The sweat rolled down the cut lines of his back and Christopher didn't even notice. His black hoodie kept the heat inside. He ran fast imagining the mountains…

…He came dancing across the water, Cortez Cortez…

His mind played the guitar rifts as he silently sang and his feet pounded…pounded…Christopher ran and felt free in his little gym sanctuary.

~***~

Ashleigh got dressed in her ratty grey sweat pants and a pink shirt that had SUPERSTAR written out in rhinestones across the front. She'd been serious about working out when she had invested $90 in cross training shoes because the salesman had said it would maximize her workout.

She had purposely arrived at 5:30 even though she didn't have to be at work until 8:00. She figured she would work out for an hour to an hour and a half, take forty-five minutes to get showered and dressed, and another half hour to have breakfast in the cafeteria. She'd seen that they had egg white omelets and turkey sausage now. She'd have time to kickback and recuperate before starting her day. But best of all, by coming so early she'd get to the gym before anyone else showed up.

The Federal Building was quiet when she arrived. No one had yet arrived to visit the Social Security Office or to have their taxes prepared. None of the workers were crowding into the building carrying their cups of piping hot Starbucks and wheeling their briefcases behind them, no mom's with strollers to drop their children off at the daycare before they dashed off to work.

There were just two guards who looked at her in surprise whether it was because they were unused to seeing the stylish woman without makeup and dressed in sweats, or because it was too early to begin scanning people in. She dug out her badge and they allowed her to bypass the metal detectors. She went to the elevators; the only set that would lead to the subbasement and nervously hit the down button.

There were lights on, thank god. She walked rapidly to the female lockers trying to remember the route; walk down the first corridor, left, left and it should be there. Viola! There it was. The lights were off in the room and she cut them on. It was clean and bright and didn't feel like a basement so she breathed easier and put her bag into one of the lockers after retrieving a hand towel and a bottled water.

She left the lights on as she left the locker room and headed purposefully for the gym. She wouldn't look at her workout as a chore but the first step into recreating herself. Ashleigh began to hear the faint sounds of music. As she got closer she thought she heard Jimi Hendrix; All Along the Watchtower. So she wasn't alone. She was kind of relieved but also a bit disappointed. She didn't think anyone would be working out this early.

She pushed open the metal doors to the gym room and All Along the Watchtower was playing at a moderate level; not quite loud but it could have been softer. There was only one other person in the room and he was running the treadmill. Ashleigh allowed her eyes to linger on the man. Damn he was big. He wore black nylon workout pants and a black hoodie, both damp with his sweat. The pants molded nicely along the man's butt. He had a great butt, like two boulders. His fists were pumping as he ran and she could tell that he was a white guy but other than that couldn't tell what he looked like.

He was a giant! She could see the muscles rippling along his back as he ran, even through the hoodie. Nice.

She moved to the mat in front of the mirrors happy that they weren't close to the treadmills and began to stretch thinking; Ugh…it's too early for this. Her tummy rumbled and she grimaced and tried to touch her toes. Her tummy got in the way so she opted for touching her knees. After about two minutes of that Ashleigh moved to the bike. Might as well start there. She hoped the man wasn't watching her but he hadn't even glanced in her direction. Good. He was just pounding away on the treadmill.

She rode the bike for ten minutes but then her legs began to ache and her chest burned. She decided to work on her upper body and moved to the curl machine set at the second to the lowest weight. She was sweating and thinking about which machine to hit next when the music stopped. She looked up in time to see the man leaving the room with a CD in his hands. His hood shielded his face and he didn't even glance in her direction. She watched him leave and when the door shut after him she went over to the radio and turned it to Tom Joyner in the morning.

~***~

Christopher hit the shower and tried not to scowl. The lady had come in making everything smell pink like flowers. Gyms were supposed to smell like sweat and hard labor. He'd seen girls like that before. They came in dressed in designer workout clothes and were all gung-ho the first day, maybe even the first week. But then they disappeared.

He'd seen her come in, using the mirrors so that he wouldn't have to turn around. She was curvy. Her stretchy sweat pants pulled across her more-than ample-bottom and he noted the way her rear-end moved when she walked. When she bent to stretch Christopher had stopped peeking, her butt was pointed right at the reflection in the mirror that he was using to see her. Her shirt had slipped up some and her pants had slipped down a bit and he could see cute pink panties and a bit of her crack.

He suppressed a growl. Why was this lady wearing pink and smelling pink invading his space?! And why was she in here so early? Well he had no plans of changing his workout time, she could just change hers if she didn't like him here.

Afterwards he got dressed in fatigues, which was his uniform while working surveillance. Christopher's workout was actually factored in to his work-day. His boss wanted them kept in tip top shape and each man was required to spend at least three hours a week working out. He easily achieved that twice over. Most were addicted to it and like him, didn't see working out as a chore. But unlike him, they preferred having an audience and scheduled their workouts around optimum female presence.

He poured himself a 32 oz size cup of Lipton Iced Tea with Citrus and sauntered in to the security room, his muscles pleasantly throbbing. Several of the guys were there guffawing and pointing. Crap…another homeless dude accosting the protectees. They'd make a call up to one of the uniformed guards to run him off.

"Yo, Beast! Check this out!" Carlos' brown face was split by a wide smile. Christopher walked over to the camera and did a double-take. The pink lady—well she wasn't pink. She was a black lady; light skinned with light hair and eyes, maybe multi-racial. But she had moved to the treadmill. She had it set to a fast walk and what the guys were guffawing about was the way her butt bounced with each step. Damn…he watched for a moment before scowling and walking away.

"You were down there with her. We were taking bets that she'd get one look at your big-ass and run." Roddy said with a smirk. "She was checking you out, dude."

Christopher had just sat down in his chair to run the reports and he gave Roddy a sharp look. "I don't want no parts of your bet, and before you ask, no I'm not going to scare her." He had a bit of a country drawl to his rumbling voice.

TK made a face letting him know that's just what they had wanted. Hell it got boring down in the basement and they found fun wherever they could. But he wasn't going to mess with a lady minding her own business when he was minding his.

"Remember that time you scared that drug dealer away?" Carlos hinted.

"That was different and you know it." They had watched the monitors and were laughing like crazy when he went up to the young thug. The dumb fuck was selling his drugs on the same corner as the freaking Federal Courthouse! How dumb could you get? Christopher had been wearing his cap pulled down low and had come up on the thug in broad daylight. He grinned and tilted his cap back.

"What you got there, buddy?" He had asked in his best redneck drawl. The young man's eyes had widened at the sight of the grinning giant with the split face.

"I-I don't know what you talking about…" He had stammered, eyes not able to leave the sight of the monster before him.

Christopher knew that his eyes had gone cold at that moment when his smile disappeared. "Well sell it somewhere else, asshole. And give me your name. NOW!"

The boy had stammered out a name, maybe it was real and maybe it wasn't. But Christopher nodded once and walked back to the Courthouse. When he got back the guys were on the floor rolling. They said the boy had about pissed his pants running away. They hadn't seen him since. Of course that was all different.

Bruce came in to the room then. He had surely heard them laughing long before but he too knew that the subbasement made a person punch drunk. It's why it alternated out with field duty.

"You idiots get back to work. I can hear you laughing like bitches all the way down the hall!" His voice was stern but each of them knew that it was more talk than anger. The men disbanded grumbling. "Sweeps aren't being made, screens aren't being monitored and reports aren't being run while you laughing assholes are watching..." He peeked at the screen and scowled. "...big bitches working out. You can see this shit on Youtube!"

Everybody cleared out except the essential people assigned to the room; which included Christopher. He saw Bruce watch the monitor for a few more moments before he made an appreciative grunt and walked out of the room.

He buried his head back into his report.

~***~

In theory, Ashleigh's plan was great. But nothing worked out as planned. She'd sweated her hair until it was soaking wet and once she got to the locker she'd had to wash it. Her hair was too short to just pull back into a ponytail and it had taken her forty-five minutes alone just getting her short hair blow dried and curled into a passable manner and then fifteen minutes on makeup and ten minutes getting dressed. She'd only had time to grab a breakfast wrap and a bottle of juice and to get up to her office where she gobbled it up.

Kendra and Lance came into her office and looked her up and down. "Did you work out?" Kendra asked in disappointment.

"I did!" She said defensively. "My freaking legs are knotted up and I'm limping," she added.

Lance gave her a doubtful look. "Girlfriend, you look like you just left the spa. Make-up and clothes are flawless."

Ashleigh smiled. Lance was so sweet, even if he thought she looked too good to have just put in over an hour on her first workout—still, he thought she looked good.

"I am not coming up here looking like those other women with the sweat stains under their arms and hair all jacked up and spending the day wafting in my own funk."

They talked for a few minutes and Ashleigh's friends finally believed her when she tried to stand in her heels and groaned in pure pain and then limped to the coffee pot.

The next day she brought hair gel so that she wouldn't have to worry about straightening her hair again. After placing her things in the locker she headed for the gym. Once again she heard music playing; The Dave Matthews Band, Ants Marching. Not quite the music you'd think about working out to but she liked the song.

Again the same man was on the treadmill. Again he was wearing all black with a hood concealing him pretty well. She pretended not to watch the way he made running the treadmill look effortless. She almost fell off the thing when she'd done it the day before.

Today she wore navy sweatpants and an oversized shirt. She did her stretching, or tried to. Her muscles were so tight that she could barely bend. She plopped down on the floor and stretched her legs, and tried to reach for her feet. Well that wasn't going to happen. She lay on her back and pulled one leg than the other up against her body. She peeked over at the sexy guy. He just stared straight ahead and didn't look at her once. Hmph. She guessed that was good. She didn't need to worry about some guy checking her out while she was straining just to touch her feet!

It took her about seven minutes to get loosened up enough to hit the elliptical machine. Ten minutes in to it and Ashleigh was asking herself, *'Why am I torturing myself like this? Who really cares...?*

And then she thought about DeAngelo and Shaunda and the woman's perfect body. Her throat tightened. Ashleigh's eyes glazed but this time not with tears but with determination. She pushed herself when she wanted to stop—when she would have stopped she just kept going. One day at a time she said this to herself when the stitch formed in her side.

A journey of a thousand miles begins with one step...

~***~

After leaving the gym and showering Christopher returned to the monitoring room. A few of the guys were there watching the lady workout but they weren't hooping and hawing because they didn't want to attract Bruce's attention. With a sigh, Christopher joined them.

"Dude, look at her go." Roddy said.

"We're taking bets that she's going to black out."

Christopher watched the woman pushing herself. She was on the treadmill again and this time she was going at a run. After a few more minutes she finally stopped and the hooping and hollering grew a bit louder as money passed hands.

"Fifteen minutes!" Someone said loudly. "That's my girl." They disbanded and went about their duties. Christopher lingered. She'd dropped down on the mat on her back. She was breathing hard. Shit, she was going to seize up doing that. Her arm was across her face. He leaned in closer.

She was crying.

Christopher's back straightened. Did she hurt herself? Should he go check on her? He was contemplating this when she pulled herself back up to her feet. She moved stiffly back to the treadmill. She started it again and got back on it!

Christopher placed his hands on his hips and watched. She was going to walk it out, he thought. That was good. But then he saw her pushing up the speed and she began running again. Damn...

Christopher tapped the controls and zoomed in on her face. Sweat and tears were evident but he could see that her brow was drawn and he saw that she wasn't going to stop until she met her own personal goal. He heard Carlos come up behind him and he quickly flipped the screen to the corridors. He didn't want any of the guys seeing her cry.

~***~

Ashleigh hurt so bad that even though she knew she shouldn't, she came straight home, popped ibuprofen, took a hot bath and then crawled into bed without dinner.

The next day when she went to the gym she was walking stiffly. Blues music was playing this time. How apropos. She looked at the giant on the treadmill. Did he even know she was there? He never even flinched when she came in through the door. He never even turned to look in her direction. Well today she planned to keep her eyes on him.

She just wanted to know what he looked like. He had to be fine with a body like that.

He generally left at six so while she was on the curling machine she kept her eyes on him. He didn't look tired even though his dark clothes were made even darker with his sweat. But his gait was steady. Six came and she saw him switch off the machine. His head was down when he headed straight for the boombox and removed the CD. She finally saw him do it. Generally the music stopped and he was half out the door before she looked up.

He must have sensed her looking because he glanced at her; just a glance. And in that one brief second Ashleigh's light brown face paled even lighter. Her eyes widened as her brain tried to make sense of what she saw. The man's face was split in half.

Jesus, she'd never seen anything like it. It was as if someone had taken a machete to him and then someone else had tried to sew the pieces back together. There was a visible seam that ran from his chin, over his lip up into one nostril. His nose was flattened and flared crookedly. The seam continued up between his brows and then ran a crooked pattern to disappear beneath the hood.

They called it a cleft palate but she'd never seen one so bad. The two halves of his face had seemed to shift; the bone structure beneath the flesh, causing his face to sink in slightly giving him a gorilla–like appearance. He also had no color. He was as white as an albino. His grey eyes were fringed in reddish lashes that looked almost non-existent. His upper lip seemed to have three distinct sections that she couldn't quite understand. He was by far the scariest looking man she'd ever seen.

He was out the door before she realized that she'd stared. She felt herself blushing and hoped that she hadn't made him feel like a monster. But he'd shocked her. She rubbed her face in chagrin. Tomorrow she would make a point of not looking disgusted. If the opportunity arose she would speak.

~***~

Christopher's keys broadcast his arrival as he unlocked his front door. Maggie quickly jumped down from where she was perched on the back of the couch, and wrapped her sinewy body around his feet. He reached down and quickly scratched beneath her chin and then put his things away. He had stopped and got carry-out on the way home and after feeding her he sat down with the newspaper and ate his meal.

His thoughts moved to the lady at the gym and he lost his appetite for the third burger and tossed it in the trash. He didn't like the shocked look in her eyes when she caught a glimpse of his face. Not that he blamed her, just that he wished someone could see him for the first time without grimacing in horror. His parent's had been too poor to get his bilateral cleft palate fixed for a long time. By the time that he was three years old it became critical as his breathing and lack of nutrition began to affect his life. The state took over and the surgery was performed for free. Unfortunately his was a very complex situation handled by surgeons not experienced in his extreme case.

After three corrective surgeries his mother could take no more and he'd been left with bad scars though his palate was now closed. Yet his teeth were crooked and several were missing. Although his hearing had been affected, it wasn't enough to keep him out of the military. And normally speech problems occurred with his condition but his voice was fine—although not often used. Christopher was pale, but not because he was albino. He was just a pale skinned red-head. He kept his hair cut short in a military fade. He was the epitome of a jarhead. He even had semper fi tattooed across his bicep. He had planned to get it tatted on his neck because he would never be anything but a jarhead, but his mother had objected and so he hadn't done it.

Christopher did a load of laundry, and changed Mag's litter box. Then he pulled out his guitar and played for a while. He wanted to perform tomorrow and hadn't practiced all week. Friday was Karaoke at The Madd Crab and he generally brought his guitar whenever he sang. He liked the music selection there as well as the people. They were a bunch of rednecks but it was a neighborhood bar with the same rednecks. Sometimes a dumb asshole would come in or a drunken girl. But most knew to leave him alone. And if they didn't learn it the easy way they learned it the hard way. His cousin had introduced him to the place because she had wanted him to sing. She used to be a bartender but had quit for a better paying job at a different redneck bar. He'd stuck around; people knew him already and they liked his singing. Plus they tended to warn the newcomers not pick fights with him.

As he ran the treadmill that night he was pretty certain that he'd gotten back down into the two hundred weight range. But he decided that he would continue to go to the subbasement gym in the mornings--and it had nothing to do with the lady who smelled like pink flowers even after she was dripping with sweat.

Christopher heard the door to the gym open. He was surprised. He half expected her to change her workout time though he no longer expected her to give up. It hadn't been a week yet but there was something in her face that drove her and somehow he didn't think she'd be easily swayed from her unknown goal.

He still wore the hood but he didn't allow it to cover his face as completely. He glimpsed her through the mirror going through her stretching. She was moving very gingerly. He hoped she understood that her muscles had to tear down in order to rebuild themselves even stronger. He hoped she didn't take the pain as a sign to give up when it was actually a sign that her efforts were working for her.

He saw her get on to the recumbent bike. She was wearing grey sweats and a t-shirt that was too big. Her hair was concealed by a cap but he was willing to bet that she hadn't combed it this morning. He liked that she didn't come in wearing make-up, though that could just be an indication that he wasn't counted into a category of someone that she would wear make-up for. Crap, why would he even care about that?

Aerosmith's Janie's Got A Gun was playing. When he was selecting the music to play this morning he wondered what she thought of the music. He wondered if she wished he would cut it down. Well she could wear a headset if she didn't like it…but she never did.

Ashleigh placed her hands on her knees and concentrated. Don't stop, girl. Keep going, girl. But she couldn't. Her butt muscle hurt! And then Bad Reputation by Joan Jett began playing and Ashleigh made a squeak of pleasure. Ooo! That was her song! She grit her teeth and squinted her eyes into slits and she kept pushing as she listened to the words sang by the baddest girl in Rock and Roll!

She got to the end of her rep and collapsed with her back against the seat, head tilted back. The song suddenly stopped and she looked up quickly.

"Good song," She said quickly as the man moved to the door. He hesitated and glanced at her.

"It is." He put his hand on the door and then stopped. "If…you can listen to it if you want. Just leave it in the boombox."

"Yeah. Thanks." He returned it to the boombox, pressed rewind and started the song from the beginning.

"Thank you," she said as he walked out the door. He raised his hand briefly in acknowledgement.

When Beast reached the monitoring room TK punched him playfully in the arm but it still hurt a little.

"What the hell was that for?"

"Making me loose ten bucks. The fat girl came back AND she talked to your ugly ass."

He shrugged and hoped he had hidden his smile. "Oh…well I didn't scare her off, that's for sure." TK clapped him on his back to show that he was just kidding. Christopher felt kind of good. When everyone had returned to their work he flipped the monitor back to the gym.

She was on the treadmill that he used. She tended to go for that one for some reason and she always ended her work-out on the treadmill. She was running, not walking. It wasn't fast and she looked like she was in pain but she kept going.

Over the next few days, Christopher noted the girl's endurance improving. She had a crappy workout routine though. Her reps were too long and she didn't pause long enough between them. She worked much harder than she had to and he was surprised that she didn't pull something with her cool down.

He knew where she worked. He'd monitored her while she left the lockers — she spent an ungodly amount of time in there. But he couldn't deny that the effort was always worthwhile. She always looked wonderful afterwards. She'd get on the elevators for the Federal building and he'd flip screens until he saw her head into the cafeteria. The eyes in the sky were amazing things. He watched her take her breakfast back up to one of the offices on the 7th floor where his camera had no access.

Christopher knew when she went to her bathroom breaks and had seen her leave for lunch. Once she carried back a bag from a fast food restaurant and he zoomed in on it and shook his head. Bad if she's dieting. Maybe it was just salad; he hoped so. He had seen her in the company of a white guy and black female. Sometimes they went out to lunch together.

Whenever he had to do sweeps or lockdown for prisoner transport he'd make sure he got back by 4:30 so that he could watch her leave each evening. At first she used to limp but not anymore. He would flip cameras until he saw her disappear into her car at one of the outdoor pay lots. As he watched her drive off, he wondered who she went home to.

CHAPTER 3

This second week of Ashleigh's workout, she hurt a lot less, but she was still exhausted at the end of the day. Sometimes she had a quick salad or opened a can of soup but most days she showered, packed her bag for work the next day and fell into bed. She prayed she would build her metabolism up soon.

However she did discover that she actually looked forward to her daily torture session. Though not because she enjoyed working out. No, she enjoyed the music. Every day the man brought something cool to listen to. When one song ended she anticipated the next one never knowing what to expect. Sometimes it was Def Leppard; Pour Some Sugar On Me. Sometimes it was Harry Connick Jr. Once he'd played Summer Madness by Kool and the Gang and Ashleigh had just stared at his back for the entire song.

The man never spoke. But he'd leave the tape or disc — whichever one he brought. Most times she'd leap up as soon as he was gone and would hit rewind to a particular song and start her workout anew. By her third week she could see a transformation in her body. There was definitely more room in her clothes, yet whenever she undressed she still saw a round belly and a big butt. She'd sigh and bypass the delicious pastries in the cafeteria and would get her soup, salad or sandwich at lunch.

Ashleigh felt weak and tired when she dragged herself out of bed Wednesday morning; two months into her workout. She'd again skipped dinner the night before and her stomach hurt because it was so empty. She grabbed a banana and ate it as she drove in to work. God, she was tired.

She put her things into the locker room and headed for the gym. She was so tired that she didn't even pay attention to what song was playing, only happy that it was something with a heavy bassline so that she could get motivated. She glanced at Mr. Mysterious, as always, pounding away on that treadmill. He never used the weights or anything else, just the treadmill.

She plopped down on the recumbent bike, too tired to even think about the elliptical. Then she began pedaling. I'm getting skinnier, she thought. Each pedal I'm getting skinnier. Each bead of sweat is a drop of fat melting off my body. Push it girl, push it…

Her ears began to ring and her body began to tremble as black dots began to form in front of her vision. She stopped pedaling and tried to stand up, but suddenly it was as if the floor had come flying up to meet her and then there was nothing but blackness.

Christopher heard the sound of a body hitting the floor. It was a pretty distinct sound; one he was familiar with since he'd caused a lot of bodies to hit the floor. The woman who smelled like pink was laid sprawled out on the floor. Christopher leaped from the treadmill, and was knelt at her side in seconds. He swept back his hood. Shit! Was she having a heart attack? He quickly checked her pulse. He could tell that it was weak. He quickly placed his hand behind her neck and made sure that her airway wasn't obstructed. She breathed fine.

Christopher looked up at the camera and gestured for

someone to bring smelling salts. Very gently he touched her cheek. Her skin was like silk and his hands were so rough.

"Hey?" He said softly. "Wake up, sweetheart. Open your eyes." Roddy and Carlos were suddenly there with the first aid kit. "Get the salts!" He commanded. TK located them and broke the caplet under her nose. The woman twitched and tried to turn her face away. She brought her hand up weakly and pushed TK's hands away. Her eyes opened and she looked up into the Beast's face.

He watched her eyes blink and try to focus. "Wha--?" She muttered in confusion.

"You blacked out, Ma'am." She kept blinking rapidly and he suddenly realized that one of her eyes was brown while the other was hazel…She'd lost a contact.

Ashleigh sat up. Three men were hovering over her and she felt instantly foolish. She'd fainted! She tried to stand and the man in black kept a hold of her arm.

"Careful Ma'am. You're not ready to stand up yet."

"I'm okay." She said in embarrassment. She touched the back of her head, and felt a lump forming. The Man in black's hand was instantly there. She looked up at him but had double vision and couldn't seem to focus. His fingers gently touched the lump forming.

"Ma'am?" His hands suddenly gripped her. "Ma'am!" and then the world went black again. Christopher caught her and swept her limp form up into his arms.

Bruce was suddenly there. "Get her inside," meaning into the secure zone. Civilians were strictly prohibited from entering it. But Christopher didn't hesitate. He carried the limp woman into their headquarters after Roddy scanned them in.

Christopher headed for the commissary. The woman's body felt soft in his arms. Her head was propped on his shoulder and he could smell her distinct aroma, beneath the flowers — fresh like baking bread. He sat in one of the metal chairs; there were no cots, no infirmary here. He propped her up on his lap carefully as everyone trailed in. They had a 16 man crew and every one of them was present and watching intently as if he carried a rare specimen.

"Ma'am?" Christopher slipped his hand behind her neck so that his thumb gently stroked her cheek. "Wake up, Ma'am. Open your eyes." He spoke softly and as if on command her eyes began to flutter open. A slow gasp filled the room.

He saw her eyes open and she squinted up at him. Everyone seemed to hold their breath as if waiting for her to scream and runaway. Instead she started blinking rapidly. When she tried to stand, Christopher gripped her gently but firmly.

"You're not ready to stand yet." She had a confused expression on her face as she looked out at the room full of men wearing fatigues. Bruce came forward.

"Ma'am, when was the last time you ate?" He demanded.

She pressed back against Christopher as she looked up into the mean face of the army guy. The man holding her rumbled. "Let me handle this, sir."

She turned to Christopher when he spoke. "Have you

eaten anything?" His voice was gentle.

Ashleigh was so confused and still half out of it. She didn't realize that she was sitting on a strange man's lap. She was just so tired.

"I think she just crashed, Sir." Christopher spoke to his Supervisor. Bruce nodded and sighed.

"Well, someone get her some orange juice. Beast, you are not to let this civilian out of your sight. Follow protocol. The rest of you; OUT!"

Everyone grumbled but left. Someone pressed an orange juice into his hands before retreating. Christopher shook it quickly and twisted off the top.

"Drink this, Ma'am." He pressed it to her lips. She squinted at him but took a sip of the offered beverage. Her stomach suddenly began to rumble and groan.

"You're hungry," he said. "Your body crashed."

And then it hit her. She'd fainted. And she was sitting in a man's lap. And where the hell was she?! Again she tried to stand but couldn't because he was holding her.

"You shouldn't try to stand. You're going to blackout again...remember? I mentioned that the last time?"

"Yeah..." She said distantly. Why couldn't she see? She rubbed her eye and gasped when something foreign caused her discomfort. She kept rubbing until she rubbed it out.

Christopher leaned forward. "Wait. You rubbed out your contact." He reached forward and gently grabbed the delicate lens from her cheek.

Ah. Her contact had rolled up behind her eyelid. She tried to take it but her hand was too unsteady. She looked at her uncooperative appendage in surprise.

"Look up at the ceiling. I'm going to put it in for you."

She nodded her agreement. Once she wasn't looking, Christopher quickly placed the lens into his mouth to re-wet it and then placed it on his fingertip. He had never done this before but had seen it done. She tried to peek at him and he waited patiently for her to look at the ceiling again. Then he pressed the lens into her eye and she quickly blinked it into place.

"Better?"

She looked up into his face, now able to see him clearly. "Better." She managed to smile. He pressed the juice to her lips and she took a longer swallow. Then she took the drink from his hands, her hands covering his for a moment and then she gulped down the orange juice spilling some down her chin. When the container was empty she belched. He hid his smile. She was still half out of it but the sugar would bring her around fairly quickly.

Ashleigh closed her eyes and placed her head on the man's massive chest. She smacked her lips and then promptly fell asleep.

Christopher was unsure what to do but he wasn't going to wake her. He settled back in his chair and held her. She felt so damned good in his arms. He looked down at the top of her head. She was so little...well she was a big girl, but in his arms she was dwarfed. He wanted to...

His arms tightened protectively around her.

Ashleigh felt a sense of relief that she hadn't felt in months. She didn't remember what all had gone wrong but so much had been wrong for so long and now it was all right. She snuggled deeper in to DeAngelo's arms. She'd missed him so much and it felt so good the way he held her in her sleep. Sometimes she knew that he'd think she was asleep and would hold her tightly against him and that's how she knew that deep down he loved her; because if he didn't why would he bother to hold her while she slept?

"DeAngelo…" She muttered softly and sighed. Christopher watched her face. He instantly hated this 'DeAngelo.' He wanted to kill DeAngelo. Some other man got to hold her and she spoke his name in that way. But then her head snuggled against his chest again and all thought left him. Damnit, why did she have to feel so good in his arms? All softness and curves…

TK walked into the commissary then. He eyed the two of them and then gave a lascivious grin. He gripped his crotch suggestively. Christopher put on his meanest expression and gestured with his head for TK to get lost. The other man silently went to the vending machines and got himself a soda. He could tell that their wordless conversation had tickled the black man who raised his ever-present sunglasses to look at the two of them and then blow him a quick kiss.

Christopher scowled but it disappeared as soon as he looked down into the woman's peaceful face. She was beautiful, she had a teeny little peanut nose and perfectly formed lips. He used to look at pictures and photographs of lips; ones with perfect cupid bows; like hers. Her face was round and girlish. He figured that she was in her late twenties. Her long lashes left dark shadows on her golden brown cheeks. She wasn't pink, she was gold and brown like hot buttered toast.

He wished that she would sleep like this forever.

Ashleigh sucked in a loud breath as if she had been drowning under water. Her hands flung out and her eyes popped open all at the same time. She was awake. She looked up into the wary face of the man and let out a squeak of surprise. Oh my god. His face...she could see it up close and clearly now. There were scars criss-crossing his face. His nose was flattened but his upper lip wasn't exactly three separate pieces as she had first thought from her brief glimpse of him, but it did have deep scars as if it had been sewn back together; badly sewn back together. His hair was cut into a very short military cut but she could tell that it was red, just like his sparse eye brows and lashes.

She realized that she was staring, but she also realized that he was allowing it. Ashleigh quickly pushed away from him. Oh my god, she had been snuggling against him! She tried to come to her feet in horror that she had made a stranger so familiar.

"I am so sorry." She said quickly. His hands were still on her arms as if he was waiting for her to fall again.

"You fainted twice." He said. She tried not to stare into his face and looked around. He dropped his arms and she realized that she was being rude by being self-conscious. She looked at him.

"Where am I?"

"This is the security area of the subbasement." He had a deep, soft voice with a country accent. "I'm Lt Christopher Jameson of the Department of Protective Services for Homeland Security."

She gave him a surprised look, momentarily forgetting about his scars. "In the subbasement?"

"Yes Ma'am," he said politely. "The employees of the Federal Building and Federal Courthouse are our protectees."

"Protectees..." She said testing the word. "Wow, I had no idea."

"No Ma'am. No one sees us. But we're here." Ashleigh smiled. That was nice to know.

"I'm Ashleigh Dalton." She blushed and tugged at her t-shirt. "And I need to really get back to work."

"Mrs. Dalton, you're not trying to exercise on an empty stomach are you?" She gave him a surprised look. And he quickly continued. "Well I see you workout each morning...and you blacked out. I figured that was why."

She blushed again and looked away. "Yeah, I guess I wasn't thinking."

"Mrs. Dalton-"

"Miss. Please, just call me Ashleigh, spelled with a gh." After all, she had just sat on his lap, and what a big lap it was. She had to look up at him as he towered above her. He was a giant. He was even bigger than DeAngelo. Big clothes concealed most of his muscles but she knew that he was perfectly toned beneath the sweatpants and hooded sweatshirt. She felt like such a slob around him. He'd probably felt every roll of fat when he lifted her. Feeling self conscious, she folded her arms in front of her.

"I'll escort you back down to the lockers. Once you get dressed I want you to visit the nurse's station in your building. You need to get your blood pressure checked and the lump on the back of your head looked at. Will you do that, Ashleigh?"

She gave him a surprised look. "Yeah-Yes. I'll do that."

He nodded without smiling and led her out the door. Several men were moving along the corridor and she instantly knew that they had been listening at the door. She looked up at Christopher who seemed to ignore it.

Several men nodded their heads at her as they passed. They were dressed in army fatigues and she was wearing sweats and a t-shirt. How embarrassing. Her cap was gone; she would have bed head!!! This day should just end. There was no way that she was going to work, she was going home and she was going to crawl into bed!

They walked down a long corridor and Ashleigh realized that he had carried her here. She looked up at him. He walked very straight and tall. She should say something.

"Thank you for helping me. I'm sorry for the trouble."

He looked at her quickly. "No trouble. Um…do you feel okay?"

No, she didn't feel okay. She felt drained but she didn't think she was going to faint again. "I'm okay." She said.

They reached the security doors and he used a card to open them. "After you, Ma'am--Ashleigh."

Why was she so tired? Christopher was watching her but she couldn't read his expression. He followed her into the corridor but instead of leading her to where the lockers were located he led her in a different direction. Oh hell she was all turned around. It felt like a maze to her anymore. But in a minute she was going to need to sit down. She hoped they would get to the lockers soon.

They reached a set of elevators and he pressed the button. She saw him look at her with a sudden frown.

"You're crashing again. You're about to black out." Concern was suddenly evident in his voice and on his face.

"What?"

He placed his hand on her elbow to steady her and led her into the elevators. "I'm taking you directly to your nurse's station." There was no room for protest. He led and she went.

"I'm feeling a little sick," She admitted.

He looked at her. "I know." She wasn't brown anymore. Now she was gray. He drew his hood on and looked down in order to shield his face just as the elevator doors opened. They hadn't used the main elevators leading to the lobby but a back elevator that was in the same corridor as the first floor nurse's station. Ashleigh had passed these elevators a hundred times and never noticed them.

The man, Christopher, had taken her hand and was leading her, pulling her forward. Maybe she was going to black out. Everything was grays and blacks…

Christopher pushed open the doors to the nurse's area and two women wearing white scrubs looked up at him in surprise. One of the women started backing up in alarm, the other looked from the man to the gray woman and she jumped into action.

"Get a gurney!" Things moved very fast. She was lying on a gurney, someone was taking her blood pressure, someone gave her more orange juice and she began to come around. A man; a doctor shined a light in her eyes and she blinked and turned away.

"Mrs. Dalton? We called an ambulance. It should be here any minute. Are you taking insulin?"

"Ambulance?!" She tried to sit up but a gentle hand was on her shoulder. She looked over and it was a man wearing a hood, Lt. Christopher Jameson. She quieted.

"Mrs. Dalton?" The doctor was talking to her and she turned her attention back to him. "Are you diabetic?"

"No. No." Why was he asking her if she had diabetes?

"You're hypoglycemic and there is a good chance that you are falling into a diabetic coma."

"Coma?"

"Basically unconsciousness due to low blood sugar." A nurse handed her a piece of toast. "Try to eat this. We can't give you glucose here. If the toast doesn't work it's the only thing that's going to make you feel better. You have to go to the hospital. We contacted your emergency contacts and they are on their way."

Ashleigh rubbed her face with shaking hands. Diabetes. The doors flew open and Lance and Kendra were suddenly there flanking her bed, holding her hands, smoothing her hair, kissing her cheeks and telling her how badly she'd scared them.

~***~

Christopher spent the morning filling out reports; incident reports, breach of security report, points of contact reports. When he was done he went down into the gym room and retrieved the CD and Ashleigh's cap. He quietly stared at the monitors, ran his sweeps, but his mind was deep in thought. No one bothered him. Carlos mumbled, "She's going to be alright, Beast."

He gave the man a surprised look. But Carlos tucked his head down and hurried away. Bruce walked into the security room later that evening. Christopher looked up from the screens waiting to get his ass chewed for leaving the area without permission.

"I got a report from the hospital. The civilian…uh the girl, Miss Dalton has been released and she's doing just fine." Christopher sighed. "Go down into the lockers and secure her property. I don't want any of her belongings getting stolen."

"Yes, sir." He stood up quickly and hurried out the door, but paused and turned back to Bruce. "Thank you, sir."

"She's a tough, cookie. She must have been feeling bad for days and came in every day and pushed herself. I didn't have men at boot camp that push themselves as hard."

Christopher nodded. He agreed.

~***~

"You two are making me hot!" Ashleigh grumbled. Lance was cuddled up in her bed to the right and Kendra to the left. He made to get up and Ashleigh gripped his shirt and pulled him back down. He chuckled when she sighed in contentment.

She'd spent most of the day at the hospital. It was confirmed; she had diabetes. Ashleigh had pulled her lip into her mouth and almost cried. The needles, the regulated diet, no more rice…She had to have PF Chang's twice a week, she just had to!

But sometimes when a door closed a window opened. DeAngelo had shown up at the hospital. He had been among her emergency contacts and he'd dropped everything to rush to the hospital and to be at her side! He had looked terrified when he saw her pale face. He gripped her hand and kissed her fingers.

"Baby, what's wrong? Are you okay, Ashleigh?" She'd stared at him in surprise. Kendra and Lance had rolled their eyes at his show of affection but had backed away — not leaving all-together, of course. But they had given her a bit of space to talk to him.

She explained about the black-out and he had blanched. "Jesus…" He had stayed with her during the diagnosis and had asked questions when the doctors explained that her A1C test was at 12 which is why she had to immediately take insulin instead of pills. He held her hand during the injections. He had even offered to drive her back home but Lance said that his WIFE would be worried about him.

Ashleigh narrowed her eyes at Lance but it was true. "You should go. My friends are going to drive me home."

DeAngelo had given her a steady look. "I'm your friend too, you know." He leaned forward and kissed her lips lightly. "I thought…I thought you would have forgiven me by now. I don't want to lose you Ash, you gotta tell me how to make this right between us."

"Okay," Lance stormed forward. "You want to know how to make everything right? You fucking disappear! You leave her alone and stay out of her life!"

"Lance," Kendra placed a calming hand on his narrow shoulder. Ashleigh couldn't believe that Lance was attacking DeAngelo like that! He was half the man's size. But in that moment he looked like he would whup DeAngelo's ass.

"You know what? I'm sick of your mouth!" DeAngelo stood up but Lance didn't back down. Ashleigh tugged his hand.

"DeAngelo…you should go."

He turned to her, his brow going up. "You're choosing him over me?!"

She narrowed her eyes at him. "You chose someone else over me!"

DeAngelo turned for the door, he paused as he left and looked at Ashleigh. "I'll call you, Ash…when there aren't so many people around," he said staring pointedly at

Kendra and Lance. Then he disappeared.

Ashleigh reached her hand out for Lance and he interlocked his fingers with hers. "Are you insane?" She asked. "You're trying to go up against DeAngelo?"

"He doesn't scare me." The smaller man said as he leaned lightly against her. He placed a kiss on her forehead. "You can do better."

"People do learn from their mistakes," she whispered.

Now the three of them were huddled in her oversized bed. They'd force fed her chicken soup and it wasn't homemade or even Progresso…but Campbell's with that one lone little square of chicken floating in salty broth and tons of soggy noodles; and she loved every spoonful! She'd had two bowls and had even begged for crackers but they wouldn't give her any.

Before that they'd watched her give herself her first insulin shot. She was so scared that Kendra almost snatched the needle from her and did it herself but Lance proclaimed that she'd have to learn to do it. She finally stabbed herself and injected the medicine — all with her eyes closed. When she opened them Lance had blanched. He gave her a shaky smile.

She dozed and when she woke up they were still there. She loved these guys.

She went to work the next day, Kendra drove her since she had left her car and then the two went down into the subbasement together to get her things out of the locker. For some reason she decided to check the gym. It was filled with toned bodies completing their before-work exercises — but Lt. Christopher Jameson wasn't present. Of course he wouldn't be present. He ended his workout at 6am; an hour and a half ago.

"What are you looking at?" Kendra asked.

"I was looking for the guy that helped me yesterday. I wanted to tell him thanks." She looked at her friend as they walked back to the elevators. "Didn't you see him in the nurse's station?"

"What's he look like?"

"Well he's a giant, at least 6'5" and he was wearing all black and a hood over his face. His face is like — all scarred up-"

"Oh my god…do you think you were seeing the Angel of Death?! You weren't that sick-"

Ashleigh rolled her eyes. "I am not describing the Angel of Death. The guy I'm talking about was wearing a NIKES hoodie and sweat pants."

Kendra pressed the button for the elevator. "Well I didn't see anybody like that — and I don't want to see anybody like that. Ever."

Ashleigh shrugged. "He was nice. He's in there every day when I work out." As the doors to the elevators opened she leaned in and whispered. "This subbasement is the base of operations for Homeland Security."

"Really?" Kendra said dismissively.

"You think I'm delusional."

The two women walked to the cafeteria. Kendra chuckled. "No. I'm just taking everything you say with a grain of salt for another few days."

They grabbed breakfast; Ashleigh had an egg white omelet and turkey sausage...which incidentally is what she had been eating from the canteen since dieting anyways. Well she planned to kick this diabetes thing. She was diagnosed with type 2 and if she got her weight down then there was a chance that she could throw away those dreaded needles.

Tomorrow was Friday. She would allow herself the rest of the week and weekend to recuperate but starting Monday she planned to be right back at the gym. Before it was about remaking herself into an image more appealing to the man of her dreams, but now it was about making herself as healthy as possible.

Christopher watched Ashleigh through the monitors as she and her friend carried their breakfast up to their office. He'd been running reports when TK announced that she was in the subbasement. Only now they called her 'Little Trooper'

"The Little Trooper's back!" Carlos had called out. Several men had come running. Christopher got out of his chair and nudged people aside, a frown on his heavily scarred face.

"She's not planning to work out is she?" Someone asked.

"She better not," TK spoke. "Or I'll be down there to spank her hiney...her very ample, nice juicy-"

Roddy nudged him when Christopher's face darkened. "What's she doing?"

"She's looking for Beast. She wants to give him a thank you kiss." Someone made kiss smacking noises and Beast reached out and swatted the back of their head. When the two women returned to the elevators everyone cleared out except Christopher. He sat down and flipped cameras until he located Ashleigh and her friend. She looked good, healthy, pretty. He was satisfied that she was alright. But he still didn't turn away from the camera.

CHAPTER 4

Monday morning, Ashleigh got out of bed early enough to make herself a breakfast of oatmeal and a slice of wheat toast. She dressed in sweatpants that were no longer quite as tight and an oversized shirt. She looked at herself in her full-sized mirror. Why was she still fat? Okay, she was smaller; the scale said it and so did her clothes but she was still round...well, her breasts had deflated. It was the one thing she hadn't minded being oversized.

Ashleigh scowled and drove to work. She had to rush if she wanted to get in a full hour. As she headed for the gym she heard the faint clanging sound of bells. She hesitated, alarms, bells...clocks? And then she realized that it was part of a song. She picked up her pace and a smile came over her face. It was the Dark Side of the Moon by Pink Floyd! Lt Christopher Jamieson was a god among men for playing Time at 5:30 am!

He was pounding on the treadmill but this time he wasn't wearing his hoodie, just a t-shirt and sweat pants. She caught her breath and her steps faltered. She had never in her life seen such a specimen of a man. His body was sheer perfection! His back formed the most perfect V down to a narrow waist and a round butt that begged to be pinched. His arms were wire tight with ropes of muscles. His short sleeved shirt allowed her to see that Christopher Jamieson was a ginger! He was covered in freckles...tons and tons of brown freckles over his pale skin.

He turned off the treadmill and lifted the bottom of his shirt to wipe the sweat from his face. Oh god…his six pack was magazine perfect, internet porn perfect, but then it instantly disappeared when he dropped his shirt back down. He gave her a crooked smile…or maybe just a smile that was crooked because of his scars.

"Welcome back. How are you feeling?" He asked in that low rumbling country drawl.

"I wanted to thank you." She said offering her own smile. "Turns out I have type 2 diabetes and I was in pretty bad condition." If not for him…well it could have been very bad for her.

His expression became concerned. "Are you okay to work out?"

"Yes, my doctor gave me a clean bill of health. In fact he encourages me to exercise. I just have to take it slow."

He cleared his throat. "Um…if you like I can give you some pointers. I noticed that you don't follow a regimen and I can suggest one that will be more effective and take half the time."

"Half the time?" She allowed her eyes to scan his awesome body before she looked down. "But I wouldn't want to take you away from your workout or anything."

"Well…" Christopher cleared his throat and she saw his face turn red. When that happened the scars on his face stood out like white stripes. She tried not to stare and focused on his eyes. He had charcoal grey eyes; a contrast in light and dark, "I could work out with you." He said hesitantly.

Of course she would accept his kind offer. Who wouldn't accept the offer of a free workout coach from a man with a perfect body? Obviously he knew what he was doing.

"Since you workout every day and I workout every day, I don't see any reason why we shouldn't workout together. It would make it more interesting; that and the music." She glanced at the boom box. Time had ended and another Pink Floyd song was playing. "I don't know that song but I know the album; The Dark Side of the Moon."

"Us and Them," he said while staring at her. "You like Pink Floyd?"

"This album is the only thing I know by the group...well except that song about the Wall. My friend and I watched The Wizard of Oz and he said that if you played this album it would be like a soundtrack to the movie."

"Ah...The Darkside of the Rainbow. Yes, it's pretty cool."

She was surprised. "You've done it too?"

"A few times, actually."

"Me too, a few times," she admitted. She had loved the experience of watching one of her favorite fantasy movies against the strange ethereal backdrop of music. It gave a new, funky dynamic to the classic. "I remember that while this song played they were dancing down the yellow brick road and the music perfectly matched their footsteps."

"Yep, remember when the house got carried away by the tornado? The Great Gig in the Sky was playing and it was almost impossible to imagine that it was only coincidence that the music and action matched so perfectly."

"I was thinking the same thing! There was cackling laughter playing while Dorothy saw visions of the wicked witch!" She exclaimed. She could barely believe that this big tough guy had confessed to watching The Wizard of Oz…and more than once. She couldn't even beg DeAngelo to watch it with her even with the backdrop of Pink Floyd's music. As a matter of fact he had said he didn't want to listen to 'white people music'. He was so dumb. Wait…did she really think that? Yeah, she had and he was!

"Ready?" He asked flashing her that crooked grin again, she smiled back.

"Ready." He made her tell him exactly what she'd had to eat this morning and he nodded in approval. And then they went through a routine that was both fun and much quicker. There were ten reps. He told her to spend only sixty seconds on each, no more, no less. Take a 30 second break between each and then start the next exercise. At first she gave him a questioning look because it seemed way too easy. After stretching they began with jumping jacks. Sixty seconds of jumping jacks wasn't really that hard — other than the fact that she'd neglected to wear a sports bra and her boobs bounced around harder than she did.

Christopher was kind enough not to look and she was very embarrassed. He had a stop watch and when he called time they just stood around and talked, about music about exercise and then they went on to the next exercise and on and on through ten exercises. She was sweating like a pig at the end but she also felt good.

"Are you okay, Ashleigh?" He asked when she leaned over her knees and caught her breath. She nodded and swiped her brow. He passed her her bottled water. "Stay hydrated." She nodded and took a long drink. "You're not going to pass out are you?" He looked concerned, worrying that he had worked her too hard.

"No." She said while straightening. "But I do have to go and check my blood sugar level. Hey, Christopher, you think we can start working out at six instead of 5:30? I'm going to have all kinds of extra time on my hands at this rate."

"That works for me."

She smiled at him. "See you tomorrow. And thanks again." She figured that he was only doing this to help her out and she really appreciated it—even if it was just because he felt sorry for the fat lady. He certainly didn't *need* to work out. He was perfect.

~***~

Christopher stood there momentarily before remembering the camera and then he tucked his head down and left the small gymnasium and headed for the security office. They had different locker rooms than the civilians and as he walked purposefully toward them he noted that not one person gave him a strange look, made offensive references or gave him a hard time for working out with the civilian. He knew they'd been watching because what else was there to do? So why…?

Damnit, they had a bet on him!

He didn't mention it and no one tried to encourage him one way or the other. But he wanted no parts of their games and was happy to be left alone. That night he stopped at the supermarket. He'd already picked up his normal groceries for the week Saturday morning. But now he needed extras, like fruit and fresh vegetables. He wasn't sure what kind…so he just picked several different kinds.

When he got home he picked Maggie up in his big hands and held her up, staring into her kitty face. "Guess what? I made a new friend." She purred and batted her kitty eyes and he gave her ears a brief stroke before letting her down. He flipped on the CD player and slipped in the Dark Side of the Moon CD while he went about his nightly chores.

The next morning while he waited for Ashleigh he looked into the camera and flipped it the bird. Then he slipped in a mixed tape that he'd just created. There was a little Joan Jett, Summer Madness by Kool and the Gang and Us and Them because he knew that she was particularly fond of those tunes. He pulled out the mats and began his stretching.

Ashleigh came in and plopped down next to him.

"Good morning."

"Morning. Um, I brought you…" He passed her a thermos.

She accepted it curiously. "What is it?"

"It's a protein drink. You don't have to drink it if you don't…want it."

"No, I do. Thanks." She said quickly, not wanting to offend the nice man but truly not wanting a protein drink. They were nasty. She took a quick sip. She took another sip. "This is a protein drink?" It was good. "What's in it?"

"Protein powder, fruit; mango, pineapple, apple, oranges, strawberries...I wasn't sure which fruit you liked so I kind of made a medley."

"You invented this yourself?"

"Yep." He grabbed his thermos. "This is what I have for breakfast every morning. Well, mine has less fruit and more vegetables. But I have kind of a strange taste. Vegetables actually taste good to me."

"Me too." She said while smirking. "I like all food — which is my big problem."

He huffed. "Yeah you say you do, but do you like brussel sprouts?"

"Yes; baked as a casserole with sliced onions and cheese. It's very yummy."

"Asparagus?"

"On the grill with slight dusting of parmesan cheese."

His eyes lit up. "Eggplant?"

"Sauteed or roasted, but best on a veggie sandwich. Believe me Christopher...I like *all* food."

"You're a foodie?"

"Yes." She gave him a sincere nod. "I would even eat a cow's eyeball if it's sautéed in butter and garlic."

Christopher cracked up laughing. "I can't quite go that far, Ashleigh. Head cheese stops me cold. I once thought I saw an eyebrow in a slice of the stuff." He grimaced. Now it was her turn to laugh.

Christopher never found much of a reason to laugh. Sometimes he thought some of the guys told funny jokes and stories and he would chuckle along with them. But with Ashleigh he actually laughed. She was funny without even trying. Every day he would bring her a new smoothie so that she wouldn't have to make breakfast before their workout. And since she loved all fruits and vegetables he would blend strange combinations and have her guess them. One day it was green grapes, green apples, cucumbers and spinach. Another day it was carrots, fresh ginger, apples and pomegranate juice.

"You must spend a ton of money on this." She said as she enjoyed his latest invention; a grapefruit, radish and pineapple protein smoothie.

He shrugged. It cost a lot but he enjoyed creating something that tasted good enough to make her eyes roll up into her head. It was his big quest.

"You should let me give you some money for this." She said. She had offered before but he had quickly declined. They had been working out together for two weeks and Ashleigh actually understood what people were talking about when they claimed to be addicted to exercising. She looked forward to getting up every morning and getting to the gym. Her body was slow to look any differently, at least to her own eye although she had resorted to pulling out the smaller outfits that she had long ago outgrown and packed away.

She had even bought new warm up pants because once while doing jumping jacks her other pair had begun to slip down and she'd had to hold them up with one hand.

Lance and Kendra kept gushing over how much smaller she was but each night she pulled off her clothes and still saw a fat woman…

"You guys, you should meet Christopher." She said as they met for lunch. She had a chicken Ceasar salad with balsamic vinegar and oil dressing, no cheese.

"You mean the scary man in the basement?" Lance asked. "No thanks."

"He is not scary." She stabbed a chunk of chicken and shoved it into her mouth hungrily. "He is about the nicest guy I think I've ever met. I kind of want to invite him to lunch with us one day." He seemed kind of lonely to her. He never said it, but he wasn't married, no children and whenever she asked about his evening the only thing he ever said he did was play his guitar. He never mentioned any other people except his mother and father.

"And he works with Homeland Security?" Kendra asked with interest. "It'd be nice to have some connections in Homeland Security."

"Well, I suppose if you are planning a career in international terrorism." She swirled a tomato in the dressing and popped it into her mouth.

"They make good money."

"I'm sure." He certainly spent a ton on protein shakes. "He was telling me that he has to go out and bust drug dealers and gang members." Ashleigh found herself grimacing. "He doesn't like talking about it but it sounds dangerous."

"Did you ever find out about his face?" Lance asked. He was eating a bowl of gazpacho and Ashleigh kept eyeing it. She shook her head.

"I don't want to ask and he hasn't offered to tell. It's obvious that he has a hairlip, but the scar goes all the way up his forehead and into his scalp."

"Maybe he got hurt while he was on one of those dangerous missions." Kendra said. She stared at Lance's soup with interest, too. "Is that good?"

He nodded. "Want some?" Both women lifted their spoons and began eating his soup to his surprise. He leaned back in his chair and smiled in amusement.

"Rick and I are going away for the weekend."

"Ooo!" Kendra exclaimed.

"Romantic weekend?" Ashleigh asked.

His eyes rolled up in pleasure. "Romantic…most definitely romantic."

"He is good for you, Lance." Ashleigh said and sighed.

He placed his hand over hers. "You're going to find your Mr. Right, Ash."

"Ivan still asks about you…" Kendra said while spooning more of Lance's soup into her mouth. Ashleigh looked suddenly uncomfortable. "Damn, I can't get enough of this. It's so good."

Lance pulled his bowl away from her. "You are gaining all of the weight that Ashleigh is losing," he said. And then his eyes got big. Kendra glanced away guiltily.

"What?" Ashleigh asked while one of her friends kept staring and the other tried to avoid the stare.

"You're pregnant!" Lance accused.

"What?!" Ashleigh asked. "But when?"

"God, you bitches! You ruined the surprise. I was going to show you the ultrasound picture! Why did you have to go ruin it?!" She suddenly giggled happily and they hugged, knocking over Lance's glass of Sangria in the process.

"Oh my god, you're going to be a Mommy!" Ashleigh gushed as they patted at the spilt wine with napkins. "Well how many months are you?"

"I am five weeks."

"You've been pregnant five weeks and you haven't told us!" Lance screeched.

"I've only been certain two weeks!" She reached out and took her two best friend's hands. "You don't think I was going to hide my pregnancy for the full nine months, did you?"

Ashleigh smiled but something inside of her dropped. Lance had Rick and they were falling in love. Kendra was going to have a baby. When was it going to be her turn?

That night when she returned home from work, she slipped off her shoes, placed her jacket over the back of the dining room chair and curled up on her chez lounge still wearing her pencil skirt and silk blouse. She got up suddenly and slipped in Some Kind of Wonderful. She smiled as she watched Watts playing the drums.

I wish I was cool like Watts, tough like Watts. I wish I was anybody but me.

~***~

"Hey. You're kind of quiet." Christopher said, his accent heavy to Ashleigh's ears. She was sipping her smoothie in deep thought. She glanced up and smiled.

"Um…acai, cabbage and mango?"

He chuckled. "Not even close."

"Not even one?"

"Nope."

"I give up."

"Green apple, a tiny bit of watermelon, pears and green tea."

"Green tea?! That's cheating. Whoever heard of a green tea smoothie?"

He smiled. "It's good though, right?"

"Delicious." He stood and then helped her up. Whenever he gave her a hands up she was again amazed by his height, and of course his big hand swallowed hers. Being a fat woman next to a man that was feet taller than you was good for the ego. She felt dwarfed by Christopher.

"What's it like being so close to the sun?" She had asked him once. His charcoal grey eyes had twinkled.

"Amazing."

They went through their workout and when they got to the tenth rep she didn't even believe it. "We're done?"

"Done."

"No way…I'm still breathing."

"Maybe it's an indication that it's time to up the reps?"

"I'm game.…um, tomorrow?"

"Tomorrow is fine."

"Bye Christopher." His eyes followed her as she walked out of the room. Christopher headed to the security door grinning and humming and when it opened three guys were standing on the other side. The smile left his face.

"If this is about y'all damn bet, I'm not interested." He brushed past them.

"Beast. There is no bet."

"Hmph." He grunted and headed for the showers.

"Beast. Christopher!" He stopped and turned. All three men were standing there glaring at him. "What the hell are you waiting for? Ask her out for Christ sakes!" A slow flush ran up his neck and enveloped his face.

"What are you talking about?"

"Dude, you've been training her for a month. The girl likes you. Why else would she drink that shit you make every morning? And no girl works out five days a week!"

Christopher looked away. "Don't turn this into a game." He turned back to them with a cold look on his face. "This isn't a game." His heart was drumming in his chest and he was angry but unsure.

Carlos stepped forward. "There is no bet. We're all routing for you, Beast. That's all. Just ask her out…or else."

He looked at Carlos in confusion. The big man flexed his muscles. He was a foot shorter than Christopher. He looked at the other two guys. They were flexing their muscles, too.

"What in the hell do you mean, 'or else?'" Christopher liked each of the guys he worked with. But he had never been threatened by any of them.

"You got three days to make something happen." One of the men said. "Or we're going to make it happen for you."

Christopher's face paled. "You guys got way too much time on your hands…"

They gave him angry looks. "We know." And then walked away.

~***~

There was nothing much worse than 16 Marines with nothing better to do than to butt into his personal business. Christopher sat back in his armchair and drank a beer, something he seldom did. If they weren't lying about there being a bet, then this was worse than he thought. Because it meant that they would keep pushing and pushing until they were satisfied.

He groaned. They couldn't understand, they hadn't been in this same position before. He knew how it worked. He squeezed the half empty bottle and tried the shut away the memory. But it replayed despite his reluctance to relive it.

Debbie Roberts lived down the street from him down in Corbin. He knew her only in passing. She had something like ten brothers and sisters and it seemed that all she did was take care of the little ones. They were always running wild and Debbie would come to their house and ask if anyone had seen this or that one.

Sometimes she would look so tired. They'd catch the school bus which was all the way down at the bottom of the hill. It took a good fifteen minutes to walk it, worse was when you had to walk up it. You actually had no choice but to be in good shape if you lived on Cobb Mountain. Debbie was certainly built nice, even for a fourteen year old.

She didn't talk much either and kept to herself. There was no such thing as poor white trash when you lived on the mountain—everybody was poor. It wasn't a word he learned until they moved to Covington. But Debbie's family was poorer than poor.

One day they were walking up the hill and Debbie just sat down. They weren't walking together, just at the same time. But when he looked back and Debbie was still sitting on the ground he went back.

"You alright?"

She didn't move for a long time, then she squinted up at him and he remembered that she had dark brown eyes and blond eye brows and the fine blonde hairs around her face was damp with sweat. "Why should I get up? Why should I walk up the mountain, take care of my mama's kids, do my homework, walk down this hill the next day, sit in school where people talk down on me? Why should I do that?" There wasn't a tear in her eye and she was asking him an honest question and waiting for an honest answer.

He swallowed. "Because you ain't never going to get off this mountain if you don't."

Debbie had pulled herself up and walked up that hill…with him. And every day after she waited for him at her gatepost or he waited for her and they walked down it and then later in the afternoon they walked up it once again.

Then at school she started sitting next to him during open assembly. There wasn't much need to talk but it was nice that she sat near him. And when he thought that he was satisfied with her silent company, she changed it by asking him about his scars and she reached out and traced a finger down the long one that ran down from his forehead. He'd given her a surprised look. No one but family and doctors had ever touched his scars.

He'd explained about the cleft palate and though she didn't seem to completely understand she was satisfied with his answer. Later that day she came knocking on his door and asked if he wanted to walk with her to the store. He did.

And the next day when she knocked on the door carrying her school books they sat on the sun porch and did their homework together. And that is how he and Debbie Roberts became friends. They didn't talk a whole lot, it was mostly comfortable quiet.

"She likes you." His brother Walt had said. Walt was a year older and had a girlfriend that he had been seeing since summer. "Why are you being a baby about it? She likes you, Chris! You're like her only friend. Just ask her to be your girlfriend."

He'd blushed beet red. He thought about her all the time, he thought about her sad eyes and her long blond hair. He thought about her skinny elbows and her beautiful legs in cut off jeans.

But did she think about him?

"Just do it." Walt said. He gathered up his nerves and on Saturday when they walked down to the spring to bring back fresh water he'd reached out for her hand.

Debbie looked at him but didn't pull her hand out of his. "Debbie. Do you want to be my girlfriend?"

She had given him a confused look. "I am your friend Chris."

"No like..." He leaned in and kissed her and she'd touched her lips in surprise. Then he knew...Debbie didn't like him like that. Debbie had never even thought of him in those terms. She made up some excuse to go back to her house. Afterwards she slowly stopped coming around after school and he stopped seeking her out.

Not long after, they had moved up to Covington Kentucky where his Dad had gotten a job at the VA hospital. Debbie didn't even say goodbye to him. For years he wished that he had just kept his mouth shut and then he would have never lost her friendship. Even if he couldn't have her as his girl, he at least could have had her as his friend.

Ashleigh's friendship was about the most important thing to him right now, even though it had only been a month. She gave him something to look forward to each day. She made him laugh, she made him think. The guys could say 'go for it.' But he liked Ashleigh and he wasn't willing to risk losing her friendship by making the same mistake twice.

~***~

Ashleigh was looking at her roots in her mirror. She hadn't been to the hair salon in weeks and her nails had long since lost their overlay. She quickly pulled on jeans, but they were too loose and even with a belt they sagged. She pulled out a box of clothes that she'd packed away. She tried on three pairs before she found one that fit her snuggly. On a hunch she pulled the jeans off and looked at the tag in back.

Size 16.

She gasped and nearly choked. Size 16?! She'd lost three dress sizes! How long has it been since she first stepped into the gym? Three months. She couldn't wait to tell Christopher! Things were happening faster because of him. She had to do something nice for him!

She paced while she thought about what she could do to show her appreciation. She would invite him to lunch with her, Lance and Kendra. He was her friend and she wanted her other friends to know just how cool Christopher was.

Ashleigh ran to her closet and began ripping down her clothes. They were getting packed up. She forgot all about going to the hair salon and about getting her nails done.

She didn't even want to buy new clothes. No, Ashleigh wanted to dig out her OLD clothes! The ones that she hoped to one day fit into again. Now 'one day' had arrived!

~***~

"Christopher, guess what?"

He looked up from where he had adjusted the mats. "What?"

"I'm down three dress sizes!"

He smiled crookedly at her, his eyes twinkling. "Now do you believe me? I told you you were getting smaller."

She clapped her hands and jumped up and down. "I believe you. I believe you Christopher! Now are you going to help me celebrate, or what?"

He paused. "Celebrate?" His smile faltered.

"I want you to meet my two best friends. We go out for lunch together at least once a week. Will you go with us?"

"With…your friends?"

"Yes."

"I'm not much of a people person."

She swallowed. "Because…of your scars?"

He nodded.

She inhaled and decided to plow forward. "Those aren't just from your cleft palate, is it?" She held her breath hoping that her question hadn't embarrassed him.

He reached up and touched his upper lip. "I have a bilateral cleft. It's a lot tougher to correct surgically. But I also had some problems with the way my skull came together...or didn't. They tried to fix that...badly. I look like Frankenstein's monster." He smiled slightly.

"Can...cosmetic surgery help?"

"Yes."

"Why-?"

"How much good is that going to do, honestly? I'll never be an Adonis. And I'm a jarhead. The time it would take for me to get surgery just so that I'll still be ugly seems hardly worth it."

He turned away and sat down and proceeded to go through his stretching. She'd upset him and it crushed her. It made her sound as if she thought he should get surgery and that's not what she had meant at all. After nearly six weeks of knowing this man his scars were just an afterthought to her anymore. Most times she forgot about them...or they seemed so much a part of the kind man that she knew that they were no longer ugly to her. It was just Christopher's face.

She sat down opposite him.

"Christopher. I apologize." She thought about the way it always made her feel when people with good intentions told her that she needed to lose weight in order to be truly pretty. "I didn't mean to insinuate that you should change anything about yourself. You are a wonderful man just the way you are."

He met her eyes. His brow knit and he steeled his resolve. Maybe...maybe it wasn't like Debbie Roberts.

"Christopher, please come to lunch with us. Will you say yes?"

He warmed and then slowly nodded. "Yes."

She smiled in relief and then leaned forward and gave him a quick hug. Christopher's hands came up to lightly touch her back. "I realize it's hard for you to meet people. But you don't have to be nervous about meeting my friends. They are good people. And I...took the liberty of explaining about your scars. So you see, you don't have to worry. You don't have to be lonely, Christopher. You got me, okay?"

Something in his body relaxed, a bit of the wall he had constructed around himself began to crumble. He nodded.

"You gotta meet my friend Kendra! She is freaking awesome. She is the matchmaker of the gods. So I'm going to give you fair warning, she will probably try to find you a girlfriend. Let her work her magic on you. I know blind dates are hard. I hate 'em too. But believe me when I tell you that if she tells you she'll find you a love interest she will do it."

Christopher's soul sank to his feet. He looked at Ashleigh and tried to hide the pain in his heart. "So if she's such a good matchmaker why didn't she find you a match?" He knew that she was single, knew that she'd just broken up with the guy named DeAngelo.

She looked down at her hands. "I guess…" Then she looked at Christopher. "I guess because I'm still in love with my ex." His eyes became guarded and he cleared his throat as he built the wall back up around his feelings.

"We better get started with the workout."

She smiled again. "Right."

~***~

The look on The Beasts face left no doubt to his mood as he stalked towards the locker room. No one met his eyes but he wasn't fooled! He was pissed that this part of his life was broadcast for their enjoyment. Now maybe they would understand and leave him the hell alone!

He pushed the door of the locker room open and it almost tore from the hinges. He stalked to his locker and the guys present glanced at him; all conversation stopped. He stripped out of his clothes and walked nude into the showers. His massive toned body rippled with unspent adrenalin. He scrubbed his body and hair and then silently re-dressed in fatigues.

He jammed his dirty clothes into his bag and then pulled his cap low over his head and went to the security room. Roddy looked up quickly from the report he was running.

"Hey, Beast," He said politely.

Christopher looked at him. "I want to punch something."

Roddy looked away quickly. "I'll leave you alone then…"

~***~

When Christopher got home, he walked right past Maggie who purred and followed at his feet. He sighed and then bent down and rubbed her ears gently.

"Sorry, Mags. I'm not mad at you." She leaned into his fingers in contentment. "Did you miss me, girl?" He stood and placed his things neatly in the closet, popped in a John Coltrane disc and then checked his messages. His mother had called.

"Son, this is Mom." He smiled, as if he couldn't tell. "I hate to tell you this over the phone but Aunt Lonnie passed away today. It was quiet and she wasn't in any pain. Uncle Ray was there and the kids." Christopher blew out a deep breath and sank down into one of the dining room chairs.

"The funeral is going to be Saturday down on the mountain. The funeral is going to be at the white church at two. We goin' to meet up at Aunt Lonnie and Uncle Ray's house early…before. They want you to be a pall bearer." His mother sighed again. Aunt Lonnie wasn't his mother's aunt, she was his mother's sister. He knew that she was holding it together for everyone else because that is what Mom always did. Aunt Lonnie was her oldest sister and she always said that she was more like a mother than a sister.

Christopher listened to the rest of the message and then quickly dialed his mother. His throat felt tight and his eyes stung with unshed tears. Aunt Lonnie had put evil smelling salves on his scars and had rubbed them in order to break up the keloids. His memories of her were mixed in with images of surgeries, soothing hands against his skin and her deeply accented voice telling them all stories about her and Mama's childhood.

He wiped his eyes and cleared his voice when she

answered on the first ring. "Are you alright, Mom?" They talked for nearly half an hour and Christopher promised that he would be over to the house bright and early Saturday morning so that they could drive down together. He hung up feeling anguished and useless.

~***~

Ashleigh's phone rang and it was a testament to the passage of time that she was surprised to hear DeAngelo's voice on the other end. Her heart dropped a little. She had been feeling so good, thinking about lunch with her friend's and her weight loss and now he had to call and stir up feelings that she wanted to forget about.

"Hi Ash, Baby."

She exhaled and looked around, tension evident on her face. "What do you want?"

"I'd like to come over and talk to you."

She was already shaking her head. "No-"

"Ash, I left Shaunda."

"What?" Her heart literally stopped beating in her chest.

"I left her. Baby, I can't stop thinking about you. When I saw you in the hospital—it killed me. I realized that I'm not prepared to lose you." Her mouth went completely dry and her legs began to shake. "Baby...I love you so much and I miss you and I'll do anything to fix this. I want to see you."

"Okay." Her voice cracked.

"I'm on my way." He hung up the phone and she sat staring into space. And then she remembered, he was on his way over now! Ashleigh leaped up and hurried into her room for something to wear that would show all her new curves. After changing into jeans and a t-shirt that hugged her boobs and flatter belly she agonized over her hair with her dark roots. God, she'd let herself go!

She was touching up her makeup when the doorbell rang and her heart began racing. Yet she walked to the door calmly and opened it. God...there he was. He was so damn beautiful. His chocolate eyes blinked as they scanned her new smaller body.

"Jesus...Ashleigh...you lost..." She beamed and opened the door for him to enter. He leaned in and kissed her cheek. "You look incredible." She shivered at the contact of his soft lips. The look in his eyes at this very moment was worth every sore muscle, every hunger pang, every drop of sweat. It was the look of desire and she didn't think she'd ever see it again.

"So. You and Shaunda are no more."

"I moved out yesterday." His hands crept to her hips and then began to glide over her butt. He grinned lasciviously. "I miss this." He said as he cupped her buttocks.

Ashleigh's brow creased and she pushed his hands away, offended at his familiarity. "Uh uh." She said. "You don't got it like that anymore. You can't just walk in here like you still got *this*. I didn't say that I was going to take you back, DeAngelo!"

He nodded and took a step back. "I'm sorry. You're right. Tell me what I need to do." She crossed her hands across her chest and turned away from him, still feeling faintly disgusted at the way he had just touched her.

She turned and looked at the fine man that stood before her; had dropped her for another woman without a warning or a second thought, and now has left his wife of less than five months.

He was such a loser.

She didn't love him. If she was foolish enough to take a man like him back, he would just do the same thing over and over. And she would deserve it. Shaunda now knew what it felt like to be her.

She looked down with a bitter smile. It didn't bring her any joy. They were just two women that had loved the wrong man.

She walked to the door and held it open. "I change my mind. I don't want this."

He gave her a surprised look. "What? Ashleigh-"

"Good luck. Goodbye. And lose my number."

He didn't make a move to leave. "Ashleigh, I just left my wife for you!"

Ashleigh raised her brow. "Maybe it's not too late for you to get her back. It's certainly too late for you to get me back." She held the door open wider for him.

His expression dropped as he searched her face. "You've changed."

She met his eyes. "I have. If…" She thought about her next words carefully. "If you ever really did love me, then…please walk away. And don't come back."

He looked at the ceiling and then shuffled slowly to the door. He looked at her, searching perhaps for the old Ashleigh that always took him back, that loved him unconditionally. But that Ashleigh was no longer present. He walked out the door.

She shut it and locked it and then let out a loud sigh.

She remembered a time when just the sight of DeAngelo brought her joy. When she couldn't wait to set eyes on him, to talk to him, when being in his presence made her feel special. She realized suddenly that feeling was still there but--not directed at DeAngelo. It's the way she felt for Christopher.

Ashleigh took a deep breath, an almost shocked breath. She woke up each morning anxious to see him. He made her laugh, he motivated her, he accepted her. He didn't give a damn if she was fat, if her roots were dark or if she went without a stitch of makeup and was dripping in stinky sweat. She smiled. Christopher…

CHAPTER 5

The next day Ashleigh smoothed her shirt down and then pushed open the door to the gym. She paused and smiled at the music. "Isley Brothers; Footsteps in the Dark."

Christopher looked up and gave her a crooked grin. "An oldie but a goodie." He was sprawled out on the mat already stretching.

Oh my god…He wore a grey shirt and lose athletic shorts. His body was amazing! His thighs were so thick that they rivaled hers! Only his was thick with muscles and not fat. He leaned forward and reached for his feet. His powerful arms bulged with tight muscles. She felt herself blush when her eyes fell on the package between his legs. It was a nice package. A very nice package.

"Ashleigh, are you going to watch me do all of the stretching?" He asked while giving her a curious look.

She jumped, her face burning bright red, and went to where he had set the pink thermos that he always used for her smoothie. His thermos was black and his concoction was not nearly as tasty as he made hers. She carried it back to the mat and sat down spread eagle opposite him. Now it was no trouble to touch her toes. Her belly didn't get in her way any longer. She took her first drink and he watched her expectantly.

"Mmm. Good. Green apple, cucumber, carrots and ginger."

He gave her an impressed look. "And parsley. Good! I can't believe you figured it out." Her eyes lingered on his lips and the way the scars swirled around in an intricate design of plains and valleys, of textures that should be explored with the tip of her tongue…

"Um," she said while shaking herself mentally. "Lunch is tomorrow."

He nodded and his eyes drifted from her. She worried that he would back out. "You're still going to come, right?"

He gave her that crooked smile again. Oh god, he had the sweetest smile. "Yeah. It's just that I'm kind of out of it. My aunt passed away yesterday."

"Oh Christopher! I'm so sorry. Were you close to her?"

"Yep. Our family is very close knit."

She hadn't heard much about his family other than that he was born in a country town and had grown up on a mountain, though not a big mountain like the Smokeys, but a small quaint place where everybody knew everybody else.

"I'm going to go down home on Saturday for the funeral."

"When will you be back?"

"The same day."

"Okay."

She was happy that he wouldn't be gone long. The thought of working out without him was unimaginable.

When Ashleigh reached her office later she informed her two friends that they would have a guest for lunch tomorrow.

Kendra gave her a worried look. It was her choice of restaurants this week. "Oh, you said he was shy. Maybe we should go some place quiet?"

Ashleigh nodded. "I think he would appreciate that." She thought about the way he ducked his head and wore his hoodie covering his face until he had gotten to know her better. It saddened her that he felt he had to do that out in public. She tried to think back to a time before she had accepted his looks and recalled being shocked by his face. She'd thought he was ugly, it shamed her. She couldn't see anything ugly about him now. When she looked at his face she just saw his sweet crooked smile and his light and dark eyes that twinkled with humor.

"Why do you have that goofy smile on your face?" Lance asked suspiciously. "When was the last time you talked to 'that married man?"

She quickly hid her guilty look. "Ah! I was going to tell you about that..."

Kendra narrowed her eyes. "You did not go and call that fool, did you?"

"I did not! He called me-"

"Oh my god!" Lance threw up his hands. "When will you ever learn-?!"

"He left Shaunda!"

"So?" Kendra said.

"I know! That's how I feel." Her friends watched her expectantly. "I thought...I don't know what I thought. Maybe I just wanted to erase away the feeling of being rejected. Maybe I have no concept of the true meaning of love. Maybe I am just shallow enough to think that love is...based on the outer package." She gave them a sincere look. "But I don't think that anymore. I don't think that at all." She smiled. "I told him to get to stepping."

Lance clapped his hands. "Good for you."

~***~

Christopher was not looking forward to lunch with Ashleigh's friends. They really looked sophisticated; everyday they dressed upscale corporate. It wasn't a matter of money, Christopher made a great living. But he was a country boy that felt most comfortable in jeans and t-shirts.

He'd watched them through the cameras as they left in the evenings or went out for lunch. They laughed and were very comfortable with each other, that was obvious. He was much more reserved, at least until he knew people.

He was supposed to meet them in the lobby in an hour. And that was another thing; he had never been in the lobby during the day except on the weekends doing sweeps. He fingered his baseball cap; right Christopher. He'd make a great impression wearing this with a pair of dress pants!

TK came into the locker room and he glanced at him warily. The black man held up his hands innocently.

"The Little Trooper asked you out."

"It ain't like that. We're just friends."

"She is fine, and she asked you out. You need to make that move, Beast."

Christopher gave him an evil look; whether it was because of his observation of Ashleigh's fine-ness or if it was because he resented his interference was unclear to the big man.

"Butt out TK. And tell the rest of them that I'm not playing their game!" He pushed past him and TK pushed back. Christopher spun with a growl. Despite his height he moved with the agility of a runner. He picked the shorter, but equally muscular man up by his shirt front. "Back off!!!"

TK clipped him in the chin with his fist, which only served to annoy Christopher more than it hurt him. He growled and slammed the man into the lockers with a bang. It brought several men into the room and when they saw what was going on they watched with interest.

TK boxed his ears and Christopher released him and drove his shoulder into TK's gut.

"Hmph!" The two men gripped each other, neither releasing the other.

"What are you going to say to her?" TK grunted out as they spun each other around the room and tripped over benches only to scramble up to smash into more lockers.

"I don't know!" Christopher grunted through gritted teeth.

"You better not…MPH!!...sit there like a damned lump!"

They were clawing at each other on the floor. "I don't know what to talk about!" TK jammed his elbow into the big man's gut and Christopher grimaced. He reached for TK's neck.

"Not my throat!" TK bellowed. "My wife is going to kill me if she sees your hand prints around my neck!" Christopher released his grip on the man's neck and slammed his fist into his eye. He smirked when TK cursed. But then the other man head butted him and damn near knocked him out!

"Damnit, TK! I got a date in less than a damned hour and you're going to bust my head open?!"

"Sorry…I got carried away." He held up his hands innocently and Christopher held his head and glowered at his friend. He made sure his head wasn't bleeding and then he pulled himself up to his feet and gave TK a hand up. Several guys got the room straightened while Christopher went to the mirror to check the lump forming on his forehead.

"You're still beautiful." Carlos said while slapping him on the back playfully. Christopher shrugged his hand away and then splashed his red face. He stared at the water as it slowly ran down the drain.

"Well what the hell am I supposed to talk about?" He asked out loud.

"You don't have to think of a topic!" Someone said. "Just don't sit there looking like a dumbass."

"Ask them what they do."

Christopher looked up. "I already know what they do."

"That's only because you're perving them." It was their word for watching people on the security camera.

Christopher blushed. "No. Ashleigh told me what they do."

"Pretend that she didn't tell you." TK was rubbing his jaw. His eye was already swelling. The guys gave him advice while he sniffed his armpits for freshness. Yeah, he was still good after his shower this morning. Someone handed him a bottle of cologne and he accepted it as if it were poison. He opened the bottle and sniffed. Not too bad. He put on a bit.

He stripped out of his fatigues and pulled on tan slacks and a white button down shirt. He felt a little less nervous after burning off his nervous energy with TK and the guys were actually giving him good advice. He guessed they knew that this was the closest thing that he'd ever had to a date.

Bruce stepped into the locker room and stared at all of his men. He didn't have to open his mouth, the party dispersed and everyone got back to their stations. He eyed Christopher and grunted.

"Take as much time as you want for lunch." Then he turned and left.

"Thanks, Sir!" Christopher called after him. He looked at the baseball cap and then placed it back in his locker. He blew out a tense breath and glanced at himself in the mirror. "Let's rock and roll."

Ashleigh, Lance and Kendra headed for the elevators to the lobby. She was only half listening to Kendra's description of morning sickness. Christ the sound of her retching was enough to fuel her diet for the remainder of the woman's pregnancy!

"We cannot have Mexican!" Kendra exclaimed. "I can't stand the smell of meat right now."

"What?" Lance said. "You can't stand the smell of meat? Earth to Kendra; every restaurant we go to will serve meat."

Kendra rubbed her forehead. "Please, Lance, don't talk about it. Please, nobody order meat."

Lance smiled. "If you make me the baby's godfather I'll do whatever you say."

She peeked at him. "God Uncle?"

"Close enough."

Ashleigh gave her a nervous look. "You want me to tell Christopher not to order meat for lunch?"

Kendra nodded apologetically and gave her puppy dog eyes. "Or…I won't be responsible for the bad thing that might happen at the table."

Ashleigh sighed. "Fine." They reached the lobby and waited off to the side. Ashleigh wrung her hands anxiously. Lance scowled at her.

"Ash relax. What do you think? That we're going to make your friend feel—HOLY SHIT!" She turned and saw Christopher coming from the back corridor. He must have come up from the elevators that he'd used to take her to the nurse's station.

Holy shit was right. He looked AWESOME. She just stared open mouthed as he approached.

"You never said he was the size of a TREE!" Kendra whispered urgently.

Ashleigh's eyes drank in every inch of him. She'd never seen Christopher dressed in anything but workout clothes and once in fatigues. His muscles filled out his perfect body in a way that made her feel breathless. He watched her as he approached, his charcoal grey eyes; light and dark never leaving her face.

"He makes Rick look like a toddler. His neck is as big as his head." Lance said under his breath. She resisted the urge to jab him with her elbow.

"Hi Christopher," she said with a bright smile once he reached the little group. Her heart was thumping like crazy.

He nodded shyly. "Hi Ashleigh." She made introductions and he shook each of her friend's hands. "Guys this is Christopher Jameson; Lt Christopher Jameson."

He looked amused and smiled. "Christopher will do just fine. I hope I didn't keep y'all waiting." He said in a slow country drawl. Kendra craned her neck up at him but she had a smile on her face as she did it.

"Not at all. We just got here. It's nice to finally meet you Christopher."

"Ashleigh said you're stationed in the subbasement. She said there's an entire battalion of Marines down there." Lance said.

Ashleigh blushed when Christopher glanced at her. Crap, she hoped she hadn't spilled some national secret or anything.

"I didn't quite say that…"

Christopher nodded. "It's pretty close to that." The group headed out the door and as Ashleigh looked up she realized that every single person in the lobby was staring at Christopher. Didn't people have better manners than to just stare like that?! Of course she had to consider that who wouldn't stare at a fine-ass giant of a man?

Kendra drove because her truck was big enough for a 6'5" man since her husband was an ex-football player himself. Ashleigh explained that due to her friend's 'delicate condition' she's requested that no one eat meat. Christopher was a good sport and readily agreed.

When they got to the restaurant he politely congratulated her on her pregnancy and as he scanned the menu he asked her what her thoughts were on bacon. Kendra nodded her consent and he ordered a BLT and a bowl of gumbo.

Lance ordered clam chowder and Kendra's eye lids began to flutter and she quickly told him no. He changed to gumbo. Ashleigh was easy, she had tuna steak and a salad. Kendra ordered the house salad. As they waited for the food to arrive Kendra looked at Christopher. Ashleigh appreciated that she looked him straight in his face; something that she hadn't even done until she'd been around him for several days.

"What's it like working for Homeland Security?" Ashleigh smiled knowing that her friend was networking. "It's not classified or anything is it?"

He smiled crookedly. "No, not classified—at least not completely." He cleared his throat and glanced at a couple that openly watched them. "It's actually very interesting. There is a lot of traveling when we're not posted. I can't really say too much…"

Lance looked intrigued. "But you've brought down terrorists, right?"

"Right."

"But you can't say who, right?"

He shrugged good-naturedly. "Mostly drug dealers."

"Drug dealers?" Lance looked confused.

"Drugs are the biggest way that terrorism is funded, that and guns."

"Oh!" Both Kendra and Lance responded.

Something occurred to Ashleigh; Christopher would go out on missions…dangerous missions. Her smile slipped and Christopher glanced at her, his brow furrowing in brief concern before he turned his attention back to the conversation. She wondered how often he had to go out on these missions.

"Christopher," she asked hesitantly, "how long are the missions?"

"They can vary. Two months is the norm. We start with briefings and then engagement and then debriefing."

She stared at him, reality hitting home. He went out and risked his life. "How often do you get these missions?"

"Well...that varies, too. We don't know when we'll get one. It's been a while and we're kind of antsy."

"Antsy?" Lance asked.

He nodded. "We're a...physical bunch. We'd be out in the field twenty-four seven if we could. Some have wives and such and I'm sure that part is hard, but we look forward to actual engagement." Christopher glanced at Ashleigh. "I do enjoy my time in the subbasement but others start going stir crazy."

"It's dangerous," Kendra said, "but thankfully we have guys like you that put yourselves out there for our country." Ashleigh's brow furrowed.

Their food came and they ate and made easy conversation, mostly centered around Christopher which kept him actively involved. He liked Ashleigh's friends. He didn't like that every single person in the restaurant stared at them, or whispered about them. He was happy that the rest of them ignored it. And as he talked easily with Ashleigh's friends he realized that he had no reason to be nervous. They were like her; good people.

When they returned to work he knew that all of the cameras were on them. He shook Lance and Kendra's hands and promised that he'd join them again some time. Ashleigh lingered with him in the lobby.

"Thanks for coming with us."

"Thanks for inviting me." They looked at each other and Christopher decided that he would just ask her. He would ask her on a date.

"Ashleigh,"

"Yes?"

The words froze in throat at the look of curiosity on her face. "I...better get back. I'll see you tomorrow."

"See you tomorrow, Christopher."

He nodded and headed for the elevators, cursing himself for being such a chicken. What if he lost her friendship because he wanted more? He didn't want to do that. Ashleigh watched him walk away.

~***~

The ride down to Corbin Kentucky was quiet. It was just him, Mom and Dad. His father had suffered a stroke a few years back and often times became confused. He had his lucid moments though and thankfully today was one of them.

Christopher's brothers and sisters had decided to meet at Uncle Ray's and he wasn't looking forward to the sad circumstances for a family reunion. He'd just been to Cobb Hill a few weeks before and every time he drove through the winding mountain roads he felt a sick sense of loss as well as joy at the memories of his childhood here.

He pulled up in front of Uncle Ray's A-frame house and let Mom and Dad out while he drove a ways down the road in order to park. It seemed that everybody on the mountain was gathered at the little house. Picnic tables had been set out along with folding chairs.

Several of his nieces and nephews ran up to him greeting him with hugs. They wanted to play football but he told them they'd get dirty. They headed away looking dejected and he called out that he'd race them down to the spring once he said his hellos. Then their faces brightened and he remembered when he was a kid and they had gatherings like this and it seemed like the most tedious thing in the world. Most of them didn't know Aunt Lonnie and the youngest ones had never even met her.

He sighed and shook hands and gave kisses to people he hadn't seen in years. His brothers and sisters came up and asked how Dad was doing and he discussed work for a bit and then he sought out Uncle Ray to give his condolences.

Ray was in the house and rocking in an old chair surrounded by some of his adult children. On his way into the room Christopher shook hands with everyone and received good natured ribbings about his size. Uncle Ray's face broke into a huge smile and he stood and gave him a hug. He was so thin now. Back when he was a kid, Ray used to be the one that towered over him, now it was the other way around and the man seemed so frail. It made Christopher sad, yet his uncle didn't appear sad at his own loss.

"Pull up a chair." Someone found Christopher a stool and he sat down in it next to his uncle. "You still in the Marines?"

"Yes, sir. I'm in it for life."

"Hmmm. Life planned out at the age of...how old are you?"

"Twenty-five."

"Twenty-five….I had three kids by the time I was twenty-five." He squinted at Christopher. "You ain't got any kids do you?"

Christopher blushed. "No, sir."

"And why is that?" He asked with a serious frown. "You ain't using that scar as an excuse?" He said while gesturing in the general direction of Christopher's face. The younger man's expression darkened. Excuse? And it wasn't just a scar, for Christ sakes! His face was deformed!

"I wasn't the prettiest man around but I still got a beauty in your Aunt Lonnie."

Knowing that it was the saddest day of his Uncle's life, Christopher bit his tongue. But he wanted to lash out and tell him that he had no idea what it was like to live in his face. Not the prettiest man around? How about living with the skull and face of an albino gorilla!

"Pretty men have women that drop into their laps. But men like us have to make it work for us."

Us.

He cut his eyes at his Uncle. Uncle Ray wasn't the best looking in the world but he'd hardly thought of that in all his life. He was just Uncle Ray. Now Christopher looked at the man that was almost as tall as him, body bent and stopped now with age. He had a nose like a squash. But he also had a smile that lit up the room and he smiled easily…even today.

Christopher allowed his anger to drift away as he listened to his Uncle speak. The older man's eyes looked distant and a soft smile appeared on his thin lips. "Lonnie used to go with a boy that ended up playing pro baseball. I thought she was the most beautiful girl in the world. Maybe not to some, but to me she was an Angel."

Ray's kids quietly listened to their Dad speak. Christopher glanced at the floor but he listened just as intently. "Why would she want somebody like me when she can have anybody she wanted? But I knew something that the pretty boy didn't." Christopher looked up at his Uncle.

"Women drop into their arms and they don't have to work for it. They don't have to learn to be funny, sensitive, a good listener and a good friend. And that's why we always got the edge." Uncle Ray focused on Christopher.

"You've developed your edge, ain't you boy?" Uncle Ray smiled. "Never mind me, Christopher." The old man's eyes drifted to a picture of Aunt Lonnie and his smile never left his face. Christopher sat with him a while longer and then stood and placed his hand on his Uncle's thin shoulders before leaving the room.

Christopher jammed his hands into his pockets as he thought about Uncle Ray's words. It seemed true; about having an edge. But he didn't think that even with this so-called-edge, he'd be able to get Ashleigh to fall out of love with her ex and in love with him.

Just as he promised, Christopher played with the kids for a while and then it was time for the funeral. They climbed into the car. There were two limos; for Uncle Ray, and his kids and grandkids. They headed to the white church;

named that because it was built of wood timbers and whitewashed. The red church was brick and they did things a bit differently; like speaking in tongues. The white church is where they had their family plot. He'd have to visit his brother Walt's grave after Aunt Lonnie's funeral. His older brother had died in a car accident at the age of eighteen. Everything was shit back then; losing Walt, moving to Covington where people made him feel like a freak, and not having his best friend Debbie.

His mom was stoic during the funeral service. He held her hand but she didn't allow one tear to fall from her glistening eyes. He wanted to tell her that it was alright to cry and that he knew that she'd always had to be strong. But instead he just squeezed her hands gently.

They walked the casket to the plot and he took the brunt of the weight. The casket weighed a ton! He thought his cousin Bobby was going to stroke out. After the internment, everyone went back to the church for a fried chicken dinner while his family lingered at Walt's grave for a while. He stayed even after they all went back inside.

He saw a woman watching him from the church stairs and he sighed and looked away. But then he saw her coming towards him and he took a second look at her, finding something familiar…

Debbie Roberts.

She still looked exactly like the fifteen year old girl that had broken his heart so many years ago. She was much too skinny and still had knobby elbows. Her blonde hair was pulled back into a bun but he could still see that curls outlined her face—just the way it did when she was a kid. She looked just as tired and her brown eyes seemed unsure. She smiled slightly.

"Hi Chris."

"Debbie Roberts."

"Well, it's Debbie McMichaels now."

"McMichaels? You married Keegan McMichaels?"

"No, Derrick."

Derrick was way older than them. "Oh, congratulations."

She nodded sheepishly. "Thanks, we have a little boy; Derrick Jr."

"How old is he?"

"Four."

He nodded and offered her a slight smile.

"You're looking really good, Chris." He shrugged almost imperceptivity. "I hear that you joined the military."

"Yeah. I joined right out of high school."

"I—" Debbie rubbed the palms of her hands nervously down her skirt. "I was hoping that I'd catch you. You were up here a few weeks ago but I didn't get to you in time to say hi."

"Oh. I didn't stay too long. It's a long drive back home. So you stayed on the mountain?"

"I did. As I got older I realized that it wasn't quite as hideous as I had once thought. Besides I want DJ to be brought up in a place where he can run and play without the city swallowing him up." She smiled suddenly. "Remember how we used to run all over the mountain? You always said you were going to be a track star but I thought you'd be a football player. You still don't much care for football?"

"No, it doesn't do much for me." All his life he'd heard comments about him and football. People took it for granted that he'd play some type of sport. But he always turned down the offers. It just wasn't what he wanted to do.

He shifted his weight. "Well, I guess I better head back in-" He said.

"Chris, remember that time you kissed me?"

He hid his grimace. "I recollect that you ran away and stopped hanging out with me."

She rubbed her neck. "I always wanted to tell you how badly I felt about that. It's still something that haunts me."

Crap. She wanted to come to terms with her own sense of guilt. He rubbed his fingers through his short hair, lightly scratching his scalp with his short nails. He was about to make up some statement about the past being in the past when she continued to speak.

"I had the biggest crush on you, Chris. That's what I've wanted to tell you. And I didn't turn away from you because of your hairlip." She looked down. "When you kissed me I didn't know how to deal with it. My mother's boyfriend used to kiss me and well...I never told anybody. But I wanted to tell you that being friends with you made things better." Christopher blinked his eyes, his mouth parting. "It gave me a place to go so that I wasn't at the house and you made me feel safe."

She tried to smile but her eyes were too pained for it to look real. "I know I hurt you when I ran off. But I didn't know how to deal with it. And then your family moved away and I couldn't ever say I was sorry. But I wanted you to know that..." She swallowed. "the only good memories I have as a kid is when I was with you. And you saved my life Chris; and I mean that literally. And...I'm really sorry for what I did."

"Debbie...Oh god...why didn't you tell me? I would have..." His stomach felt like it had dropped to his feet. But anger was slowly blossoming inside of him.

"You were my friend, and that's what I needed." She smiled then and this time it touched her eyes. "I remember running with you in the mountains, and getting water from the spring, and lying in the grass looking at the clouds. And those are good memories and I want to thank you."

He reached out slowly and let out a deep sigh as he pulled her into his arms and hugged her. She clung to him and then pulled back and looked up into his face.

"Did you ever get married, Chris? Did you ever meet a girl?"

He sighed. "No. I was too shy."

"Nobody but me knew you were shy, Chris." He watched her quietly. "In school they all thought you were too cool to bother with them. You never looked scared, you just looked like...you didn't care. It made you very cool."

He laughed bitterly. "Right."

"I know you cared, Chris. I'm saying that no one else did."

He stared at her for a long time and then touched her chin so that she looked him right in the eye. "What ever happened to your mother's boyfriend?"

"He died a few years back; drunken accident."

"How long did he hurt you?"

"The funny thing is, Chris; he stopped when I started being friends with you. I believe that he thought I'd tell you."

"I wish to hell you had."

She shook her head. "I could hardly even tell myself."

He hugged her again. "I'm sorry Debbie. I'm sorry that we lost our friendship."

"Me too, Chris." She pulled out of his arms and then she quickly stood on her tiptoes and gave him a brief kiss.

"I better get home. But I'm happy I got a chance to see you." She walked away and then turned and waved.

"Me too, Debbie." He called. *Me too*.

~***~

Christopher glanced up nervously when Ashleigh walked into the room. She always came in looking full of energy and ready to tackle the workout without complaints.

"Good morning. I know people always ask stupid things like, 'How was the funeral.' But how was the funeral?"

He grinned. "It was actually a very nice funeral as far as those things go. I got to see a lot of family that I hadn't seen in a long time. And I had a long talk with my Uncle Ray—it was his wife that passed. I also got to see an old friend. How was your weekend?"

She made a face, reached for her thermos and then plopped down across from him to begin her stretching. "Boring."

He cleared his throat and untwisted the top off his thermos as if in deep thought, or perhaps stalling for time. Finally he just looked at her. "Ashleigh, I was wondering if you might want to have dinner with me...sometime." There! He'd said it. He felt nervous sweat beads begin to form on his brow.

"Okay."

Christopher blinked. She said okay? Did she hear him? She just said, okay...

"Okay?"

She nodded and her eyes were bright and big and beautiful. He smiled.

"Okay." He nodded once and they continued stretching.

When Ashleigh left the gym room she couldn't wipe the pleased smile from her face. She sighed and entered the office and faced her two friends.

"Christopher and I are going on a date."

Kendra and Lance exchanged brief looks. "Well it's about time." Kendra said.

"It was pretty obvious that you're crushing on him." Lance said. "Does this mean that you'll stop saying 'Christopher this and Christopher that?' all damned day?"

Ashleigh's eyes bugged out. "Crush? You are crazy. I mean…I like him but that is far from a crush…"

Kendra patted her belly and looked miserable. "You were making goo goo eyes at him all during lunch the other day."

She turned red. "I mean, so what if I am crushing on him a little. Is it a big deal?" She looked expectantly at each of her friend's; especially Kendra.

Lance rolled his eyes. "As long as it means you're over DeAngelo then I'm pleased as punch. Besides…he's got a damn nice body."

"Hell yeah…" Kendra said. "He is…scary looking with the scars, and I'm not sure what was up with the lump on his head, but it's obvious that he's a really nice guy."

Ashleigh smiled. "I forget about those scars. Well maybe that's not true…" She began to feel warm. It wasn't that she forgot about them, necessarily, but found herself wanting to run her fingertips over them and then her tongue…She gushed and caught Lance scowling at her.

"God, you need a cold shower."

Kendra stared at her with half narrowed eyes. "You are nasty. I know what you're thinking."

Ashleigh shook her head in denial but then ducked her head and hurried to her office in embarrassment.

CHAPTER 6

Christopher took the good natured ribbing because he really had no choice. But at least he had avoided whatever plan they had created in their idle time to get him and Ashleigh together. He ran his reports, did his sweeps and transported the prisoners all with a goofy smile on his face. Was he the cool guy? The idea made him chuckle out loud several times. His shyness scared people away...

And poor Debbie. Good thing that child molesting asshole was already dead or he'd kill him. He actually wished that he was alive so that he could torture the bastard and THEN kill him. Beast popped his neck and several prisoners were unsure of what to make of the giant, scarred, guard that smirked one minute and scowled the next. One thing was for certain; the sight of him alone assured that none of them would be stepping out of line.

That night Christopher stopped at the grocers. He could take Ashleigh out...but why do that when he could have her all to himself if he cooked dinner for her? He picked out the things he wanted to make and then he went home and dusted although he was fairly neat due to his military training.

That night when he got on the treadmill, it wasn't the mountains that he saw but the sway of Ashleigh's hips when she walked and the smile that she easily flashed. God, he knew he had it bad for her. He had it so bad that he even contemplated leaving the subbasement just to say hi to her when she lingered in the cafeteria or went for a break. He was the cool guy, right? Well if he was so cool then why didn't he feel like it?

Ashleigh spent her evening shopping for new underwear that wouldn't fall down around her ankles. And then she wondered what Christopher would think of white lace, or did he prefer black translucent nylon? She couldn't believe that she was thinking like this about her friend!

But then again she could. She remembered being cradled in his arms half in and out of consciousness and some man had called him Beast. He'd said Beast take care of her, or something in that vein.

Ashleigh stared grimly into space. Once upon a time she only cared about how someone looked, how good she looked, how good they looked together. Ashleigh knew the truth; when it's all said and done it wasn't Christopher that was the Beast, it was her.

He was just a beautiful man waiting for someone to see past his outer wrapping.

~***~

The plan was for Ashleigh to meet Christopher at his place Saturday evening. He wanted time to make a good dinner and not to just whip something up after work so he opted for Saturday. He wouldn't tell Ashleigh what was on the menu and reminded her that she was the one that had said she liked ALL food.

"Well if you can cook the way that you can whip up a smoothie than I'm not worried."

He had just given her a mysterious smile. "I do fair to middlin' in the kitchen."

Her brow quirked up in humor. "Um…I don't know what middlin' means. Is that another country phrase like, 'I'm fixin to', or 'over yonder'?" She hid a grin.

"Oh pardon me. I forgot I was talking to a city girl," he said while watching the stop watch. "Time." And they began their next set; jumping jacks. It was the set he most looked forward to, and anguished over. The way her body parts moved beneath her clothing as she jumped caused him to worry about her seeing certain of his body parts becoming 'happy.'

But then he began thinking about the camera and how many of the guys were becoming 'happy' as they watched her ample breasts and rear-end bouncing up and down. She was definitely losing weight, but her ass was not going anywhere, and that thought made him want to smash the camera. He would have to tell her about the camera. Once, when he'd turned his back he'd caught her briefly adjusting her bra and he almost lost it at the idea of someone else perving her while she was doing that.

After he called time and they waited the thirty seconds for the next set he decided to casually mention the camera.

"Hey, did you know that there is a camera in here?" Okay, maybe that wasn't so casual.

Her face took on a surprised look. "What? Where?" She looked around.

Christopher gestured to the ceiling and she saw the little black ball no bigger than a golf ball nestled into the ceiling tiles. "They're all over…and some you can't even see." He decided that he would not tell her that the only reason he had mentioned it was in case she wanted to put her boob back into her bra after jumping jacks when she thought no one was watching. Somehow he thought that might freak her out.

"Christopher! There aren't cameras in the lockers are there?!"

"Time." He said and paused in the workout since it didn't appear that she was interested in them at this moment. "No, there are no cameras in lockers or restrooms, that's prohibited actually."

She searched his eyes. "Promise?"

A brief look of surprise crossed his face. "Of course." As if he would allow someone to watch her in the bathroom and locker room!

She seemed satisfied. He didn't mention that pretty much everything else was open to them including the outside circumference of the two federal buildings. The private offices did not have security cameras; like Ashleigh's, but the SSA and TAC offices had them. She did not look very happy as she glanced at the camera.

"Don't worry," he said after they resumed the set. "There's...probably no one even watching. I mean...it's a security camera and they know I'm down here so no need to watch." He was surprised that he was even able to say that lie so convincingly. But he didn't like seeing her anxious about it.

"That's true," she responded, relaxing again.

~***~

Saturday seemed to take forever to come. Ashleigh always dressed very upscale for work and so this time chose to dress casually for her date. Date. She beamed. What was it about Christopher that made her feel so happy? Well for starters she felt very attracted to him. He was so gentle and soft spoken and yet there was something powerful about him. She felt safe with him. She somehow knew that he would always have her back. But in regards to the attraction; she'd never met anyone so perfectly put together.

She slipped on jeans that hugged her butt. Next was a polo shirt and she liked the way it made her look like she had a waistline…wait, she DID have a waistline now! Ashleigh giggled and checked her hair and makeup, and then she hurried to Christopher's house.

She knew the area that he lived but used her GPS to find his house. She pulled into the driveway of a single story ranch style house. It was very well maintained; the lawn was completely weed-free and perfectly green. His shrubs didn't have a leaf out of place. He even had a neat flower bed with huge hydrangeas and Ashleigh tried to picture him on his hands and knees planting and weeding. It was just too weird imagining him out of the subbasement.

She rang the bell and not five seconds later the door opened. Her eyes drank him in as his swept over her. He wore jeans and a USMC shirt that showcased his huge arms. One thing she appreciated about Christopher is that while he was tall and well muscled, he wasn't some 'roided-out' looking monstrosity.

"Hi Ashleigh." His broad smile almost made her melt.

"Hi." He stepped aside and let her in. She inhaled deeply in appreciation.

"Oh my god. Something smells great."

"Ah…yes, we'll get to that in a moment. You didn't have any problems finding my house did you?"

"Nope. Garmin Nuvi got me here safely and soundly," She said referring to her GPS device. She looked around in amazement. He did not live in some bachelor's pad. Christopher's house was warm and welcoming. Music that she didn't recognize played softly over the stereo. He had hardwood floors with a huge area rug that made her want to kick off her shoes and sink her toes into it. An orange tabby walked over to her and when she bent down to pat it it darted away.

"She's shy," he explained. "I'll show you around." He led her from one well decorated room to the next. He showed her a bathroom that was huge and had the biggest tub she'd ever seen.

"I had to special order that." He said. She looked up at the ceiling. There was a skylight. "I put that in." He said.

She looked at him, impressed. "You did that? That's really nice looking."

"Thanks, but it was easy. It came in a kit." Still, she could barely change her own light bulbs. Lord forbid if a fuse tripped or a pilot light went out. Then she'd be screaming for DeAngelo. Well, she'd have to learn to be more self sufficient. Maybe Christopher would show her some home improvement tricks.

He led her back into the hall and pointed out a room that

had been converted into a gym. There were free weights, treadmill, mats and a 42 inch wall mounted flat panel television.

"Nice."

The next room was his bedroom. There was a King sized bed which didn't surprise her, but the pretty decorations did; matching comforter and curtains, artsy portraits on the wall, and nice, huge furniture with simple lines and uncluttered surfaces.

"Are you an interior designer in your spare time?" She asked, only half joking.

He smiled and shook his head. "No…I just have a lot of spare time on my hands. You should see this place at Christmas." He actually planned out how the tree would be decorated months in advance. Every year he did something different; either purple and gold, red and silver and once he did nothing but white. He also loved putting out lights and carving pumpkins at Halloween. He always had plenty of visitors during the holidays with his big family but…it wasn't the same as having his own.

Last was the kitchen. Ashleigh gasped. "Christopher…" She took in everything from the metal finish on the appliances, to the granite counters and dark wood cabinets. He even had a six burner, gas stove with a grill!

There was a kitchen eating nook beside a wonderful bay window…and she just wanted to stay forever! She looked out the window into a large wooded back yard with a deck and simple but nice furniture.

"You have a great house. I really love it." Her condo was pretty but it was also staged. Her place wasn't meant to make people feel warm and fuzzy but to impress. She had expensive white furniture that had to be cleaned professionally twice a year because wearing certain colors could easily mar the fabric. There was lots of glass and silver…and coldness.

"I'm happy. I want you to be comfortable." A shiver ran up her spine and she smiled shyly. He watched her for a moment and then led her into the kitchen.

"So. Are we ready to eat?"

"Yes!" Was her enthusiastic response. And she was pretty sure that she had guessed what he had cooked. It smelled like…Thanksgiving dinner.

He opened the oven and closed it back. "The cornbread needs a few more minutes." He lifted the aluminum foil that covered a Dutch oven and she saw 4 perfectly roasted Cornish hens.

"Four?"

He smirked. "I figured you'd eat one, right?" She nodded. "And I'll eat three."

She gave him a surprised look. Oh, yeah he was HUGE.

"Wild rice stuffing."

"Yum."

"Baked sweet potatoes." He lifted the lid from a simmering pot and she saw collard greens. Her brow went up.

"You know how to cook collard greens?"

"Yep." He picked up a slotted spoon and stirred them. "I know how to grow 'em, pick 'em, clean 'em, cook 'em…" He winked at her, "and eat 'em. Remember, I grew up in the country." She wasn't likely to forget with that sexy accent of his.

"Soul food is no different than country food," she said.

"I don't know if I agree with that."

"Really?"

"Unless you eat muskrat and raccoon."

"Uh…can't say that I have, you have?"

"Yep, ate it often when I was a kid; muskrat with gravy and rice. It was good. Raccoon…eh…you had to boil the hell out of it and get every bit of fat and glands off of it. More trouble than it's worth and it still had a…funky taste. Not too bad with beans, though." He went to the fridge as she listened aptly. And then she found herself checking out his butt in his jeans. Running the treadmill everyday sure made for a fine ass…

"What would you like to drink? I got diet soda." He'd picked it up with her diabetes in mind. "Unsweetened tea." Though he preferred his sweetened. "Beer, and bottled water."

"Bottled water." He grabbed two and a stick of butter. He picked up a potholder and then pulled a black skillet from the oven. Golden brown cornbread sent an unbelievable aroma through the air.

"My Mama uses an iron skillet to make cornbread, too!" She said.

"This is the only way to do it, Sweetheart." He liberally buttered the top of the cornbread. She hid a grin when he said Sweetheart. She liked hearing it coming from him, it gave her the warm and fuzzies.

"I'm hungry, Christopher." She said while staring at the cornbread.

He reached into a cabinet for plates and passed her one. "Dig in." He didn't have to tell her twice. His plate was piled high with food so she didn't feel bad about placing an entire Cornish hen on her plate with loads of greens and a butter and brown sugar topped sweet potato. Christopher sliced the cornbread and heaped it onto a separate plate and placed it on the table along with hot sauce, salt and pepper. Ashleigh grinned at the sight of the table. Damn, he ate like her family.

They didn't talk, they just ate. That's the way it's supposed to be. She wanted to kick off her shoes and tuck her foot under her.

"You make greens better than me." She admitted, her cheek bulging with food as she carefully spoke. "And that's not Jiffy cornbread mix."

"Jiffy is good for desert with some butter and jam, but when its dinnertime there ain't nothing like white cornmeal cornbread."

After dinner he quickly put away the food while she watched him. He had warned her not to expect desert and she said that she didn't have room for another bite.

"Thanks for dinner." She said shyly. "You are a really good cook."

"I like to eat and if I wanted to eat good I had to learn to cook. Good food to me is food I grew up on. Can't get that from McDonald's." His low country voice did something to her. She just loved the sound of it.

"Can I help you with dishes?"

"Nah, I'll load up the dishwasher in the morning." He led her into the living room. "What do you want to do? Watch TV, listen to music...I can play some guitar for you."

"I've been wanting to hear you play!" She sat down on the couch and he moved to the stereo and turned off the music. A guitar was tucked almost behind the entertainment center and she hadn't seen it before. He sat down next to her.

"What do you want me to play?"

"You're good enough to take requests?"

"I don't normally take requests." Each week he selected two songs to play at the Madd Crab each Friday and if someone really wanted to hear something special he'd do a third.

He strummed, nothing in particular but it still sounded really good. She tried to think of a song, but wasn't sure of his ability.

"Did you play as a kid?" He nodded. "I bet it made you super popular."

"Nobody heard me play but family. And I was not super

popular. I was like that creepy kid in the movies. Remember that movie called My Bodyguard?"

She nodded. "I know every eighties movie ever made—well at least the ones with a teen cast."

He gave her a half smile. "I was like the big kid that everybody avoided and was afraid to talk to. Only thing is that he wasn't really all that scary in the end." A brief frown passed his face before he chuckled. "I would have much rather been a character in a John Hughes film. At least the underdog always got the girl."

Her heart leaped in her chest as her eyes grew big. "Ducky didn't get the girl."

"He did in the way that John Hughes had meant for it to be made. In actuality Molly Ringwald pushed him to change the ending because she said that no one wanted to see Andie and Ducky get together. She said that everyone would want to see Andie and Blaine together."

Oh my god...he knew the characters. She was going to have a heart attack...she was going to die right here and now. He knew Pretty in Pink!!!!

"You like John Hughes movies?" She asked hopefully...please please please...

"Yep. I like any movie where I could..." He stopped and blushed.

"Pretend to be the character that wins in the end?" She whispered.

He met her eyes. "Yeah." He glanced down and his fingers began to strum The Psychadelic Furs tune; The Ghost in

You, except his version was a gentle soothing croon. Ashleigh stared incredulously but she didn't make a sound. He began to softly sing and his voice was amazing.

"…Inside you the tims moves and she don't fade. The ghost in you…"

Ashleigh's mouth turned as dry as the Sahara desert as she stared at Christopher.

"…she don't fade…"

She was frozen and the world seemed to stop, and all there was was this man singing this particular song to her — this song of all songs; from a movie that defined her life.

"...Ain't it just like rain. And love is only heaven away..."

Ashleigh leaned forward and placed her lips on his. This man was her soul mate. This was the man of her dreams. This is the man that she had been waiting for.

There was no doubt in her mind. She wanted Christopher to be hers.

His hand moved up to cup her face at the same time that he drew in a surprised breath. He returned her kiss but then leaned back slightly to look at her. Ashleigh's eyes stared deeply into his and he saw nothing there but desire. He pulled the guitar strap from around his neck and placed it on the floor and then urgently pulled her back to his lips.

"Ashleigh…" He sighed. His heart felt like it would explode from his chest.

She drew back slightly and he died a little until he felt the warm tip of her tongue tracing his lips and his body surged! He didn't move, just allowed her to explore his lips with her soft tongue. Finally he met her tongue with his own. She sighed and it was almost his undoing.

He was kissing Ashleigh.

He captured her lower lip and then released it long enough to slip his tongue between her lips. Gently but insistently he began to explore her warm mouth. He had never done this before. He had never done anything remotely close to this. But he allowed his instincts to take over, as well as his need to taste her.

Christopher's mouth and lips against hers caused her body to warm, her skin ultra sensitive to his every move. Ashleigh's arms went around his neck and she felt Christopher begin to tremble. He pulled away from her and pressed his forehead against hers as he tried to catch his breath. She kissed his face, her lips moving along each line, each ridge, each crevice. She kissed his eyelids and the tip of his nose and then she rose up to kiss his brow and the scar on his forehead.

Christopher could barely catch his breath. His big hands rested on her hips and each kiss of her lips felt like the healing touch of an Angel. When she finished kissing him she hugged him, her head falling to his shoulder.

Christopher's arms went around her possessively, holding her tightly against him. He knew that he was holding her tightly, maybe even too tightly. But he couldn't help himself. He just couldn't let her go.

"Hmm." Ashleigh sighed in perfect contentment. "It feels so good with your arms around me like this." She felt him shift his position and then he was looking down at her face where it was now against his chest. She felt his fingertips tracing her face, running along the bridge of her nose and then over the cleft in her lip.

"Your lips are so perfect." He said softly. And then she felt his soft mouth kissing her lightly. "You are so damn beautiful…"

She opened her eyes and gave him a serious look. "Christopher…you are the one that's beautiful." She lifted her head. "And not just on the inside. You're beautiful on the outside, too. To me…you're perfect."

She could see several emotions move across his face before his eyes half closed and his light eye lashes created a frame through which she could see the eyes that she loved so much. And they watched her with a little bit of trepidation.

"You say that to me…and if you're not careful you might end up stuck with me." It was a warning.

"You're making this difficult." Her eyes never moved from his face. "I think that's what I'm trying to tell you. I want to be stuck with you."

Christopher surprised her by sitting up and gently pushing her back, but he did place his hands carefully on her shoulder. His expression was very serious as he studied her eyes.

"Ashleigh, Sweetheart, I can see myself falling head over heels in love with you. And if you don't think that you can feel the same way for me than please tell me now because I absolutely cannot be the only one that feels this way—"

"I absolutely feel the same way."

He stopped the smile that was about to spread across his face and his brow gathered. "And your ex? What about him? Because a week ago you said you still loved him...and if you do, I get that-"

"But he came over the other day." Christopher's jaw clenched tensely. Already he felt protective of her. "I thought about it, about getting back with him. But when he touched me I finally realized that I was just in love with...the memory of loving him. I don't feel anything for him anymore; not love, not even anger." Ashleigh frowned slightly. "I never told you this because...it would make me seem really stupid. But my ex married another woman while we were dating." She looked down at her hands feeling her face flame. She felt Christopher's fingers beneath her chin and he made her look at him.

"Why would that make me think less of you? He was the fool."

She met his eyes sincerely. "I was the fool. I thought that because I was fat, that I couldn't ever have the man of my dreams. And I let him cheat on me...and every time he did, it picked away at something in me and made me feel less. And then I felt like I needed someone like him to make me feel good enough." She placed her hand on his. "But you make me feel good enough no matter how I look."

"I think you're beautiful, even before you lost weight I thought that." He finally smiled. "And I don't care about the stupid people in the world! Sweetheart, you are all mine." He pulled her into his arms and kissed her passionately. My girl, he thought. My baby. Mine.

Christopher and Ashleigh kissed and when they got tired or out of breath they would stare at each other and talk in whispers about matters of the soul; whether it was youth, movies, or soft words of love, whatever was in their souls. Then they would kiss again until Christopher pulled back, cleared his throat and looked suddenly nervous.

"Ashleigh, will you stay with me tonight?"

She ran her fingers along the back of his massive hand and felt him shiver. Oh, I'm such a slut…

"Yes."

His heart was pounding when he pulled her into his arms and hugged her…a bit more gently this time. He placed a kiss on her forehead and then took her hand and led her to his bedroom.

"I need to use the bathroom." She paused when they reached the bathroom.

"You can use the one in my room." She followed him not realizing that he had an ensuite bath. Christopher turned on the light in the bedroom now that it was night. And then he led her to the closed door of the private bath.

She looked around in awe. The large bathroom was masculine with brown marble counters, gold fixtures and chocolate and tan walls. There was a stand-alone shower and another huge bathtub, this one a Jacuzzi tub. Again his counter was bare of anything except in this case, a soap dispenser and a matching tooth brush holder containing one toothbrush. She already had plans to add her own.

While she used the bathroom, Christopher used the other. Maggie had come out from hiding and followed at his feet back to the bedroom. He stopped at the door and picked her up, giving her a quick rub under her chin.

"No, you can't come in tonight, Mags. And you're going to have to warm up to my girlfriend." He whispered the last before letting her back down to the floor and closing the bedroom door. Ashleigh came out of the bathroom then and met Christopher's eyes shyly. She'd taken her insulin before leaving the house and was okay until morning when she would need her first dose of the day.

He came forward and took her hand. "I have…a condom in my wallet. But it's probably so old-"

"I'm on the pill."

He looked deeply into her eyes at the trust she was showing him. "I'm regularly tested because of the military so I'm about as clean as clean can be." She nodded, satisfied.

He led her to the bed and began pulling down the covers. She helped. They were on opposite sides of the bed watching each other when it was all done. Christopher reached down and swept off his shirt. Ashleigh's lips parted. She'd never seen him without a shirt. The pale skin of his chest was dotted with freckles and a sparse covering of red hair. She'd never seen red chest hair before and felt an urge to reach out and run the palms of her hands over it.

She pulled off her polo shirt and carefully placed it on the end of the bed. She was wearing the black nylon bra that she'd just bought and the sheer material tinted the image of her nipples and aureolas. Christopher's eyes moved from one breast to the other and she felt her nipples harden beneath his gaze. He groaned softly and hesitantly began to undo his jeans. When he pulled them off his boxer briefs outlined a magnificently thick and hard penis that curved across his body.

Ashleigh could hardly breathe. She had never seen a man built so perfectly! An auburn trail ran from his belly button down to his briefs, a bit darker than the hair on his chest. She swallowed and unbuttoned her jeans. She had never liked this part; when she had to get undressed in front of DeAngelo and she would imagine that he wished she was someone else…

Christopher's cock jumped when Ashleigh came out of her jeans. She; with her toasty brown skin and the black see-through nylon underwear that showed her hardened nipples. And when she was just down to panties and he could see that she was hairless and the slight impression of her slit, he could honestly wait no longer. He moved to the bed and she followed, about to reach behind herself to undo the bra but he stopped her hand. He didn't want her to remove the enticing material. The two of them knelt on the bed facing each other and Christopher ran his hands up her sides until his thumb was level with her breasts. He allowed them to gently stroke her dark, raised flesh and then he gave in to his desire and leaned down and kissed each hardened nylon covered tip.

Ashleigh's body arched forward and she gasped, a quiet moan escaping her lips. Christopher pulled back enough to examine her now wet nipple through the nylon. He used his finger to lightly tease it, watching as it grew even harder and rose even more. Ashleigh groaned low and long when his mouth covered her again and he sucked the nipple gently into his mouth.

"Oh god…" She cried softly. He moved to the other and repeated it while his hands travelled up her thigh.

Ashleigh had wanted to touch his chest for so long and now she could. She ran her hands over his hard pecs and the little bit of hair caused her palms to tingle. His chest was hard and soft, especially when he flexed a muscle. As he continued to kiss and suck her nipple, Ashleigh let the tips of her fingers move down and across his abdomen.

His hands began to tremble again and he paused in his nipple sucking to take a deep breath. He glanced down taking note of her light brown hands and the way it contrasted with his much paler stomach. He suddenly looked up and sought her lips. He would never tire of kissing this woman. He placed a gentle hand behind her head holding her in place as he urgently kissed her.

Her hand dipped lower, finding his hard shaft straining against the material of his briefs. She stroked his length, amazed at how long he was. How many inches had it taken for her fingers to finally reach the flair of his tip? Ten? More?

Christopher's body jerked when he felt her fingers against his shaft, and his mouth parted as he panted and tried to catch his breath. Ashleigh continued to kiss his opened mouth even when he groaned softly at her touch. Her fingers stroked him repeatedly and his own hand moved between her legs, seeking the warm place where her thighs met.

He lightly touched her nylon covered sex. It was wet. With a loud groan he sunk down onto the bed and kissed a rapid path down her belly until his head was buried between her legs. Ashleigh heard her own low moan. She quickly came up on her elbows and she spread her legs for him. She felt him lathe kisses across her mons and breathing became a task.

"Christopher!" She screeched when she felt his tongue tracing a path along her sensitive slit. At the sound of her cry he hooked his hands beneath her and pulled her closer. And then she felt him sucking her through the nylon and she fell back; arching, her legs splayed apart. She gripped his head, holding him in place and thrust upward, rolling her hips against his mouth and tongue.

Christopher lapped at her delicious fountain. He'd never tasted a woman but her juices combined with the aroma of her sex turned him mindless. He tugged her panties aside and saw her perfectly hairless pussy and lips, glistening with their intermingled juices and he allowed his mouth to fall onto her again. This time his tongue found her clit and he favored it lovingly as if it was his own special prize.

Ashleigh tried to cry out but couldn't find her breath, her eyes rolled and her mouth was opened in a silent scream. He ate her like a man that loved it, not like a man mindful of bringing her to orgasm. And because of that he was bringing her too quickly. However, she wasn't of a mind to stop him. Her head went back and she screamed her explosion of ecstasy as she pulled his face deeply against her, her hips rolling against his wonderful mouth and tongue.

"Christopher Christopher Chrissss….! Cummingggg! Oh GOD BABY!"

He only pulled her closer, working her rapidly, pushing her over and over. When her body finally went limp, he pulled her hairless pussy lips into his mouth one last time and then placed a kiss on them before moving up the bed. He wiped his mouth on the back of his arm and then pulled Ashleigh against his chest. She went with absolutely no resistance, her half closed eyes appeared glazed.

He pressed kisses against her forehead and she snuggled against him. "Mmmm that felt so good Christopher." She rubbed her hand over his chest and then down further where she wrapped her fingers around his stiff shaft. He gasped and tensed. Her fist moved up and then down. He was incredibly hard. As she looked down she noted the skin covering his penis was red and lined in veins.

Ashleigh wanted to see him and came up and took in the sight of her brown fingers wrapped around his 'pole'. She'd never been this close to a white man's penis. His was pale skin combined with reds and pinks where she was used to brown skin combined with purples and black.

She leaned forward anxiously and swiped her tongue across the mushroom top, tasting his slick precum. She swirled her tongue around it as she gripped him in her fist.

He bucked his hips. "Ash!" He cried out loudly. And then it was his turn to throw his head back as his mouth flew open in a breathless yell. He clutched the sheets instead of her head and tried to control his movement. Christopher felt her warm mouth gliding down his length and he fought to keep his hips from slamming forward.

"Ohhhh Ashleigh!" He yelled. He bit his lip and finally gripped her head, his fingers burying into her hair. Ashleigh had never put anyone into her mouth quite this long and she felt herself gagging several times to her chagrin. She had always prided herself on knowing how to please her man. She wanted Christopher to never ever think of another woman's mouth on him. She doubled her efforts, working her fists up and down the portion of his shaft that her mouth would not reach. She sucked and lapped and teased with her tongue, reveling in

Christopher's responsive cries and groans of pleasure.

"Mmmm, you like it, baby?" She crooned as she popped his mushroom shaped tip in and out of her mouth.

"Oh god Ashleigh, YES! Please don't stop..."

She pushed her mouth down over him as far as she could and he was literally partially down her throat. She cupped his testicles as she came up for air. Her effort was rewarded with a strangled cry of pleasure from Christopher. She felt his hands on her shoulders and he was pulling her up.

"I need to cum!"

"Cum in my mouth-" She said as he continued to pull her up.

"No, inside of you!" He pushed her gently onto her back and covered her with his hard body. She had time to hope that he knew what to do with that big hard thing of his...otherwise it could really hurt, but then he was slipping it gently into her slick opening. She was swollen from her recent climax and he felt very big, but he slid into her carefully, though he didn't pause not until he was fully inside.

Once inside Christopher rolled his pelvis against her, creating a delicious friction that made her gasp as the pleasure fully awakened in her once again. The combination of his thick girth stretching her, and the friction of his pelvis rubbing her caused her to whimper and clasp her legs around his rock hard body.

Christopher concentrated on anything but the explosion building in his loins. "Ashleigh! I'm going to cum...!"

He pulled out of her slightly and then pushed back inside, repeating the move again and again and then he felt her fingers digging into his shoulders and he fought not to climax until she did. Please, baby, cum now…cum now…He thought.

Ashleigh screeched and her legs tightened around him as her body clenched like a fist around his shaft obliterating any remaining restraint that he had. His body pumped fast and hard as he orgasmed. When the first shot of semen left his body, he keened out something that was a mixture of her name and an animal wail.

His pumping hips finally slowed. He could feel the semen that he'd just so recently deposited inside of her gliding out to pool along the bed sheet. He was too weak to do anything about it. When he collapsed he at least was only half on top of her body.

They lay like that for a long time until Christopher lifted his head. "Are you okay? I didn't hurt you did I?"

"No…" She said breathlessly. "It felt so good."

He grinned and rolled out of bed. She watched him walk naked into the bathroom. She perked up at the sight of his magnificent back and ass…and calves and thighs. She heard water running and he returned with a wash cloth and towel. He sat on the bed and gently washed her body with the warm damp cloth. She lay back in comfort feeling her body dragging her towards sleep. He covered the wet spot with the towel and then pulled up the blanket to cover them. He spooned her, pulling her back flush against his body.

She turned her head and he kissed her lips, rubbing his

hands along her belly which still pooched out but he liked it, he liked rubbing the soft skin there.

She was curious and so decided to ask. "That wasn't your first time?"

He grinned good-naturedly. "Was I that bad?"

"Hell no!" She said honestly. He was great which is why she had to ask. She had assumed, due to his shyness that he'd never been with a woman. But he knew exactly what he was doing…and he did it exceedingly well.

"I'm not a virgin, but I haven't done it very much." He didn't want to tell her that he'd been with whores a few times. Overseas, whores were much more readily available because you didn't have to find them, they found you. The first time he'd just allowed someone to suck him. She was pretty and it had felt good. The next time he decided to go all the way. He had used a condom but still worried about crabs. Someone on the team always came back with a case of them.

The blank look in the woman's eyes had made it difficult, especially when he considered that if she wasn't a druggie then she was probably some poor lady trying to make ends meet. He'd done it once more, years later, searching for someone whose eyes didn't look half dead. But it still hadn't given him what he needed and he hadn't been with a woman since.

He pulled her closer and buried his face into the back of her neck. "You're the first person I've ever made love to, though."

He felt her hands gently cover his arm where it enclosed her against him.

~***~

Ashleigh woke up several hours later to the feel of Christopher's hard pipe nestling against the crack of her ass. She paused, listening for the regular sound of his breathing. He was asleep. She sighed and pushed back against him innocently, hearing him grunt lightly and come awake. His arms instantly tightened around her and she felt his lips lightly kiss the back of her neck.

Ashleigh beamed. He kissed her even when he thought she was asleep. That was her true definition of love.

In the morning, Christopher slipped into her from behind, his lips locked onto her neck and shoulder while his fingers plucked and stroked her nipples. It was slow and sensual and when he came inside of her for the second time he thought about how wonderful it would be to wake up like this every single day.

They showered, doing nothing more than washing, kissing and touching. Ashleigh indicated she had to go home as she was overdue for her insulin. He hated to see her leave at the same time that he wanted her to get home and take her injection.

He explained that he was going to dinner at his parent's house as he did nearly each Sunday, and would give her a call later in the evening. Later when he was cleaning the dishes in his kitchen, he mentally kicked himself for not inviting her. He realized that he was moving fast but it wasn't too fast for him. He already knew that he intended to have Ashleigh in his life as a permanent fixture…as long as she wanted him. And he planned to do all that he could to make sure that she'd always want him in hers.

He found his mind drifting back to Uncle Ray's wise words. And then when he thought that she'd had enough time to get home he called her.

"Ashleigh. Would you like to go with me to dinner at my parent's house?"

She didn't hesitate. "Yeah, I'd like that."

"I…miss you already." He sighed.

"Me too." Was it crazy? But having sex made everything so clear. Christopher was everything she needed in a man. He told her that he'd pick her up at about five and then told her that he loved her. He felt it and he said it and that was all there was to it. But when she said that she loved him he smiled in disbelief at his fortune.

Ashleigh stood there with lights twinkling in her eyes and a smile on her face. *I am loved for who I am and nothing more.*

She floated through her home before noticing that she had messages from both Kendra and Lance. She knew that they were going to have something to say about her not coming home last night. Well she was grown and single! Deciding to take care of them both with one phone call, Ashleigh made a 3-way call.

"Guess who has a boyfriend again."

"That was fast work." Kendra commented. "Are you sure you want to take that step, Ash?" Her voice held a touch of concern that surprised her. "He's pretty big. If you break up with him you may have to enter the witness protection services."

Ashleigh found herself smiling. "Maybe...maybe I won't ever break up with him."

"Ashleigh," Lance said. "You're not talking about...marriage, are you? I mean it's only been one date."

"Lance, he told me that he wished his life was a John Hughes film."

Lance began screaming through the phone line. "Don't toy with me, woman! You didn't start the conversation with, 'Hey do you like John Hughes films?' Did you?!"

"No, he brought up teen movies first. He told me he was the big quiet guy from that movie My Bodyguard."

Lance began screaming again and panting 'Oh my god, Oh my god.' "You must marry him. Marry him now!"

"You two are insane." Kendra said not appreciating their obvious fixation on teen movies.

~***~

Ashleigh wore a pretty dress that was both nice enough to meet parents and attend church, but was also complimentary to her newly curvaceous body.

Christopher arrived a few minutes before five and she showed him around her condo. He was thoroughly impressed, complimenting her on her style. Ashleigh thought Christopher looked very sexy in khaki pants and a button down shirt. They spent a few minutes kissing until the bulge in his pants began to grow noticeably and it was either stop now or arrive late for dinner. They decided to stop...for now.

Christopher's parents lived in Covington Kentucky and he prepared her for a rather large gathering. He had four brothers and sisters but only two lived in Kentucky. One of his brothers had died several years before and there would be a few kids running around. He wanted to prepare her for his father. He'd had a stroke years before and it had caused some permanent damage. He warned that he might repeat the same thing over and over or act confused…or he might be perfectly okay.

Ashleigh could tell that he didn't tell her any of this with any sense of shame and she loved him even more for that.

He directed her attention to points of interest as they drove; the High School, his first job, the house where a certain relative lived. She listened intently to every word. He could have been reading the yellow pages and she would have been enthralled. His voice just did it for her. She pictured slipping her hands down his pants as soon as they got back to her house.

They finally pulled up to a small two story house on a street that overlooked a factory on one side and a Quickie Mart on the other. She figured that the people who lived on this street didn't make a lot of money but all of the homes were well maintained and the yards were kept up nicely.

He pulled in behind a mini-van and gave her a quick wink before rushing around to open her door for her. Several kids were playing stickball in the side yard and came running when they recognized Christopher.

"Uncle Chris!" They yelled, jumping on him. For a minute she worried that some of the bigger ones might hurt him but he didn't even seem to feel their leaping and bounding bodies. For a moment they ignored her while they tried to bring down their giant uncle.

"Hey guys! Timeout!" He bellowed and his voice left no doubt to his seriousness. "I want to introduce y'all to someone. This is Ashleigh. She's my girlfriend."

"You gotta girlfriend, Uncle Chris?" A little girl that appeared no older than four peeked up at him.

He lifted her up like she was a teeny doll, which is what she appeared in his big hands. "Yes I do, Rachel. And you guys have to be on your best behavior around her. Do we have a deal?" Everyone said, 'Yes, sir.' "Tell her hi."

"Hi, Miss Ashleigh." Ashleigh grinned and returned the greeting.

"If you're good I'll come out and play touch football with you for a little while after dinner; me against all of y'all."

"Is Miss Ashleigh going to play?" One of the kids asked.

Her eyes got wide. "I'll just be a cheerleader."

Christopher took her hand and led her up the side stairs. He knocked once and entered. A group of women were sitting in the kitchen talking and they all looked at him happily, their curious stares finally resting on her. She gripped his hand and plastered on a nervous smile.

"Hey everyone." Christopher pulled her after him as he entered the kitchen where she could smell something good cooking. "This is Ashleigh; my girlfriend."

You could have heard a pin drop. To Ashleigh it felt like forever but in actuality the quiet lasted just a second or two. A woman was moving forward. She could have been in her early fifties, maybe late forties. She had a huge smile on her face and looked enough like Chris that it left no doubt that it was his mother even though she was a little thing. She gave him a kiss and a hug.

"Hi Mom."

Mrs. Jameson turned to her next and gave her a hug too. "Now where did you come from?"

Ashleigh wasn't sure how to answer that question because she wasn't exactly sure what it meant.

"Mom, Ashleigh comes from my job. She works in my building."

"Well you sure are a pretty girl. Ashleigh, is it?"

"Yes, Ma'am."

Christopher introduced her to the other ladies in the room. There was a sister-in-law, an aunt, his sister Alma, and two cousins. The ladies seemed friendly and they asked her several questions about where she lived and what she did. Alma asked her what she wanted to drink and she asked for a bottled water and got a glass of iced water instead.

Christopher took her hand and led her out of that room and into a family room. Several men were sitting around watching ESPN. At least with them, they didn't come to a complete silence although it was pretty plain that they were surprised to see a woman with Christopher. She hoped the surprise wasn't due to her being black. She realized that he hadn't mentioned her coming, or her color.

Ashleigh's eyes fell on a frail looking man that looked like he was old enough to be Christopher's grandfather. He was white haired and slouched over with eyes that seemed rheumy and glazed. This had to be Mr. Jameson.

"Hi Daddy." Christopher leaned forward and gave his father a hug. The older man looked at him in surprise before smiling.

"Walt? Where you been, son?"

Christopher tried to mask the pain in his face but not before Ashleigh saw it.

"I'm Christopher, Daddy."

"Christopher? You back home from The Marines?"

"Yes sir. Dad, this is my girlfriend Ashleigh."

Mr. Jameson turned to her and smiled, offering his hand to shake. "Nice to meet you Ashleigh. Y'all sit a spell and have some dinner."

"Yes, sir." Ashleigh responded politely and someone pulled up one of the dining room chairs for her to sit down in. The ladies came in from the kitchen while Christopher introduced her to his brother Butch, an uncle and the husbands of the two cousin's that she'd already met.

She wanted to remember their names but knew that wasn't going to happen. She had to at least remember Butch and Alma since they were Christopher's siblings.

They sat around and talked for a while and Ashleigh

could see the way Christopher relaxed in a way that she'd never seen him relax before.

"You two been together long?" Alma asked." Butch tried to discreetly scowl at her. But Ashleigh didn't mind the question that had been directed at her.

"Not long, but I knew him for a while."

"Okay." She looked at her younger brother. "Cause he ain't never said nothing about a girlfriend."

Christopher turned to her from his conversation with the two cousins. "Consider this me telling you about my girlfriend."

His mother changed the subject and mentioned a family reunion that Uncle Ray wanted to have. Dinner was served a few minutes later and Ashleigh offered to help but the aunt told her to relax and that she was company.

Dinner was a hodge podge but everything looked good. There was fried corn, meatloaf, coleslaw and potato salad, cottage cheese, canned pears and green peas. Alma had burned the dinner rolls as she was too busy slyly watching Ashleigh.

The kids sat at a card table and it brought a smile to her face as she remembered being relegated to the kids table. Ashleigh saw that Mrs. Jameson had to feed Mr. Jameson. His hands didn't seem to cooperate. Although he did make every attempt to feed himself it only resulted in green peas rolling around on the table and meatloaf being dropped into his lap.

Christopher engaged his father in casual conversation about the game that had just been on. His father favored a team that hadn't been playing.

Mr. Jameson looked at Ashleigh curiously. "Now who is this?"

"This is Ashleigh. She's my girlfriend."

"Honey, that's Christopher's girlfriend, Ashleigh." Mrs. Jameson explained distinctly while wiping his lips with a napkin.

"Do I know you?" He asked in confusion.

Ashleigh swallowed a bite of meat loaf. "We just met, Mr. Jameson."

His eyes cleared and he smiled again. "I remember. You're one of them colored kids that lived down at the bottom of the hill."

Everyone at the table grew quiet, even the kids at the card cable looked on in surprise.

"Well," Ashleigh cleared her throat, "I don't belong to that particular colored family. I belong to a different one. We didn't live on the mountain but in Cincinnati."

"Ohhhh, okay." he said. "But they were a good lot. The father died so it's a good thing that their not your kin." He tried to spoon an entire pear wedge into his mouth and it landed in his lap with a plop. Mrs. Jameson grabbed it and then peaked up at Ashleigh and mouthed, 'thank you.'

Ashleigh glanced at Christopher whose face had gone pale.

After dinner there was brownie cake and ice cream.

Ashleigh passed and Alma frowned. "You don't like cake and ice cream?"

Ashleigh didn't immediately answer, surprised by the question although it wasn't delivered in a bad way—it was just the question itself.

Christopher looked at his sister. "Alma, she doesn't want ice cream and cake."

"Fine." She sulked like a child. "She can speak for herself," she murmured. Christopher was just staring at his sister.

"I have diabetes."

Alma scooped up a large bowl of ice cream and a big slice of brownie cake and cut her eyes side-ways at Ashleigh as she ate it.

Christopher stared at his sister.

After dinner the ladies wouldn't allow Ashleigh to help with the dishes and made her go outside with Christopher to help the kids burn off their energy.

"Oh my god, Ashleigh," he said when they were alone on the porch. "I had no idea my Dad would say something like that. I've never even heard him use that word before—"

"Relax, baby. You guys reacted more than I did. He had a stroke but I can still tell that he's a good person."

"Come on Uncle Chris, its getting dark!" The kids began yelling for him. He gave her a quick kiss and bounded down the porch stairs. She pulled up one of the porch chairs and watched the way he thoroughly enjoyed himself with the kids. Mr. Jameson and one of the male cousin's came outside with her to watch them play and to hoot and cheer.

Mr. Jameson told her a story about a furnace and some goats and she pretended to understand. Christopher looked up at her and gave her a questioning look and she raised her hand and waved letting him know that everything was okay. He got tackled by four kids and Ashleigh grimaced but he seemed to love it.

Mrs. Jameson came outside to check on her husband and Ashleigh thanked her for dinner. Alma pulled up a chair and watched the kids. "That little one is mine." She said to Ashleigh. "I hope my brother doesn't squash him."

"He's being very gentle." Christopher picked up one of the kids and tossed them to the grass and Ashleigh's eyes widened. But the kid just leaped back to his feet laughing all the while.

"So you work for the government too?" Alma asked.

"Yes. I work in the Federal Building where Christopher is stationed."

"Well it's a damned shame how that President is screwed up our government." Ashleigh's back stiffened. "Almost might have been best if they had shut down the whole damn government."

"Alma, you don't know what you're talking about." One of the men scowled. "Without the government how do you think Buddy's going to continue to collect his social security?"

Ashleigh clenched her teeth and then looked at Alma.

"And Obama didn't create these problems. They existed before he came in to office."

"Oh Alma!" Mrs. Jameson snapped. "Don't start up about President Obama."

Mr. Jameson huffed. "Barack Obama is our President. It don't matter if you voted for him or not. Now that he's in office he's our Commander and Chief. Your brother risks his life for his boss; and that's the President, as well as for all us Americans. You don't talk against the President of the United States in my house!" Mr. Jameson glared at his daughter and when he didn't receive a response he tried to stand up. "Where's my belt?! You go get my belt right this instant, young lady! You have been asking for a butt whupping all evening!" Alma's face reddened as her eyes grew big. Her father pointed angrily to the house. "Go on. Get!"

"Yes, sir." Alma got to her feet and went into the house. If she returned with a belt Ashleigh thought that she might just sit there and laugh. Instead she gave Mr. Jameson a smile. Christopher was suddenly on the porch studying Ashleigh's face, trying to find out what was going on. Ashleigh's grin told him that she was okay and that's all that really mattered. But he decided it was time to go and the two of them bid the family goodbye.

Mrs. Jameson pulled her into a tight hug. "You're welcomed here any time, dear." Then she whispered, "And don't mind my daughter. She won't be so impolite next time you come, not after Christopher lays into her. And I got a thing or two to say to her myself." She pulled back and looked at Ashleigh. "You will come back won't you?"

I have to, she thought, because I intend to be in

Christopher's life for a very long time. "Yes, Ma'am. I intend to come back."

Mr. Jameson gave her a brief pat on the back while still wearing a broad smile. She didn't know if he was lucid or not but told him that it was nice meeting him, and meant it.

As Christopher drove her home, he reached for her hand and pulled it to his lips to kiss. "There is normally not that much excitement, I promise."

"Christopher I won't ask you to apologize for your family…if you don't ask me to apologize for mine. You'll have to meet them, too, I guess." It was strange seeing such a look of fear cross his face.

CHAPTER 7

It was just after nine o'clock when they reached her home. She gave him a look, and ran her hand along his massive thigh as he parked. He returned the look and it was filled with yearning. They walked hand in hand to the apartment, moving fairly quickly and as soon as the door was opened Ashleigh pulled him inside, pushed her body against his and slid her hand down into his pants, rubbing it up and down against his fully erect penis.

He grunted in surprised approval and then gripped her by the shoulders and kissed her urgently. He walked her to the couch; the expensive, white couch, and pushed her back until he was covering her, grinding his hard cock against her.

With a loud cry of need, Ashleigh began pulling at his clothes and hers. Not wanting to take the time to remove them all together, Christopher pushed her dress up and her panties down while Ashleigh tugged at the zipper of his pants until she had them just down over the round of his ass. Christopher rubbed her breast through her clothing while she managed to kick one leg out of her panties.

"Damn sweetheart," He groaned, "You are so sexy. I've been thinking about this all evening…" His lips moved from her lips to her neck and shoulder where he lapped and nipped as he rolled his hips against hers.

"Please…I need you now!" Her body throbbed! She

slipped her hand between them and rubbed him urgently. "Please Chris, please…"

He rolled slightly to the side and gripped the base of his shaft, guiding himself into her slick opening. He was careful yet quick as he rolled back on top of her and pushed fully into her body.

Ashleigh threw her head from side to side in ecstasy. He never teased by dipping in and out of her, he always went straight home. When he pushed into her like that it felt so incredible; a pleasurable pain. He stretched and pushed against things that sent her mind reeling in desire. Only then would he pull back only to rock forward, grinding the base against her clit as she shrieked out in pleasure.

Christopher thrust in and out of her quickly but not roughly. He was big and knew it. He didn't want to hurt her. Even with the incredible feeling of pleasure he held back enough not to lose complete control. She liked it when he pushed into her fully and so he kept doing it, even as he buried his face into her neck and tried to keep his head, Christopher thrust deep and then twisted his pelvis for optimum grindage. Each time he did that, she would shudder and cry out loudly gripping and pulling at his back and ass.

And then her satiny hot canal spasamed and gripped him hard and Christopher's cries of pleasure joined hers.

"Oh god…Ashleigh!" His body took over. She was so tight, she squeezed and pulsed and he lost the small grasp on his control. He pulled out almost fully, only to slam back into her with a loud grunt. Ashleigh's thick, sexy thighs gripped him, her legs wrapping around his body so that he had to slide up inside her in order to hit home.

"Oh baby...!" He cried out hoarsely. Sweat dripped from him and onto her as he thrust rapidly into her. Suddenly his toes curled and he cried out again. "Ashleigh!" He could barely think as his pace quickened and the first shot of semen invaded her.

Ashleigh's hands roamed his body as she felt his hot semen flooding her. It was like being on a wild ride; her body rocked with his rapid thrust. Finally, panting as if he'd run several miles, Christopher went limp.

Ashleigh hugged him and gave him a tired grin. "How do you do that so good?" He pulled up his head weakly and looked at her.

"Good?"

"Excellent. You do...really excellent." She spoke shyly.

He kissed her. "I just want you to feel good."

She rubbed his naked buttocks and he flexed his muscles there. After a moment he slipped his spent penis from her and came to his feet pulling up his pants and tucking into place.

Ashleigh quickly followed suit, not wanting to ruin the couch. She hugged the big man, her head only reaching his chest. And when his arms went around her she felt wonderful and so loved.

~***~

The next day Christopher arrived at work. He was already dressed in workout cloths, as he did each and every morning. He headed to the security room lockers not able to keep the smile from his face. Once he reached them, each man present turned to him expectantly.

"How was your weekend, Beast?" Carlos asked.

"It was alright." He said casually. "Went to my parent's for dinner on Sunday."

TK scowled. "You do that every weekend!"

"Well this time I went with my girlfriend."

"Oh damn!" Roddy punched him in the arm. "I was about to ask how you could possibly manage to screw up dinner with a girl that stares at you like the little trooper does."

"Little trooper?" He asked curious about the nickname.

"She doesn't wimp out on her workout." Lem said. He was as tall as Christopher and just as physically formidable. "She pushes herself just like a Marine."

Yes she does.

He got out of there pretty quick, not just because he was anxious to get down to the gym to see his girl, but because the guy's pornographic comments about his weekend was really too close to home. He knew that they weren't being disrespectful but he had no intentions of confirming anything that he'd done to her, giving credence to their theories about big bottomed girls, or shedding light on whether once you go black you never came back.

He entered the darkened gym room, cutting on the over head lights and setting down their individual thermoses. He slipped the c.d. into the player; Warren Zevon, and then he pulled out the mats. He was stretching and thinking about how this morning his body had yearned to nestle into Ashleigh's soft, hot canal when she walked into the room. His dick lurched and he suppressed a groan.

Damn, he couldn't walk around with a hard-on just at the sight of her!

She smiled so soft and sexy.

"Hi Christopher. Did you miss me?"

Was she reading his mind…or the bulge in his pants?

He chuckled and came to his feet. "Um…yes." She reached out to give him a passionate kiss and hug and he cleared his throat before she could. "We're being watched."

And then she remembered the security camera. Damnit! She had spent the entire morning fantasizing about kissing Christopher! He took her hand in his and gave her a chaste kiss on the cheek.

"Ah…." She said. "Okay."

"Sorry." He murmured while gesturing to the camera with his head. "I really don't want the guys getting all hot and bothered watching you kiss me."

She smiled and retrieved the thermos containing her protein drink. She could see by the slight bulge in Christopher's workout pants that he was the one at risk of becoming hot and bothered.

"We better get cracking then. I might need you to help me with something in the locker room…where there are no cameras."

His eyes darkened. Wordlessly he began the time clock. At

the end of their workout they went through their normal routine of cleaning up and putting everything back in order. As they headed out, Christopher followed Ashleigh instead of heading down the corridor towards the security door.

Ashleigh grinned as he followed her into the locker. Only once or twice had she ever seen another woman down here this early. But as soon as the door shut behind them she reached over and turned the lock. She did a quick sweep of the small locker and shower area while Christopher stood nervously by the door.

She came to him, surprising him by leaping into his arms. He gripped her easily and felt her legs wrap around his waist. Her lips were immediately on his and his body flared to life. She felt so good pressed against him. They kissed that way, passionately exploring each other's mouth.

"Christopher...I want you."

His response was a quick grunt as he lowered her to her feet. "Sweetheart...you're driving me crazy." She quickly pulled down her workout pants and turning her back she gave him a look with half hooded lids and then bent at the waist.

Christopher gasped at the sight of her golden brown ass and sexy slit and the way that her nether lips swelled in evidence of her desire. He groaned, knowing that he sounded like an animal but not able to help himself. He reached into his pants and withdrew his erect penis with one hand while holding onto her hips with the other. He guided himself into her opening.

"Oh god...." He groaned as her tight satiny walls gripped

him. Ashleigh had her hands braced on her knees and she leaned back slightly against him, pushing herself further onto his dick.

"Christopher!" She yelped when he sank fully into her. He hesitated until he felt her ass wiggling slightly back and forth. His eyes rolled to the back of his head and he began pounding her with hard strokes.

He sounded like he was running a race as he panted. Each thrust brought a responsive cry from her as they went at it fast and furious. Ashleigh adjusted her stance, planting her feet and trusting that Christopher wouldn't let her fall face first to the floor. She felt his big hand rubbing her ass and then his knees bent and he dipped upward into her with a long ragged groan.

"Baby! I'm going to cum!"

"Yes Chris! Cum…" She groaned. His knees felt weak as his dick swelled and then an explosive shot blasted from him and he began pumping his semen into her. Christopher cried out and then repeated the sound a second later when Ashleigh's body fisted around his cock and began pumping him as she orgasmed.

He continued to work his hips against her until she was panting and quivering and then he pulled his spent dick from her. Ashleigh straightened and stumbled but was prevented from toppling over by Christopher's strong arms around her waist. He turned her and pulled her into his arms for another kiss which he delivered slowly, languishing in the feel of her tongue against his.

He pulled back suddenly. "I could do this forever Ashleigh. But-"

"…but someone will eventually try to come in." She said. And plus his semen was gliding down her inner thighs and beginning to congeal.

"Right." He kissed her nose and lightly tapped her ass enjoying the feel of it bounce beneath his palm. Mmmm. "Get showered, okay? And I'll call you later."

"Alright." He watched until she gathered her shower kit and went into the separate shower area. Then he unlocked the door and quickly left. He headed down the corridor knowing that he was going to catch hell from the guys for not immediately coming back.

Christopher showered while listening to the guys ask him questions such as if his sweep of the ladies lockers proved secure, and other comments less tasteful. He blushed and tried to figure out a way to control his desire for Ashleigh each morning. It would just be impossible to watch her exercise; the way her body moved, to hear the way she breathed, to smell the fresh sweat on her body and not to be completely pulled into that direction. They were definitely going to have to come up with some way to control themselves during work hours.

The two made plans to meet at Ashleigh's house after work. She got off earlier than he did and decided she would showcase her talents in the cooking department by making him a home cooked meal. She didn't have much time for anything too fancy but broiling some steaks in the oven, throwing together a salad and roasting some potatoes would take no time.

She hurried to the door when she heard the bell ring and the sight of Christopher in his military fatigues made her heart beat speed up. He grinned and removed his cap.

"Hi Sweetheart. Food smells good."

He looked so formal standing there at the door. She ushered him inside and stood on tiptoes to kiss him.

"Come in, babe."

"Thanks for cooking. I could have brought something over."

"No trouble. I gotta check the steaks. Be right back." She headed for the kitchen and Christopher lingered in the living room taking in everything. She had great style. He walked over to a bookshelf where there were photos of her and her friend's from work. He easily recognized them. There was another of an older man and woman. The woman was slender, but otherwise looked just as pretty as Ashleigh—only with a much lighter skin tone, and he assumed it was her mother. The next was Ashleigh as a kid missing one of her front teeth and looking no older than seven or eight. She was a pudgy, cute kid flanked by two scrawny but cute girls; her sisters judging by how closely they resembled each other. Ashleigh didn't talk much about her family so he wasn't even sure if she even had siblings.

He picked up the last photograph. It was of Ashleigh with a handsome black man. They were evidently at some type of club and Ashleigh was absolutely gorgeous with her hair done up perfectly and her makeup flawless. She was wearing an evening dress that showed off a set of beautiful, thick legs in high heels.

He studied the man. He was fairly tall, though not as tall as he was. He was very good looking; the type of good looking that made for movie stars and models. DeAngelo. His brow furrowed. They really looked good together…

Christopher quickly replaced the picture when he heard Ashleigh's return and picked up a c.d. and pretended to be reading it.

She slipped her arms around him and looked up at him as if he was...perfect. "MMM. You ready to eat? I'm starving." He could feel the tension leaving his body as he looked down at the woman that he had fallen so deeply in love with.

"Yes Ma'am, I am." He smiled and thought about Uncle Ray's words. '*The good looking guys didn't have to work for women's attention. They just dropped into their laps.*' Christopher knew that he would do anything necessary to keep his sweetheart interested in him and only him.

After dinner they made quick work of cleaning up the dishes.

"Want to watch a movie?" She asked.

"Yep. Hey! Do you want to do the Darkside of the Rainbow?"

"I don't have the movie. Lance does." She said in disappointment. "I can borrow it from him and we can watch it this weekend."

"Sounds like a date."

They looked through her movie collection together. She had a lot of classics; Hitchcock, Fred Astaire. He picked up Heavy Metal.

"No way... Heavy Metal. I haven't seen this since I was a kid!"

"Do you want to watch it?"

His eyes lit up. "Can we?"

She chuckled and pulled it out of his hand and slipped it into her disc player. They got comfortable on her chaise, she was tucked securely in his arms. And then she hit play and her amazing surround system and high definition television caused his face to beam in delight. Hell yeah! Heavy Metal in surround and high definition! During the opening scene when the belly of the spaceship opened releasing the 1960 Corvette into outer space…and it landed with a parachute and the driver just drove off, Christopher kissed Ashleigh's neck in appreciation.

"You are the coolest girlfriend in the world." His face froze. He'd called her his girlfriend. To her face. How did she feel about him referring to her in that way?

"You are the bestest boyfriend." She said and snuggled deeper into his arms. He sighed…Alright Chris…stop being so damned insecure. This woman loves you. She's said it and she's shown it. He rubbed his thumb over her knuckles and allowed the stones that he had built around his heart to take one last tumble and to fall away completely.

~***~

The next day Christopher sat in his truck and dialed his sister's number…again.

"Hi Chris." She answered, her tone was uncharacteristically clipped.

"Alma." He drummed his fingers along the steering

wheel. "Thanks for taking my call." He said sarcastically. Alma worked but he knew her hours. She was avoiding him. "So what was that all about with Ashleigh?"

"What?" She spoke evasively.

"Alma, don't play games with me. You were very rude to Ashleigh."

"I-"

"And when did you become a racist?!" There was silence. "Look. I have a chance at happiness for the first time in my life. So I don't know why you don't like Ashleigh — and I don't want to know why because there is no goddamn reason why you shouldn't! All I care about is that when she comes around you don't even dare to look at her funny!"

He had never, in his life, raised his voice to anyone in his family. Christopher loved hard and held on to those people that he loved very closely. He would never hurt anyone that he loved with words. But he wouldn't tolerate anyone disrespecting Ashleigh either. Period.

Alma cleared her voice. "I hear you, Chris." She sounded sad. "Bye then." She said.

He felt suddenly guilty. "Bye Alma." The phone went dead in his hands.

Damnit, Alma was his tough, older, kick-ass sister that never let anybody bully him. Well...until he got taller than her. Then he was the one that made sure that her mouth didn't get into trouble. He didn't really have to beat anyone up. All he had to do was to walk up and glare at them.

"Fuck!" He dialed his sister. "Alma!"

"What?!"

"I'll see you Sunday!" He growled. "And I love you!"

He hung up.

~***~

"We're going out to Bartini's after work." Lance announced. Ashleigh looked up from her computer where she was doing more daydreaming than work. "Kendra's going to Bartini's?" She frowned.

"I'm just going for the non-alcohol variation." She explained.

"Ah. Gotcha. So you're going to pay six bucks for half a glass of fruit juice."

"Hmph." Kendra said. Her normally pretty face turned down into a scowl. "Ask Christopher to come, then since I know you can't do anything without him present."

Ashleigh turned to look at her friend surprised by her snippy tone. "I was just kidding. What's wrong with you? Baby hormones?"

Kendra sighed. "It's just…you're so buried up under him anymore. Why do you have to get so wrapped up in a man, Ashleigh?" Ashleigh opened her mouth to say something but wasn't sure what there was to say. "I mean I have Jeffery, Lance has Rick and we still make time for our friends."

"Is this because I skipped our weekly lunch?" She'd skipped it to have sex with Christopher...yeah, okay that was probably pretty bad. They had been together a week and it was pretty intense. Last Friday they were even supposed to have gone to the Mad Crabb to see him play guitar during karaoke...but they hadn't made it out of bed. "Gee, sorry. I guess I thought you guys would share in my excitement at meeting someone special."

Lance raised a brow. "Honey I'm rooting for you guys. But I don't want you to lose yourself in loving him." Did they really think that she was so pathetic that she HAD to be with a man? God...is that what she showed people? Ashleigh slowly stood and walked out of the room.

"Ashleigh?!"

"Please don't be mad, Ash!" Lance said.

She went to the elevator and stabbed the button and once she was in the lobby she headed for the canteen and straight for the vending machines. She fed a dollar bill into the machine and pressed the button for a Hershey bar. She peeled the paper back and ate half of it as she stood there.

God...it was so good. It had been ages since she'd allowed herself to enjoy a candy bar. She ate the other half a lot slower, just staring at nothing. She searched her pocket for another dollar and fed it into the machine and bought a second candy bar. This time, though, she went to the ladies room and ate it in secret.

Christopher's brow was knit with concern as he watched the monitor. He'd seen her shoveling the first candy bar into her mouth and wondered how much candy she might be allowed to eat. When she got the second one his back bristled. No way that she should be eating two.

Christopher rubbed his chin, his brow still gathered darkly.

~***~

Ashleigh returned to the office a few minutes later. She felt calmer although a bit guilty about the candy. She shouldn't have done that, but couldn't deny that it had calmed her. She now knew that Lance and Kendra thought that she used men like a crutch and she supposed that in some ways that had been true. With DeAngelo she just wanted to be made to feel beautiful. But it wasn't like that anymore. She wanted Christopher because he was her — just flipped inside out.

Kendra quickly came to her feet, her face filled with guilt. "Ashleigh...I didn't mean...I mean-"

"Kendra, what do you want to say?" Because she could clearly see that her friend had something she wanted to get off her chest.

Kendra gave her a thoughtful look. "Ash...*why* are you with Christopher?"

Lance got up and walked right out of the room as if shit was going to start flying.

"What do you mean?" Ashleigh wanted her to say what she meant. If they were going to have this conversation then she wouldn't make it easy by filling in the blanks for her.

Kendra wrung her fingers, her face full of concern. "Don't you think...you're jumping into this kind of fast?"

Ashleigh shrugged, her gaze on her friend steady. "I've been friends with Christopher for months even if we just went on our first date less than two weeks ago. How is that fast?" Yes, some people dated to find out if they were compatible. But with her and Christopher that first date just signified something they had already figured out; they both wanted to be with each other.

"Ashleigh, where do you see this going?"

"Where…any relationship goes, Kendra. I want to nurture it and allow it to keep growing. What are you getting at?"

The pretty woman took a deep breath. "Ash…do you think that you and Christopher…fit?" Ashleigh just watched her friend. "I'm saying that…are you sure that you didn't just jump into this thing with Christopher because of how you and DeAngelo left off? I mean, you're all hot and heavy with him-"

Ashleigh scowled. "No. He is not 'rebound guy'. I wasn't *trying* to fall for Christopher. But I couldn't help it because he is like no other guy I've ever met."

"And babies? What about babies? Your babies will probably have cleft palates. I looked it up, and it's congenital, you know? And it's not just a cleft palate that he has. Christopher has cranial facial deformities. His skull is smashed in! That is not a cleft palate, there's other things wrong with him!"

Ashleigh stared at Kendra in surprise.

"I'm just saying…nobody is going to look down on you if you back away from this guy. Or if you just want to fool around with him because…he's got a fucking great body! But Ashleigh, you don't want to MARRY this guy!"

Kendra rubbed her eyes and felt tears on her fingers. She cursed as Ashleigh watched her silently. Then she reached for tissues and wiped the tears from her eyes. She looked at her best friend.

"Well…cuss me out, hit me but do something!"

"How hard was that for you to say?"

Kendra sighed and more tears gushed from her eyes. "I've been wanting to say it for days. I just didn't want you to hate me…"

Kendra started crying. Lance came hurrying back into the room. He looked from one friend to the other. He loved them both, but Ashleigh had a special place in his heart because he knew what it was like to be an outcast of society. Kendra was a sweetheart but she had no clue. She was perfect.

Ashleigh took a deep breath. "I want you both listen to what I have to say. And don't interrupt me. I'm not angry because you feel that way, Kendra. Because I used to think in those terms too, maybe we all do. I know that when I go places with Christopher we will always be the center of attention. I already know that I have to come to terms with that.

"I also know that I can't think that way anymore. I was so concerned about looks that I stayed with a handsome man that had no capacity to love. I discounted your friend Ivan without even trying to get to know him because he wasn't my 'image' of beautiful. And once upon a time, I would have never considered a man that had the facial deformity that Christopher has.

"I know now that I felt very ugly. The world makes you feel ugly. Your friends when they say, 'if only you would lose weight,' are really saying, 'you are not as good as the rest of us.'" Kendra gave her a hurt look. "Oh, they don't mean to hurt you or pass judgment or call you ugly. But in my case, I put two and two together and what I came up with is that I wasn't good enough. But, as long as I could have beautiful men loving me I could pretend.

"I wish I knew then what I know now; it doesn't matter what people look like on the outside, because if you love them they are beautiful." She smiled. "Christopher is beautiful. I'd rather have him with a facial deformity then have DeAngelo with a perfect one." She nodded at Kendra.

"You don't need to define my beauty for me anymore. Your definition doesn't meet mine anymore because I think Christopher is beautiful and that's why I love him, not because of how he looks."

Kendra used her wet tissue to dab at the tears in her eyes. "I really come off as shallow. But it's certainly not what I meant." Kendra met Ashleigh's eyes. "But I guess I am. I didn't realize how judgmental I was being. I'd…like to get to know Christopher better. Can we get together and do that?"

Ashleigh nodded. "I'll talk to him about it."

Lance came forward and placed his hands on both of their shoulders. "Group hug?"

Corny or not, the three friends hugged and Kendra gripped her extra tight. "I'm sorry, Ashleigh, if I ever made you feel ugly. I love you. I didn't mean to hurt you."

"I know and that's why I let you."

Lance sighed. "Sometimes I feel awfully left out because I'm not a black woman."

Kendra pinched his cheek. "But you are in your heart."

"True." He nodded.

~***~

Ashleigh preferred spending time at Christopher's house in the evenings because his home was just so much more comfortable. They had gotten into the habit of her sleeping over and even though they couldn't drive in to work together since they had different quitting times, they could satisfy their morning 'desires' for each other and therefore create a more productive workout session in the gym, without overwhelming sexual tension...and without running the risk of becoming exhibitionists.

Because she got off work earlier, she had time to go home and pack her bag for the next day. She had learned to leave a supply of insulin in Christopher's refrigerator so that they didn't have to end their lovemaking just for her to go home to medicate.

As usual, he was at the door before she got a chance to ring the bell. He pulled her into his arms for a brief hug and kiss on the forehead. "Hi, sweetheart. Hope you're hungry because dinner's cooking."

"Mmm. Good, I'm starving." He pulled her inside and kissed her intimately. Ashleigh ran her hands up his back. After a few minutes of that Christopher went into the kitchen to check the chili. Maggie the cat moved cautiously towards Ashleigh who crooned a soft greeting.

She didn't dare try to touch the feline for fear that she would dash away like she always did. Maggie blinked green eyes at her and then scurried away. The cat did not like her.

Ashleigh went into the kitchen and watched her man as he cooked. "Hey, is it cool if my friends get together with us sometime?"

He looked up from where he was stirring the simmering chili. "Yeah, that'll be fine. As a matter of fact I was going to ask you to come watch me play at the Madd Crab Friday." He had already missed one week, though it had been worth it. He suppressed a smile at the memory of what they had been doing instead of listening to karaoke. "If you think they'd want to come along then they're welcomed to join us."

"That's a fantastic idea." She watched him cook, her body beginning to tingle at what lay beneath his clothes. She was already anticipating what was going to happen later tonight.

"Sweetheart," he glanced at her, "have you checked your blood sugar levels yet?"

"Not yet." She looked at him curiously.

"Maybe you should check it now."

She shrugged. "Yeah, alright." She grabbed the items that she needed and pricked her finger. Christopher turned off the chili and pulled bowls down from the cabinet.

"How is it, Sweetheart?" he asked as he ladled chili into bowls.

"It's a little high."

"Oh? What did you eat today?"

She walked into the kitchen. "Oh…you know; your shake, chicken salad on lettuce for lunch…"

Christopher stared at her. "Is that all?"

Ashleigh's eyes darted away and her cheeks turned red, even despite her brown skin. "Yes…and some unsweetened tea."

His baby was such a bad liar. But she was lying and he didn't like that. "Come and eat, honey. There are beans in the chili so that should help with your carbs. Did you already take your insulin?"

She met his eyes again and nodded. "Yep." She pulled up her chair and stirred the hot chili. He watched her for a moment and then began to eat. Ashleigh did the dishes while Christopher took care of some quick chores and then they went to bed.

Their lovemaking was another intense session filled with plenty of grunting and loud passionate moans. Afterwards he kissed the back of her neck where she was spooned up against him. "I have to workout, baby."

Ashleigh looked at him in exhaustion. "You didn't consider that a workout?"

He pulled himself out of bed with a soft chuckle. "I need to hit the treadmill, it just helps me to sleep. And yes, that was quite a workout. Truthfully, if we keep that up, neither of us will need to hit the gym again."

"Alright." Ashleigh pulled herself out of bed and reached for her panties.

"What are you doing, sweetheart?" He asked quickly, thinking she meant to go home. He intended to love on her a little more after he worked out.

"I'm going to watch you workout...I mean, unless you mind."

"I don't mind." He said in relief.

She paused as she pulled on her shirt minus the bra. "Can you workout in the nude?"

"Will that please you?"

"Very much so."

"Then yes I can."

She had the biggest grin as she walked into his workout room. She positioned herself in front of the treadmill and as he began to run Ashleigh was unable to remove her eyes from the sight of his bouncing penis and balls. He watched her watching him and smirked. Then his penis thickened right before her eyes and she met his eyes. He winked at her.

She decided that tonight she would get some more practice deep-throating him.

~***~

Christopher didn't know how he'd gone all of these years without the joy of sex. Now the least little thing made him hard and horny. Once Ashleigh reached under the sink for the dish soap and her gorgeous ass seemed to call to him and he wanted to slip her pants down and slam into her hard and fast.

But that wasn't the only way he liked it. He liked pushing into her softly as she begged him for more. He loved being with her and not just sexually. He enjoyed holding her in his arms while she fell asleep. He loved watching her on the treadmill as she found a pace that suited her. He loved the way she watched him as if there was nothing wrong with him.

But he worried, too. And maybe that was the nature of love. He worried about her health. He worried that her ex might try to come back into her life, he worried about them being out in the open and how the constant looks might affect her, he worried about meeting her family — because she had already met his twice and she had made no more mention of him meeting hers...but more than anything he worried about the lie.

~***~

Friday came and Christopher knew that he should be nervous because Lance and Kendra were bringing their significant others. But Christopher was just excited that Ashleigh would finally get to see him perform on stage. He sang for her almost every night but he really liked karaoke night and he looked forward to sharing it with her.

They met the others at the Mad Crabb. He had advised Ashleigh to tell her friends not to go in without him and so they all met up in the parking lot behind the old building. Jeffery; Kendra's husband was a big man and so was Rick, both having experience in professional football. But when they saw the big white man stepping out of his truck, even they were in awe. He was bigger than them *and* more cut.

Rick began to roll his head and flex his shoulders and Lance nudged him discreetly with his hip. Rick looked down at the smaller man and grinned. Yeah, Rick wasn't used to being the small man in the crowd. He'd been forewarned about Christopher's looks but didn't see anything about his face that affected him. He'd smashed guys in the face and seen them look worse than that. He was more concerned about how much the man bench pressed.

They shook hands and Rick greeted Ashleigh again, surprised at how different she looked from the first time that he had seen her. If only he knew that he was partially responsible for her new weight loss.

Rick was asking Christopher if he had played any sports when Jeffery and Kendra reached them. Jeffery shook his hand and eyed him in appreciation of his physical size. Jeffery didn't think in terms of beauty; only in the context of what it would be like to go up against him on the field. Christopher wasn't a guy that he wanted to go head on against, that was for sure.

"Nice to meet you." He gave Ashleigh a brief hug in awe at her weight loss but knowing that he shouldn't mention it or it would be misconstrued as him saying that she was fat. Jeffery knew all of the pitfalls in giving a woman compliments and mentioning weight was strictly off limits.

Christopher moved his guitar case to his left hand and placed his arm around Ashleigh. "Let's head in. The bar is kind of redneck. There's nothing classy about it. But they're good folks and the live band and karaoke is pretty entertaining."

"Karaoke?" Rick said warily.

"Don't worry, Big guy," Lance said while giving him a quick hug. "We won't force the world to hear you sing." Rick grinned and placed his hand on his lover's shoulders as they headed to the bar but he removed it a moment later and Lance felt slightly sad at the loss of contact. They couldn't be affectionate in public the way that Kendra and Jeffery could, or even the way that Christopher and Ashleigh could, especially not in Covington Kentucky when it wasn't just race but also the added issue of homosexuality.

The little bar was obviously popular because through the large picture window could be seen a nice sized crowd. A band was playing a rendition of Sweet Home Alabama.

Kendra mentally squared her shoulders. She didn't think there was any way in hell that she would have fun here but the point was not for fun, the point was to get to know her best friend's boyfriend and to stop being so judgmental…which meant not making fun of the fifty year old lady wearing a mini skirt and tank top…

The bouncer greeted Christopher enthusiastically, before he cut through the happy, dancing, drinking crowd and led the small group to a table that wasn't littered with too many empty beer bottles. Several of the regulars slapped his back in greeting and a waitress came by to quickly clean up and take their drink order.

"Hey Chris." She said with a curious grin. "You having a beer?"

"Hey Myrna. Yep. This is Ashleigh, my girlfriend." He made quick introductions of the other people at the table while Myrna scrutinized the pretty black girl. She was happy to see that he had someone. She had thought that he was a loner due to his scary face. The owner of the bar had even approached him to be a bouncer but he'd declined stating that he couldn't, he might hurt someone too badly. It was obvious that he was a real nice guy.

At first Christopher worried that Ashleigh's friends wouldn't like the place but after several beers and laughing at the expense of drunken karaoke performers, they warmed up and got comfortable. Jeffery and Rick mentioned football training camp and wanted to know what The Marine Corps workout was like. Christopher described it and everyone at the table was in disbelief. Christopher talked about going down to Georgetown as a kid to watch training camp and Rick quickly invited them all down this year to watch the team.

Christopher gave Ashleigh a look that said he was interested. She beamed at the idea of taking a weekend trip with him.

"Yeah, thanks a lot, Rick. We'd love to come down and watch." She said.

"That is if he doesn't keel over from heat stroke." Lance said with a severe expression on his face.

"Baby," Rick said earnestly, "there have been a lot of changes since Korey Stringer's death. I promise you that I will be alright."

"Hmph." Was his short response, because it wasn't just that. He wouldn't be able to go down and hang out like all of the other player's significant others. Rick wasn't 'out'. Lance was going to have to stay hidden away in a hotel. And when they played he wouldn't be able to be

VIP...Not that he was looking for that. But he wanted to be able to cheer his man in open just like any other person.

Kendra and Ashleigh picked up on Lance's mood and Ashleigh felt ashamed that she had been so wrapped up in her own troubles that she had not considered Lance's. Ashleigh saw Rick reach under the table and grip Lance's hand in his and Lance's expression relaxed.

They called Christopher's name to perform and Ashleigh became anxious. He had let the small group select the song that he would do and though he'd had to decline Lance's suggestion of Sir Mix-A-Lot's I Like Big Butts, they had made good recommendations.

Ashleigh quickly rubbed his back as he headed for the stage. Several of the regulars called out his name as he sat down on the stool and began to strum. Lance whistled shrilly through his fingers and Christopher blushed but grinned happily. He took a deep breath and began to sing Ordinary People by John Legend.

There was not a peep to be heard. All conversation stopped in the bar which hadn't been the case with the other karaoke singers—even the good ones. But Christopher's voice and style was captivating. The soft crooning was a contradiction to his appearance. One would never suspect that such a big strong man would have such a gentle and beautiful singing voice. When he finally stopped strumming and singing there was a prolonged silence and then simultaneously everyone began to applaud. He stood shyly and nodded.

When he returned to his table he was surprised to see everyone there standing and clapping loudly. He was used to people's happy response to his performances but he'd never had people waiting at his table to give him slaps on the back--and from his own girl...a sweet kiss. He decided that he liked having friends.

They stayed longer than he ever had before. Normally he was home by midnight. He'd perform his two songs, have a beer, sit and watch for a while nursing club sodas and then head home. But tonight they stayed until closing. Ashleigh drank two beers which is one more than she would normally have and was feeling very 'relaxed'. The same with Lance and poor Kendra was stuck with iced tea due to her delicate condition. Her two friends still managed to cajole her into getting up on stage and making a huge mess of Single Ladies by Beyonce. Of course Lance took the lead; looking very Kurt from GLEE!

They were no worse than any of the other drunk performers and actually got nice applause. Jeffery and Rick couldn't be convinced to go up and perform, however, since they were the designated drivers they weren't drunk either, which was a very good excuse.

At last call they all walked out of the bar, happy and promising to get together again before training camp.

"Wait here." Jeffery said to Kendra. "I'll bring the car around."

"We may as well wait together." Lance said. "You guys are the designated drivers anyways."

"True." Rick said and the three huge men left their dates at the sidewalk in front of the bar while they went around back to retrieve the cars.

Kendra squeezed Ashleigh's hand. "I like him! He's a wonderful man." Her eyes were bright and Ashleigh beamed. "He's so in love with you, Ashleigh. His eyes light up when he's looking at you. He listens to every syllable that comes out of your mouth. He is entirely focused on you even when he's talking to everyone else."

Lance nodded in agreement. "But I see the same thing with you. When he sings your expression changes and it's almost like there is no one else in the world."

Ashleigh had a thoughtful smile. She was about to speak when something made a loud thunk sound and Lance grabbed his face and went down to his knees.

"GET OUT OF HERE FAGGOT!"

There was a group of four or five young white men across the street. One of them had thrown a rock at Lance and it had hit him in the face! Kendra quickly went down to her own knees to check him. Ashleigh was staring in disbelief at the laughing men. One of them glared at Ashleigh and flexed his wiry muscles.

"What the fuck are you looking at, Nigger?!"

Ashleigh's mouth dropped in shock. Lance shook Kendra loose and stood up quickly. Blood was streaming down his face but he pushed the girls behind him.

"What the hell is wrong with you?!" He screamed. "You could have hit these ladies and one of them is pregnant!"

"I'm going to hit *you*, faggot." The leader said. He looked mean and full of hate even though he couldn't have been twenty-five years old. The rest of them trailed behind him as he crossed the street towards them and Ashleigh gripped Lance's arm and then she pushed Kendra behind her. Things were about to happen fast and she didn't want Kendra hurt.

The sound of several car doors slamming could be heard and guy crossing the street very nearly got run over by Rick who stopped his car with a screech of tires and didn't even bother to shut the door when he exited. The rednecks took in the two big black guys that were heading for them and the one huge white guy with the scary face, and it dawned on them that they had selected the wrong three people to harass tonight.

They held up their hands trying to plead innocent but the sight of Lance's bloody face said otherwise. Rick's eyes were red like demon eyes as he went barreling at the leader. He caught him at a dead run right in his middle.

Jeffery looked like a crazed bull as his nose flared while he breathed in ragged breaths. With lightening speed that seemed unnatural from such a big man he caught one of the men that thought he could run past. He slammed a big ham sized fist right into the side of the man's head…and he was out cold.

Christopher's face was like a mask. His eyes had gone dark, his expression was drawn in rage. He had one man by the back of the neck and the other by his upper arm. They looked like two children that had misbehaved in school instead of two grown men caught in the middle of committing a hate crime.

He slammed them into each other and Ashleigh grimaced at the sound of bones snapping. The men began screaming and crying. Christopher did it again. One was knocked out the other was holding his broken nose and teeth and moaning in agony.

He dropped the men quickly when he saw that Rick was slamming his fist repeatedly into the face of the leader who was now unconscious. Lance was hanging on his lover's arm, trying to pull him back but Rick neither felt him nor heard his cries to stop. Jeffery and Christopher rushed forward and grabbed the enraged football player, pulling him away from the battered, limp form of a man that would probably never be recognized again…if he lived. It took Lance throwing his arms around Rick's neck and holding on to him for the large man to finally snap out of it.

Rick gasped when he realized that Lance was hugging him and trembling. He blinked at the sight of his hurt lover. "Oh god, baby. Oh god, you're bleeding. Let me see, baby! Are you okay?" Lance was trying to tell him that he was okay and Myrna burst from the bar where everyone was gathered at the picture window watching what had just transpired. She grabbed Christopher's arm.

"You and your friends got to get out of here now, Chris! The cops are on their way!"

Christopher was frowning. "I'm not going to run away. We did nothing wrong."

"You said you can't fight because you're a Marine." Myrna said quickly. "Your hands, aren't they considered weapons?"

Christopher paled.

"We got to get out of here." Lance said in a shaky voice. "We can't have this in the papers…" The Bengals already had a bad rep without something like this appearing in the papers.

The bartender came out then. "Get your friends out of here Chris. Leave this no-account trash for the cops to deal with. They probably got warrants anyhow and have been nothing but trouble around the neighborhood. You get your people home before the cops cause you trouble."

Jeffery had a protective arm around his wife and was already leading her to their car. Ashleigh had sobered completely and was already giving Rick instructions to get Lance to the Emergency room. They were all going to meet at the ER and there was no longer any doubt of sticking around. Lance was hurt. They had to go.

As they drove to the hospital Ashleigh could see that Christopher was upset. His muscles seemed to bunch and he was glaring at the road. She reached over and placed her hand on the white knuckled grip that he had on the steering wheel and he took a deep breath and looked at her. She was surprised at the depth of pain she saw in his eyes.

"I'm so sorry, Ashleigh."

She shook her head in confusion. "Why?"

"I should have been there. I should have never left you alone." Anger seemed to take over his expression. "I heard what that guy called you. I wanted to kill him. I wanted to do to him what Rick did."

"Baby, it's not your fault-"

"Nobody is ever going to use that word against you while I'm around. EVER!"

She saw the muscles clenching in his jaw as he glared at the road again, gripping the steering wheel tightly. "Ever." He said more to himself. "Not against my woman, not against our children, not against our friends."

Ashleigh stared at him.

His woman, his children, his friends.

She gently pulled his hand from the steering wheel and when he released his strangle hold on it she kissed his knuckles hearing a slow breath release from his body.

"I wasn't scared because I knew you'd come back. I knew that everything was going to be alright, Christopher, because you were coming back."

Christopher bit his lip. He was a Marine...and more than that, he fought terrorism. He loved his job, he loved the reason he did his job. But what if...one day he wasn't able to come back?

~***~

Sunday they went to Christopher's parent's house and she noted that he was still subdued. She didn't want him to feel so bad about Lance, or bringing them to a redneck bar, or whatever it was that was causing him anguish. Lance was going to be perfectly okay, despite having a slight concussion. And no one blamed him one bit.

Alma had indeed apologized for her actions, under her brother's watchful eyes and then she had retreated to the kitchen...and had basically not acknowledged her since. They still didn't let her help in the kitchen, regulating her out to join Christopher and the other men. They treated her well and she was happy that at least Christopher had a family, although she didn't necessarily feel included. Her father and mother were divorced. Mama had moved to Tennessee and her father was remarried and living in Florida. She had two sisters who were just a phone call away...which was the best way to keep it.

As they lay in bed Sunday night, Ashleigh ran a soothing hand over his brow. Christopher closed his eyes and turned his face towards her. She traced his brow and then down his nose where a lot of the damage to his face was centered. Christopher had no bridge and therefore had a concaved look. Her fingers moved over his lips where scars created raised lines...perfect for exploring with the tip of her tongue.

She leaned forward and did just that. They had already made love twice but Ashleigh already felt like they could go for number three...

His hands came up to cup the back of her head and they kissed. After she withdrew she stared at him, his hands still there on the back of her head. She lay down and snuggled against him and he closed his arms around her protectively. She needed this type of love from him, where there was no judgment, no expectation to be someone else, where she could learn how to be just Ashleigh. This is the type of love that was slowly healing all of the damage that she had heaped on herself all of her life; from the time that she was the fat one in the family and Mama kept putting her on diets that didn't work...because she had secreted candy away and would binge when no one was around.

Even DeAngelo didn't know about it. Every time he stepped out on her with one of his many pretty slender girls, Ashleigh always found solace in food and fantasy; movies where the ugly duckling turned into the swan.

And now, for the first time in her life, she didn't care about being a swan. Christopher had shown her the value of the most important beauty of all; internal beauty. Ashleigh closed her eyes and pressed her lips against

Christopher's neck and that is the way they fell asleep.

CHAPTER 8

The first thing Monday morning, Christopher marched into his Commander's office. "Sir...I need to talk to you about something pretty important."

Bruce Koepke sighed. He liked Beast. He didn't want to lose him, but he already knew what he wanted to ask.

"Beast, you're a heluva Marine. You know that or you wouldn't be on an elite force. I don't want to lose you, son."

Christopher could barely meet his Commander's eyes. Finally he relaxed his formal posture and looked steadily at the older man who was more than his Commander, who was his friend.

"Bruce, I'm a Marine for life. That's never going to change. But...I can't go out on missions anymore. I'm not going to quit The Marines...but I want to step down from the DHS."

Bruce frowned. "TK, some of the others have spouses, girls, kids-"

"Yes, sir." He looked uncomfortable. It wasn't easy to talk about his facial deformity and how it makes you take a step away from the rest of the world, until you didn't even feel like you belonged. "When I didn't feel like I had anything else, I always had The Marines. I always fit in here. When my father...couldn't even remember my name I had the guys here—and you. The team is about as close to me as my own blood family.

"What made me into a person fit to serve in this Special Task Force is that's all I had and I put everything into it. But now...I got something else. It don't mean that I don't want to serve my country, or my protectees. It don't mean I won't deploy when I'm called. It just means that I don't want to go out on any more special missions."

Bruce studied him and then nodded once. "Damnit, son...start putting in for other jobs then. I'll start the paperwork to remove you from the duty roster. Are you sure about this?"

"Yes."

Bruce stood and shook his hand and clapped his back. "Well, if you found something that you love more than The Marines, I'm happy for you, Chris."

He nodded and his face broke into a happy smile. "I have."

~***~

Bruce told him that it might be best not to mention to the rest of the team that he would be reassigned. It bothered him that the guys might be mad at him or even feel that he was letting them down. He couldn't think of a better group of guys to work with. And he didn't like holding back from them, but there was no need to create tension over something that was purely a personal decision.

Also, he didn't feel the need to mention it to Ashleigh either. They had never discussed his missions in any detail and he didn't see any reason to tell her about his decision until he had at least found a new position. He hoped he could find a post nearby. He could even see himself being stationed at the airport...though he would miss watching Ashleigh on the monitors—not that she would be happy knowing that he had been perving her at every available moment. But he didn't think he was doing it in a stalker I-got my eye on you kind of way...well...maybe he was. But it was done more to give him joy and not to keep tabs on her, though he had seen that she hadn't returned to the vending machine for more candy bars.

Over the course of the next few days it seemed that everything was falling comfortably into place. Ashleigh noticed that the tension had left Christopher; he joked and laughed again. And Christopher was contemplating some very important steps into his future; first step was the career change from special forces and then next...he wanted to make his relationship with Ashleigh permanent. He realized that they were still new and he worried about her feeling rushed but he also knew that he wanted to live with her for the rest of his life. He'd known that after the very first night they'd made love.

One day after his talk with Bruce, Christopher walked into the lockers and the guy's all turned and looked at him. His brow gathered and he quickly thought back to what he and Ashleigh had done during their workout. They hadn't done anything overtly sexual had they? No, he was very mindful of the damned security camera and now that they spent most mornings with each other, that problem was generally satisfied before even arriving to work.

He shrugged and frowned. "What? Don't tell me you guys got another bet on me?"

Carlos gave him a snort. "We never had a bet on you." He looked away quickly. Christopher's frown deepened.

"Then what?!"

TK was the one to answer. "Commander just announced that we got called on a mission."

Christopher's face paled. "When?"

"Seven days."

Christopher swallowed. It had only been a month since he had asked for a change of position. It hadn't been enough time to find a new post...And now he understood why the guys were giving him 'the look'. They looked forward to missions so it wasn't that. It was because he was in a new relationship.

You never wanted to be sent on a mission right after getting married, having a baby, starting a new relationship. The superstition was that something would happen to you and sure as shit you'd leave someone a widow or fatherless. He didn't buy into the superstition but...he couldn't deny that he had seen it happen time and time again; whether it was because the guy's mind was preoccupied, or because he was trying to be too careful could very well be the reason. Regardless, being in a new relationship was the kiss of death on a mission.

He left the lockers and went straight to Bruce's office.

"Sir, I heard we're scheduled for a mission."

"Christopher...I couldn't get you off the roster in time. You're going to have to serve this one."

His charcoal eyes were dark and troubled. "What if I'm able to find a new position before we ship out?"

Bruce shook his head sadly. "You'd still have to hit the best qualified list and get selected before you could be considered in a new position; and that's the only thing that's going to get you off the roster. Just to BQ takes two weeks alone. I'm sorry son. My hands are tied."

Christopher thanked him and left. Damn.

One more mission.

That night Christopher took Ashleigh out for dinner. He preferred eating at home even if they picked up something and carried it back. Although, preferably he liked cooking for them and that way he had leftovers for lunch the next day and could make sure that Ashleigh was eating healthy. But he wanted to tell her about the news some place nice.

Ashleigh was excited about going out. More than anything she was just happy to dress in something other than sweats for her man. She put on a sexy red dress. It was size 14 and she thought that she could have worn it in a size 12. Now she was allowing her mind to accept the fact that she was no longer the fat girl. Yes, there were a lot of people that would look at her and still see someone that could stand to shed more weight. But luckily, that is not how she saw herself.

They sat in a dimmed restaurant that had a candle on the table and soft music playing in the background. She smiled. "Baby, what do you think about the six of us renting out a house for the weekend when we go down to Georgetown? That way Lance and Rick can be discreet and Lance won't feel so left out with us there."

Christopher had been quiet and thoughtful when Ashleigh spoke. He looked at her. His mouth drew down at the corners. "Sweetheart...I'm not going to be able to go to Georgetown."

"What? But why?"

He reached for her hand. "We got called on a mission. It starts in seven days."

Ashleigh's mouth dropped open. A mission; with guns and fighting and terrorists...and of course she couldn't stop her mind from recalling all the news around Bin Laden's capture and death. Would Christopher be involved in something like that?

His hand squeezed hers. She looked at him, her eyes troubled. "Christopher..."

"Sweetheart, I've been putting in for a change of duty. I asked to be removed from the task force. But this came up before my Commander could get it to go through. But this will be the last mission I'll need to go on. Just one more, honey. Okay?"

She gripped his hand. "How long?"

"Two months."

A harsh breath left her. She watched his eyes. "What are you going to be doing?" She had brought up his missions before but could tell that he didn't like talking about it with her. It was still kind of vague to her.

"We're not going to know that until we get briefed."

She didn't speak for a moment and then she swallowed.

"Will you be going to places like Afghanistan of Iraq or will you be staying in the states?"

He shook his head slightly. "I don't know, Sweetheart."

"Have your missions ever been in places like Iraq?" He didn't answer. "Do you really fight terrorism by going after drug dealers and gang members, Christopher? Or do you actually hunt down *real* terrorist like Bin Laden?!"

He reached out and stroked her cheek. "Sweetheart, I do exactly what I told you I do." She was studying his eyes but found that she couldn't read them; he was just looking at her with love and sincerity. "I can't tell you exactly what I do because it's classified. And when I don't share these things with you, it's not because I'm trying to be secretive. It's because what I tell you might risk your life, my life, my team's life...and the safety of our entire nation."

She cupped her hand over his and kissed his palm. "I understand." She closed her eyes and nodded. She wouldn't ask him again. But of course it made it worse...not knowing just how dangerous her man's missions were. She gazed at him, noting his big toned body and she remembered the look of his team. They were big and in top physical condition. Guys like that weren't just sitting around drawing up plans. Guys like that are who carried out those plans...

"And you're not going to have to go on any more after this?"

He nodded. It caused him so much anguish to see her so distraught. "I won't be placed on missions, no, but I'll still be active. You understand that don't you? I can still be deployed-"

"I understand that. It's the…missions that…" that required him to do things that were extra dangerous, things that others couldn't, things that no one could know about…

He watched the emotions cross her face and wished he hadn't taken her to a restaurant and that they were back at home where he could pull her into his arms and kiss away her fears. He looked down at the remainder of his partially eaten meal.

"Do you want to just get boxes and take the rest of this home?"

Ashleigh nodded. He paid the bill and they went back to his house. His brain couldn't stop wondering if he should have asked her to marry him weeks ago. Yet that would have definitely fed into the superstition. And he couldn't ask her before leaving--that wouldn't be fair to her if…It would feel like a desperate move to reassure her that he would return. And Christopher didn't picture asking her to marry him in that way.

~***~

While Christopher fed Maggie, Ashleigh picked up the guitar and began plucking absently on the strings. He peeked into the living room before joining her on the couch.

"Do you want me to show you how to play?"

She shook her head. "No." She passed him the guitar. "I want to hear you play."

He placed the strap over his shoulder and watched her. He played several love songs before he realized that she was on the verge of crying. Christopher abruptly stopped.

"Ashleigh, baby, I'm sorry! I was trying to make you happy not sad." He had already placed the guitar to the side and pulled her into his arms where she buried her face into his massive chest.

She tried to chuckle but it just came out like a sorry croak. "I'm okay. I just…two months is so long." Damnit…she knew that she sounded like a whiny baby and that's not what she wanted, especially now that she had grown accustomed to seeing him every single day. She didn't want him to think she was one of those needy people that didn't know what to do without a man constantly at her side, though that is pretty close to how she was feeling. She wanted him to focus on coming back safely…not on her emotional stability.

He rubbed her back and sighed. "Two months is a long time. But it'll go faster than you think." She suddenly moved her hand beneath his shirt and his muscles tensed at her soft touch before he melted into butter.

"I think we should make every single night memorable." She looked at him with open desire. Christopher silently nodded his agreement before he leaned forward and kissed her, his hand moving behind her head. There was desperateness to their kissing. Ashleigh's hands clutched him and when he stood, lifting her, she wrapped her arms around his neck without breaking the kiss.

Christopher carried her to his bedroom and partially covered her with his body as he lay her down on her back. He sat up on one elbow and looked down at her. Her lids were heavy and half hooded as she, in turn, watched him.

"I love you; more than anything." He whispered.

Her breath caught in her chest and the tears that she had been fighting finally sprung into her eyes. She wiped them quickly and sniffed back tears.

"I'm sorry. I'm sorry-"

"Don't cry Ashleigh…" He showered her face with kisses; attempting to kiss away her tears. With trembling hands she reached between them and pushed one down into his pants. Christopher sighed and lifted himself up enough to undo the button and pull down the zipper. Ashleigh gripped his semi-hard cock while his eyes closed and his own breath became strained. She quickly craned her neck forward and kissed his jaw until he turned his head so that she could kiss his lips. She kissed him hard and frantically and Christopher rolled onto his back, eyes still closed. Ashleigh moved on top of him and he could hear her soft cries of desire, passion, sadness…

And then he felt the kisses trailing down his torso and suddenly her tongue jabbed at his frenulum and he groaned. Her hand on his shaft was firm, causing it to quickly swell. And when her warm, wet tongue danced around the sensitized head, Christopher's body began to tremble and his hips thrust forward. He licked his lips and blew out a loud breath, resisting the urge to bury his fingers in her hair, resisting the urge to fuck away his misery.

Finally he cupped his hands on each side of her face and thrust gently in and out of her mouth. Ashleigh groaned, her eyes closed in deep concentration, tears wet on her lashes.

"Love you, Ashleigh…" He moaned. "Love you…"

She released him and he opened his eyes to see her tugging down her panties and hiking up her dress. There was a lost, anxious expression on her face as she quickly straddled him. Christopher's lips parted at the sight of her. She was pure sex. He should have fucked her mouth. It's what she wanted. With a groan she lowered herself onto him. He saw her grimace and he didn't move, though the feel of her tight passage made standing still nearly impossible.

But once she'd lowered herself completely and her round ass was flush with his testicles, Christopher reached forward and gripped her hips, holding her in place. He rolled his pelvis against her and then he thrust upward repeatedly, each move punctuated by a loud grunt. Ashleigh's hands gripped his wrists, holding him while she threw her head back and sought his rhythm, matching it. Her hips rolled counter to his clockwise.

The friction was maddening. Ashleigh brought herself up and Christopher's hips followed. He thrust, seeking her heat, his hips moving quickly, withdrawing enough only to thrust back into her rapidly.

"Oh yessss!" She dragged, her eyes closed in ecstasy. "I need you…" she groaned. "Chris, I need you, baby…"

Christopher clenched his teeth; biting back a whimper, and then he buried his fingers into the soft flesh of her hips and held her tightly. His hips moved smoothly in long deep strokes.

"Oh Sweetheart…" His heart was pounding in his chest. Ashleigh suddenly leaned forward, planting her small hands on his shoulders. Her eyes bore into his in an incredibly raw and open manner in which she seemed to be trying to absorb every nuance of him.

Her rhythm quickened, he could hear the sound of her ass slapping his pelvis each time she slammed down on him. His breath was just a series of shudders, whimpers and moans. No one but this woman had ever made him feel this way; almost overwhelmed by the act they were sharing. Ashleigh's tight grip on his dick matched the grip that she would forever have on his entire being.

He knew that a man should always wait for his woman to cum, but no one had ever fucked him so hard and so thoroughly and Christopher's body suddenly tensed and then he was awash in an implosion of pleasure. He almost couldn't see as stars shot before his eyes.

He grunted in a series of short breaths and then one loud growl. "Oh fuck! Baby, I'm going to cum!"

"Yes, baby! Cum…fill me up…need you…" She cried, her eyes boring into him her body working him even more rapidly. Christopher's big hands gripped her ass, the bouncing continued as she worked her body faster over his. It felt like he was having a seizure as his semen exploded from him and then pumped rhythmically, flooding her. Suddenly her fingers tightened into fists, gripping his shirt and he saw her eyes become glassy and far away, mouth falling open silently.

And then he heard her scream.

Christopher tightened his grip on her rapidly bouncing bottom and slammed into her even though he was at the tail end of his own orgasm. He dug one foot into the mattress and used it as leverage to jack hammer into her canal and her loud cries became staccato intermingled with words. Soon her movements slowed and she collapsed panting on top of him. He kept his spent cock buried inside of her until the act of her falling on him forced him out. His arms went around her body and he held her, cocooning her.

It suddenly dawned on him what she was crying as she came; *need you need you…*

~***~

Ashleigh had fallen asleep there on top of him still fully dressed; they both were. After holding her sleeping form for a long time, he finally shifted her onto the bed so that he could go to the bathroom. When he returned with a wet cloth he was surprised to see her watching him.

"Hi, Sweetheart."

She smiled. "Hi." He cleaned her while she spread her legs for him. He loved her smooth mons. She waxed regularly, but sometimes he wondered what her hair would be like down there. It would be something nice to explore. They snuggled in bed, her head on his shoulder. His body was her most comfortable pillow.

"I'm going to be the best Marine girlfriend. I promise." She said, almost as if she was convincing herself.

"Going to be? You've already achieved that." They'd only been dating for a little over four months but already he felt like Ashleigh was a permanent fixture.

Her hands moved along the hard plains of his chest and her nails gently scratched at his auburn chest hair.

"I'm going to make you cookies and brownies. Hell, I'm going to be sending care package big enough for you to share with everybody-"

He looked down at her. "Sweetheart…it's not like being deployed. We're on a Special Taskforce. We don't get any care packages. We can't even have a cell phone or write home. When I'm away for those 2 months you won't be able to contact me at all."

Ashleigh stopped breathing as she looked up into his face.

"You can't even call me to let me know that you got there okay?"

Had the moment not broken his heart he could have smiled at the innocence of her question. He killed people. She worried that he might not arrive safely? It was so unbelievably sweet. If only she understood…and thankfully she didn't.

"No, baby. We won't get our cell phones back until after debriefing."

"I can't even send you letters…" She whispered.

He pulled her against him. But all she could think is that she was so addicted to him. His smell; masculine and clean soothed her to sleep each night. His touch, his presence, and the sight of him; the open love in his eyes, his crooked smile, all helped to reassure her that she was worthy of being loved. Two months without her Christopher would be hell on earth.

~***~

Lance had a thoughtful expression on his face as he watched Ashleigh. She fidgeted with her ink pen and tried to look as if she was paying attention to the conversation, but he knew that this mission of Christopher's is all that was on her mind right now.

"Why don't we go out Friday?" He said and then quickly added, "but not to that karaoke bar. I mean like to a place that has less racism."

Kendra's lips curled as she gave his hand an affectionate rub. Even though it had been months he still had a faint scar right at his hairline and might always have it. "Yeah, someplace less Ku Klux Klan would be nice." They looked at Ashleigh who frowned when she realized that she was the center of attention.

"What?" Her brow was gathered as she had only been pretending to listen.

Lance didn't give her a hard time about it. "We should all get together before Christopher ships out. Maybe we can get together this Friday."

Ashleigh opened her mouth and then allowed it to snap shut. "We're…going to be kind of busy." A red blush began to creep up from her neck.

He rolled his eyes. "You two will have to take a break in order to eat, right?"

She frowned at him. "Just long enough to run into the kitchen to get bottled water and a snack cake." She rubbed her chin. "I could buy a cooler…"

"Okay, Ashleigh, TMI. Just enjoy your boyfriend this weekend. I think we'll understand." Kendra smiled.

Christopher continued to search for jobs that week. He wanted something lined up when he returned because he was not taking any chances of being stuck on the roster again for another special assignment.

Each night Ashleigh made the evening memorable, just as she promised. They made love in places and in positions that he'd never dreamed he'd do comfortably. And he enjoyed every second of it. But each day brought them closer to his ship out date. He tried to prepare her as much as he reasonably could. He explained that the entire team would gather at the subbasement sometime in the later afternoon on Monday. They would fly out together and he would return 60 days later.

They had to suspend their workout session in the basement because he and the crew spent most of their time conditioning. A shadow crew had come in to take over where Christopher's team left off. The shadow crew wasn't with The Marines but were trained security personnel, though there were only seven of them. But along with the normal Federal Building and Federal Courthouse security there were never any problems transitioning out.

On Sunday, the two were forced to take a break from loving each other. Christopher wanted to visit his parents one last time for dinner before his mission. As they sat around the dinner table, the family all lowered their heads and prayed for Christopher's safe return. Since Ashleigh watched his every move, she saw a shadow cross his face.

After dinner Christopher, his brother Butch and a cousin; Nick, all played with the kids while the rest of them sat on the porch and cheered. One day, she thought, he'll be playing with our kids like that. And the thought made her both happy and sad.

~***~

They drove in to work together for the first time early Monday so that he wouldn't need to leave his car in the underground parking garage. As they walked down the street hand in hand, she plastered on a smile. Ashleigh had tossed and turned all night and he had barely slept because of it. Well…that wasn't true. He wouldn't have slept regardless.

"One last kiss?" She requested once they were in the lobby.

He leaned down and kissed her. "That doesn't have to be the last one." His softly accented voice made her smile tremble around the edges as she fought back her sadness. He didn't need to be a witness to her anguish. She would have to put on her big girl panties just like every other wife, mother, and girlfriend had to do when they had a man that served in The Armed Forces. "We can meet for lunch if we can do it early; how's that?"

She beamed. "Really?"

"Yeah, if we can stay close, maybe just to the cafeteria?"

She stood up on her tiptoes and kissed him excitedly. "Yes! What time?"

His hands went around her much smaller body. "11:30?"

"Perfect!" She said happily and released him. Now it was okay for her to go off to her office because this wasn't actually goodbye. She looked over her shoulder and saw him watching her. "See you in a little while. Love you!"

He smiled crookedly. "I love you too, sweetheart." As soon as she was gone the smile slipped from his face only to be replaced by a look of determination. He headed straight for Bruce's office. He'd been thinking of something as he lay in bed last night. And if his Commander would agree then he wouldn't be going on a mission.

"Beast...You know I can't take you off the mission-" Bruce had a look of sorrow on his face that normally showed nothing but control. He knew that Christopher was dating the little trooper. All men that had new girlfriends, frightened wives or mothers came to him and asked the same thing. He had to tell them no.

"That wasn't what I was going to ask, Sir."

Bruce gave him a curious look. "Okay. What?"

"I want a different mission. Well not really a mission but-"

Bruce was already shaking his head. "Beast...Christopher, you don't want to do that, son. If you leave this team you have to learn a whole new one. They know you and you know them. Another team won't."

"Let me explain." Christopher began to pace as he tried to form the right words. He'd never had to speak about this to anyone and the words weren't easy. But he must have been convincing because when he finished speaking Bruce stared at him.

"Yes." He was nodding his head. "It's well within your right, son. I'll need to make some calls but no one can deny your request If it's what you want then I'll make it happen." Bruce

smiled. "I suppose the little trooper will be relieved. What does she think about it?"

"I wasn't sure what you'd be able to do it. We're going to have lunch before we ship out and I'll tell her then."

~***~

Ashleigh was talking on the phone with a member of her analyst staff. Her eyes kept darting to the clock. Damnit! It was already 11:17 and Gloria was still going on and on about non-work related stuff. Why did people go into details about their personal business?! Why couldn't she understand that no one in their right mind needed a detailed accounting of your weekend when all you did was hang out with the same man that you've been married to for twenty years and go out to eat at the same restaurant you went to each Friday???

Gloria wasn't exactly her boss but high enough on the food chain that Ashleigh had to consider her exit strategy very carefully.

"...so the bartender is single and he's such a nice guy. I think his wife died in '07...wait, maybe it was '08. Because it was the same year that Bob and I bought the Tahoe--"

"OH MY GOD!"

"What?!" Gloria exclaimed.

"There's a...fire! FIRE DRILL! I gotta go. Talk to you later!" Ashleigh quickly disconnected the phone and then she sighed and shook her head. Her eyes darted to the clock. 11:22! Damnit! She darted out of her office.

"Where are you going?!" Kendra yelled as she rushed past her office.

"Lunch with Christopher!"

"Tell him we said bye!" Lance yelled.

But Ashleigh was already down the hall pressing the button to bring the elevator. Gloria had ruined her plans to have lunch already purchased and set up at one of the corner tables where no one ever sat. It would have given them more time to spend sitting with each other instead of standing in line waiting to make their purchase. She rushed to the line and grabbed a tray, loading it with things that she knew Christopher enjoyed. She kept glancing at the entrance so that she wouldn't miss him, happy that her plan appeared to be working. He hadn't arrived yet. She had time to quickly set their meal out and when it was all set she glanced at the clock. 11:35. Oh hell! Now he was late.

At 11:40 her anxiety had built. This was eating into her time with him! Worse is that she had darted out of her office without her cell phone. He probably got held up and had left her a message. But at 11:45, when he still hadn't shown up Ashleigh forgot all about the food that she'd purchased. She went straight for the elevators to take her down to the subbasement. Maybe he'd gotten preoccupied. She should get her phone but decided she'd head downstairs and knock on the security doors just in case he got sidetracked. If she didn't get an answer then she'd go up and check her messages.

Ashleigh used the elevator in the back corridor near the nurse's station. When she pressed the button to bring the lift, the door immediately opened and she was happy that she wouldn't have to wait for it. She pressed the button for the subbasement nervously, knowing that it was stupid to be worried. But she couldn't help it. Christopher had never been late before...god...what if he'd been forced to ship out early?!

"No no no," she moaned. When it reached the subbasement the elevator doors didn't open. She looked around quickly. Why weren't the doors opening? She pressed the button indicating 'door open'. Nothing happened. Real fear hit her and she quickly pressed L for the lobby. Nothing happened. She quickly pressed 7, for her floor. And still nothing happened.

The air froze in her chest. She was stuck in the elevator! Ashleigh had a very real fear of small enclosed spaces. Elevators were bad for her, but made tolerable only due to the fact that she would be in one for less than a minute.

She looked around the small compartment frantically as if another exit would magically appear, and then she slammed the sides of her fists against the closed elevator doors. "Hey! I'm locked in the elevator!"

Was this a lockdown? Well why hadn't she heard any alarms or seen any flashing light? Well that was easy; they didn't put lockdown warnings on the main floors.

"Hey!" She bammed on the door again, feeling panic well up inside of her. Then she saw a control panel near the buttons and she opened it expecting to see a telephone like in the movies. There was a button that said PRESS IN CASE OF EMERGENCY.

She pressed the button three times. "Hello? Is someone there?" Ashleigh did that for the next five minutes but there was no one on the receiving end.

She began to feel as if there was no air and had to close her eyes and convince herself that just because she was trapped in a small, enclosed area didn't mean there wasn't any air. And how long did that lady say lockdown was in effect? Five or ten minutes as they transported prisoners?

Okay. She could probably do a few minutes. Oh why had she not gone back for her cell phone?! Idiot! Ashleigh rubbed the tension from her neck as she prepared to wait it out.

~***~

Five minutes passed and the doors still didn't open; well what she assumed was five minutes. She didn't wear a watch and yep…the cell phone was still upstairs on her desk.

And that's when she began to worry. Was there a real emergency? Yes because lockdown was only a few minutes and it had already been more than that considering how late Christopher was. What if there was a real fire??? Had karma come back on her for telling that lie to Gloria?

Oh Jesus! She was trapped in the elevator during an emergency. The panic crept up on her like wicked little fingers. Sweat began to roll down her body and the air in the elevator suddenly became hot and stale.

"Help! Someone, I'm trapped in the elevator!" She began bamming on the door again and this time she didn't let up.

"Christopher!" She screamed. "I'm in the elevator!"

After five minutes of that she was exhausted and she moved into the corner to sit down and hold her knees tightly.

Calm down, calm down. She chanted to herself as she began to rock. No one has ever died due to being trapped in an elevator. Even if…god forbid, I'm trapped for a few hours, someone will eventually have to wonder why this freaking elevator is still locked.

She tried to rationalize her way through the panic. Christopher is expecting her. Yes. He was going to find her and he wouldn't like knowing that she'd been scared of a little old elevator. She began to relax by small degrees. He was going on a dangerous mission, and she could tell that he didn't want to go. How much faith would he have in her if she couldn't even handle something like this?

She opened her eyes and unclenched her fist, taking in a soothing breath. Yes…better. Have faith in Christopher. He'll get you out.

Time stood still, becoming endless to her. The only thing she could do was to think about pleasant things; Christopher and her friends, the love fest that she'd had this past week…Her head was buried in her hands when the elevator door finally did open. She jumped to her feet immediately only to be surprised by a man wearing army fatigues standing in the entrance with a concerned look on his face.

It wasn't Christopher but she'd seen him before. He had been one of the men present when she had fainted; some type of commander. It didn't matter to her, he was in Christopher's troop and she recognized him. She gripped him in relief, clinging to him as if he was a lifeline.

"The doors didn't open. I was trapped," She explained nearly hysterically while physically shaking. She felt his hand patting her shoulder stiffly.

"Yes, Ma'am." He cleared his throat, seeming uncomfortable. "There was an incident at The Federal

Courthouse."

"Is Christopher okay?!"

The man gave her back another awkward pat. "He's okay. Everything is okay. Shots were fired but we controlled the situation. Everyone is okay with no casualties."

She looked past him out into the empty corridor. He had somehow caused the doors to be frozen open and she wanted to be on the outside of this elevator, but more than that she didn't understand why Christopher wasn't here now. "Where is he?"

"Lt Jameson came to me earlier today and requested that I take him off this mission and that I give him another." Her eyes got big, hopeful. Bruce resisted his urge to smile as he continued to stare down at her. He didn't think that she was aware that she was touching his shirt fronts, but he was...very aware.

"I complied with his request." Bruce didn't feel as if it was his place to give her the details. That was between her and Beast. "I spoke to him right before he shipped out and he asked me to tell you that he explained everything in a message on your phone and that everything is going to be okay..." Bruce cleared his throat and blushed, "and that he loved you. I'm sorry that he couldn't give you the message himself but has already shipped out. Once I notified his new team of the change they were able to assemble quickly. They'll be able to get started later this evening."

She stared at him in horror. Christopher...was gone?

"I didn't say goodbye to him..." She stared at him and the anguish in her eyes melted his military stiffness. Bruce rubbed her shoulders gently and gave her a sympathetic look. When he spoke again his voice was gentle.

"Lieut--Christopher was going to explain everything during lunch with you and due to the incident at the Federal Courthouse he missed that lunch. He did ask me personally to tell you not to worry and that he is going to be okay and that he loved you. Unfortunately, that's all I have. I need to prepare my men to ship out...but I want to tell you personally."

Ashleigh came to attention. "I have to get upstairs! I left my phone on my desk. And may I have your name please?"

"Chief Warrant Officer Bruce Koepke, Ma'am." He used a card to scan into the security box and pressed the 7th floor, surprising her that he knew which floor she worked on. He made no attempt to leave the elevator, riding up with her and she was thankful. He must have seen the panic on her face.

Once the doors opened she dashed out and remembered to thank him just as they began to close. He was big, gruff but his expression softened momentarily before he nodded and disappeared behind the closing doors.

Ashleigh hurried into the office. Lance craned his neck at her and Kendra came out of her office.

"God, Ashleigh...if you and Christopher are going to do it at work can you at least clean yourself up afterwards?"

She paused long enough to yell over her shoulder. "I was trapped in the elevator!"

Lance and Kendra came into her office while she was searching for her cell phone.

"You've been gone for nearly two hours." Lance said. "Gloria called asking if the fire drill was over. I told her yeah but we had to attend a safety meeting—*what are you doing*?"

Ashleigh looked at him frantically as she pulled items from her purse. "I missed seeing Christopher! He shipped out already!"

"Oh no…" Kendra said.

She located her phone and quickly dialed into her voicemail. She heard Christopher's voice and held up her finger for her friend's to be quiet.

"*Babe*?" The reception was cutting in and out, which is the reason they normally texted. The subbasement just couldn't get a clear signal. "*Call me back as soon as you get this!*" Then the phone went dead. She went to the next message which was just a minute later.

"*Sweetheart, where are you?*" He was cutting out bad. "*Babe…emergency Federal C…house. Ashleigh…mission! Baby, DON'T WORRY! OKAY? I got my mission…so you don't have to worry. I…active. Can you…me, Sweetheart? I'M NOT…! I gotta go, they…my phone. I love…and sorr…you! Two…okay? I love you!*"

Ashleigh was squeezing the phone tight. She replayed the message three times but didn't make much more sense out of the string of words that she could make out. Lance and Kendra listened and Lance thought he was saying that he got his mission changed.

And then Ashleigh remembered that is exactly what his Commander had said. "I need to talk to the guy that got me out of the elevator!" They offered to go with her but she was already back out of the room and heading for the elevator, completely forgetting that she had just recently sworn herself off them.

Ashleigh's heart was beating a mile a minute and she wanted to cry. She couldn't believe that she had missed him! She didn't get a chance to tell him goodbye and how much she loved him, how much he meant to her. She had saved it all for when she would see him at lunch. She felt tears stinging her eyes. He'd changed his mission for her. She would have never asked him to do that. He shouldn't have changed anything! Maybe that is what gets soldiers killed…what if her stupid fear and needy attitude got him hurt?

Ashleigh was openly weeping when she got back down to the subbasement. She hurried to one of the security doors and began knocking on it frantically.

"Commander! I need to talk to you, please!" Ashleigh knocked and looked around for one of the security cameras. She waved at it frantically trying to capture someone's attention. But after ten minutes it was evident that no one was coming.

Ashleigh replayed Christopher's message again as she headed back upstairs and to the canteen. She went to the vending machine and got a candy bar and ate it while she replayed his message, trying to understand or maybe just wanting to hear his voice.

~***~

Lance watched Ashleigh pick at her salad. "Honey, if you

don't eat you're going to get sick. You have to eat when you have diabetes."

Ashleigh shook her head and offered him a smile. "Sorry. I guess I was daydreaming." She took a bite of the wilting salad and felt like gagging.

Kendra cleared her throat. "Do you want us to come over tonight?"

Ashleigh shook her head. "You two came over Monday and Tuesday." Now it was Friday.

"You don't have to spend the weekend alone." Lance said while sipping a glass of wine. "Rick and I were thinking about throwing some steaks on the grill…"

Ashleigh shook her head. She wouldn't be good company and she didn't want her friend's to think that she couldn't manage her first weekend alone without Christopher. She was not going to turn into a basket case. "I'm going to hang out at Christopher's place and maybe take care of some yard work."

"You?" Lance's eyebrow quirked up.

"Yes me. I'm not going to mow or anything. Christopher already took care of that. A lawn guy is coming over every other week to do that. But I can make sure no weeds pop up in the garden," even though the garden was perfect with not a weed in sight. During the week it would be easy. She could come in to work, finish up cases, hang out with her friends but on the weekend she knew that she'd be lonely. So she was going to fill it by searching for a weed to pick.

Ashleigh had learned more about the shadow crew that had replaced Christopher's team. They were brought in by the Federal Protective Service whenever the men went out on missions. Also, she had learned that you didn't just go around announcing that the secret marine crew stationed in the subbasement was currently out on a mission. She learned all of this from the guards who were more than a little reluctant to speak to her about security issues — but who did anyways because they had seen the odd couple together long enough to know that they were in a relationship. Eventually Ashleigh stopped the questioning when it became obvious that the guards knew less than she did. She would just have to do what every other wife and girlfriend had to do; wait.

Ashleigh 'unofficially' moved in to Christopher's house. She had been going over there every day in order to feed the cat but during that first weekend without Christopher she had returned to the neat house with enough clothes to last her several weeks — not to mention what was already over there. She hadn't made plans on exactly how long she was going to stay, but when she packed she just didn't stop until she had two suit cases and a tote filled with her personal care products.

"Hello?" She announced when she arrived, not wanting to alarm the cat and get jumped. "Maggie?" The cat evidently knew that it wasn't her Daddy coming in through the door because she was hidden, just as she had done all week long. Ashleigh immediately placed fresh food and water in her dishes and waited a few feet way to see if the cat would become interested. But there was no sign of the little feline that still didn't like her.

Ashleigh put her things away neatly. She didn't think Christopher would mind that she emptied two of his drawers and pushed some of the items aside in the closet.

She wasn't planning to redecorate or anything, although she didn't think he would mind if she did. She turned on the stereo and smiled when she recognized some of the music that he'd just recently listened to.

She took a deep breath and felt suddenly good. It felt like Christopher was still here; the house, the sound of the music, the faint smell of the food that he cooked — this was all Christopher.

~***~

"Ash...have you been working out?" Ashleigh looked up from her computer. Lance was standing in the door to her office looking as if he'd rather be somewhere else.

"What?" She said, trying to replay what he'd just said. Working out. "No. Why?" She swept her bangs out of her eyes and pushed them behind her ears. Her hair really had gotten too long to be considered short and cute. It was more like long and scraggily.

Lance stared at her. "You kind of picked up some of your weight again and...I know how hard you worked on it..."

She hadn't worked out in the entire three weeks that Christopher had been gone. It had been fun because Christopher was there. But now she didn't even want to go into the subbasement. Ashleigh scratched her thigh where the material of her pants seemed tight and itchy. She sighed. "Yeah...I guess I slacked off over the last few weeks. I'll get back on track." Lance lingered and then nodded and left her office.

Ashleigh waited a few moments and then glanced at the door which was cracked open. When she was sure that no one was around she slipped a candy bar out of her desk drawer and quickly ate half of it.

When Ashleigh got back to Christopher's house that night she went through her nightly ritual. "Maggie? Mommy's home." The cat just didn't come out for her. She knew that it was around because in the last three weeks she'd seen the litter box filling up and needing to be changed. And each night the food and water needed to be replaced.

Ashleigh scowled as she changed the litter that night. "At least I could get a quick meow in thanks, Maggie." She said. After dumping the offending article she washed her hands and changed out of her work clothes and into one of Christopher's USMC shirts. It was like a dress on her but the main thing is that each of the shirts smelled of him even though they were freshly laundered and folded away neatly in his drawers.

Still it was what he worked out in and still held a hint of his masculine smell. She had no problem picking up that smell and bathing in it. After changing she headed for the kitchen to check the pantry knowing that she wouldn't find what she really wanted to eat. She wanted roasted Cornish hens and collard greens and baked sweet potatoes smothered in brown sugar and cornbread made from white cornmeal. And then maybe some jiffy cornbread for desert, smothered with butter and jam.

She scowled again as her stomach tumbled. She was so hungry that she wanted to just shove food down her throat. She wanted to wallow in chocolate and drink buckets of syrup. She wanted pudding and and and...

Ashleigh lowered her head into her hands. She couldn't do this every day, if she did it would kill her...

Every single day Ashleigh had been eating PF Chang's and pizzas and pastries from her favorite bakery. Then she'd get sick when her blood sugar couldn't regulate what she was pouring into her system. Sometimes she'd pray to god not to let her go into a diabetic coma as she lay in Christopher's bed sweating with her heart beating a mile a minute. She'd promise to be good but the next day she'd begin the cycle all over again.

Ashleigh slowly lifted her head and stared into the pantry. She reached for a bag of cookies.

She ate until there wasn't any more and when she reached the bottom of the bag it surprised her. She stood there at the counter panting at the empty bag of cookies. She quickly crumbled it and darted into the bathroom. She lifted the toilet seat and shoved her finger down her throat until she had regurgitated all that she'd eaten. When her stomach was empty all she could do was lay on the floor panting, she felt something warm and furry touching her foot. She pulled her head from the bathroom floor and saw Maggie rubbing against her before she darted away.

Later that night Ashleigh went into Christopher's weight room. She put music on and then stared at the treadmill. She hadn't worked out in three weeks and in that time had gained over 10 pounds. Every day she felt sick and listless. Worse is that Christopher would be home in a month and a half weeks and she looked a hot mess. Ashleigh climbed onto the treadmill and began slow. She felt her body quiver as she pushed it but once she caught her second wind she remembered the way the endorphins would flood her system. She turned up the speed. She listened to the sound of her feet pounding on the deck of the treadmill. Her blood was racing through her body and her lungs burned. It felt good.

Maggie jumped up on the weight bench and watched her. Ashleigh gave her a quick nod. This is the sound that both of them had missed; the pounding of feet on the deck of the treadmill.

~***~

Ashleigh got out of her car Sunday afternoon. She had roamed around Christopher's house missing him and had a desire to do something that would make her feel even closer to him. Now she was wondering what in the hell she had been thinking. She lingered there for a moment and considered getting back in though she said she wouldn't do that. But she considered it. Then one of the kids called her name.

"Miss Ashleigh!"

She plastered on a smile and headed to the little girl; Rachel. "Hi Miss Ashleigh! Where's Uncle Chris?" The other kids surrounded her in curiosity.

"Your uncle is still on his mission."

"Aww." They began to disburse. Rachel stuck with her and slipped her little hand into Ashleigh's.

"I don't like when he goes away for a long time." She said. Ashleigh gave her small hand a gentle squeeze.

"I don't either." The two of them headed for the side door and Ashleigh took a deep breath and knocked briefly before poking her head in. "Hello?"

Five sets of heads turned to her and each person gave her a pleased smile. Mrs. Jameson wiped her hand on a towel and hurried forward.

"Come in, child." Then she frowned. "Christopher's not back yet--?"

"No, Ma'am....but I thought I'd come by and keep his place for dinner...if that's okay."

Mrs. Jameson hugged her briefly and nodded. Her eyes were sad and happy both at the same time. It must be tough being Christopher's mother. It must be tough being Mrs. Jameson with her husband and being poor for so long, losing one child already.

Ashleigh rubbed her hands together after greeting the other ladies present. "I want to help cook, please. When Christopher comes home I want to know how to cook the food he likes."

Alma had her hand in a sink full of collard greens and she quickly picked up a towel and began drying them.

"You can clean these greens then-"

"Alma you are going to clean the greens." Mrs. Jameson spoke.

"Mama, she said she wants to help-"

"Alma Mae." Her mother said sharply. And Alma turned with a sulk and plunged her hands back into the sink of greens.

Okay…something just wasn't quite right with Alma, Ashleigh decided. Mrs. Jameson gestured to the ground beef that was in a bowl.

"I'll show you how to make the meatloaf. Christopher loves my meatloaf!"

Ashleigh loved the meatloaf too. She could have eaten two helpings but reminded herself that her man would be back in less than a month and a half and she intended to look damned good for him.

They retreated to the front porch after dinner. Mrs. Jameson talked about the first family reunion that they would have in ages. They had pushed it back a few weeks so that Christopher could attend when he returned.

"Uncle Ray wants the family to stay together. Now that some of us older ones are passing on he wants the younger ones to remember the family." Mrs. Jameson explained. "It's going to be a weekend thing. We got enough family still on that mountain so that everybody's going to have a place to stay. Ray's kids offered to stay in the trailer out back. He's going to put out a tent for some of the young boys. I'm sure they going to want Christopher in the tent with them but you two are going to take the den off of the kitchen-"

Ashleigh cocked her head at Mrs. Jameson's words. She'd said, 'you two,' as in she was included.

"Um…did you say for the weekend? On the mountain?"

Mr. Jameson was rocking in his seat. "Yep. You can visit your kin-folk at the bottom of the hill."

Alma snickered. "Daddy, she ain't trying to be bothered with Cobb Hill Mountain. She's a rich girl."

Rich? Is that what Alma thought.

Mrs. Jameson gave Ashleigh's hand an affectionate pat. "You'll come."

She gave Alma a haughty look. "Yes. I'll be there."

Mr. Jameson nodded. "You probably miss the Furnace, too. It's goin' be hottern' hell."

"And the goats will stink to high heaven." Alma said.

Ashleigh was about to ask about this furnace and why goats were in it when Mr. Jameson had a bad coughing spell and had to be taken inside. Ashleigh made sure he was okay but then indicated she needed to go and thanked them for dinner.

Christopher's brother walked her to her car, even though it was just parked at the curb.

"Thanks for coming." Butch said. He was in his early thirties and was nearly as tall as Christopher but rail thin. He wore his hair short but it was more auburn than red. He too was pale and covered in freckles and his eyes were emerald green instead of the charcoal gray of his brother's but their resemblance was unmistakable.

"Sorry about Dad. I'm sure Chris explained about the stroke."

"It's not a problem. I do understand."

"It meant a lot to my mother that you said you'd come down home with us. She don't really show it but she worries about Chris more than she does anyone else in the family; including my father."

She wondered if Christopher knew about that. "It's not a problem," she assured him.

Butch opened the car door for her. "See you next week." He waved while she drove off.

~***~

Ashleigh spent each evening running the treadmill. Every night Maggie came out of her hiding place to watch her. Maybe she thought it was Chris but stuck around to watch the show. And she sure did put on a show. Every night Ashleigh would run until she stumbled from the treadmill and collapsed onto the plush wool rug. Most nights she was able to drag herself back up and climb on it again, eeking out a few more minutes before her body literally gave out.

In the morning she'd get up, make a smoothie using one of Christopher's remembered recipes and she'd head to the gym. The first time she'd gone in after so many weeks of neglecting the place, it felt like Christopher's ghost was there and she'd been almost too overwhelmed. But then she slipped in a c.d. and she climbed on the treadmill and she began to run. Every day she would turn her mind off and picture Christopher. She pictured his steady form, running, barely looking out of breath; his muscles flexing with each movement of his arms and legs, his torso straight his head facing forward. Or she'd see his naked body, his cock bobbing, hardening because he knew that her eyes were glued to it. She'd meet his eyes and they would be dark with desire. He could have stopped then, and made love to her but he never did. And it seemed that the longer he prolonged it the better it would be when he finally did climb down from the treadmill. They'd make love while he was still wet with sweat, most times never making it to the bed and either falling to the carpeted floor or with her pushed up against the treadmill.

Ashleigh would begin to forget the world around her. She would look down in amazement when the timer on the treadmill stopped after half an hour. It amazed her the first time she had run at a steady pace for half an hour without even realizing it. She began setting the treadmill for forty-five minutes and still there were days when she was so lost in thought that she was surprised when the machine came to a stop. As the weeks moved on, Ashleigh's body transformed even though she didn't know it.

One day she climbed off the treadmill and saw that two guys were there working out. Two sets of eyes watched her with open interest. She only felt annoyed that they were violating her sanctuary. She quickly retrieved her c.d. and left, not caring in the least that she had left them without music. Maybe they should find another place to work out and ogle women who weren't interested.

The next day her feet pounded away on the treadmill. Her breath came out steadily and her pace was even. She didn't know that her body was tight and toned. There was no a roll of fat and her belly didn't need sucking in. She wasn't small she wasn't big but she was toned. She didn't know that the man in the gym watched her ass until he could barely complete his own workout. How could a woman be so curvy yet so tight with such a wondrous ass? He watched her with interest and then walked to the boom box and pressed stop, a self-assured smirk on his face.

Ashleigh pulled the safety line causing the treadmill to come to a stop. She looked over her shoulder while wiping a thin sheen of sweat from her brow. It had been nearly two months since Christopher had shipped out and wasn't due home until Monday. It was only Wednesday but still she looked over her shoulder with excitement. Maybe he had come back early!

She frowned when she saw the muscled man standing by the boom box, grinning. He was pumped with huge swollen muscles. His head was shaved and he had striking blue eyes and a blondish goatee. He stood at about 5'10" and wore lycra workout pants and a sweat shirt with arms cutout. It said USMC just like Christopher's shirts did.

Her attitude perked. Had his troop returned, after-all?

"Sorry." He said, though it was obvious that he wasn't. "But you were so deep in your workout that I didn't know any other way to get your attention." He walked towards her and offered his hand. She looked at it momentarily before shaking it. "I'm Tom Kardel. And you are?"

"Are you with The DPHS stationed here?" She asked, ignoring his flirtation.

"The…what?"

Ashleigh glanced at his shirt. "You're not with The Marines stationed here?"

His brow furrowed. "There are Marines stationed here?"

She gestured to his shirt. "USMC."

"Oh I got this at a sporting goods store."

"Oh," she said in disappointment. "Can you put the music back on?" She requested while turning her back to him.

She rolled her neck hearing a satisfying pop and then started the treadmill back up and resumed her run. The music never resumed and when she thought to turn around again Tom Kardel had left.

"Asshole."

On Sunday Ashleigh sat in Mrs. Jameson's kitchen with the other ladies. She'd come every single weekend since that first time she'd shown up hesitantly on the doorstep like a little stray kitten. Surprisingly, it wasn't out of a sense of duty. This family made her feel closer to Christopher in the sound of their accented voices, the stories they told about him, and the resemblance that they all bore to each other. And in turn, she began to learn and understand them. For instance, she found that they weren't just regulated to the kitchen to cook for the men. The kitchen was their gathering place. They drank their coffee or soda, had a slice of cake or pie and they talked about the happenings of the past week. They were funny, and sweet and entertaining and best of all they loved having a new person to tell their old stories to.

Ashleigh was making the meatloaf as she listened to tales about the wildcats that sound like women screaming and ghost stories about people who had died but then been seen walking in the woods. This was the thing that she missed with her own family. She would see her parents and occasionally her sisters but her aunts and cousins never got together.

"Ashleigh you got too much onion in that meatloaf." Alma said. Ashleigh looked at Mrs. Jameson who shook her head indicating that it was okay so she ignored Alma.

"What time will Christopher get home?"

"Well..." Mrs. Jameson seemed to be in deep though. "Normally he gets home in the afternoon. He calls me and lets me know he's home." Mrs. Jameson winked at Ashleigh. "I guess I'll get the second call this time. Just make sure he does remember to call me. I'm sure his mind will be completely on something else."

Ashleigh grinned. Tomorrow her baby would be home. The two month wait was finally coming to an end. She'd spent most of it trying to get her body back to something Christopher would be proud of and found that she had surpassed herself. She had an athletic body that *she* could be proud of. In just nine months Ashleigh could now look in the mirror and be happy with what she saw — not that she had. She couldn't count even one single time that she'd been happy since Christopher's departure.

Counting down the last final days of his return was agonizing. She had spent the weekend dusting and vacuuming his already spotless house. Maggie had followed her around until she'd pulled out the vacuum and then the poor cat had gone back into hiding. It had taken months but the cat had finally warmed up to her.

She focused her attention back to the present. As was the ritual, they had gone out to sit on the front porch to watch the kids play for a while. Ashleigh found herself alone with Alma as Butch and his cousin Nick played stickball with the younger ones and Aunt Edith and cousin Patricia brewed coffee and sliced up cake for everyone while Mrs. Jameson was busy helping Mr. Jameson in the bathroom.

Ashleigh tensed and glanced at the slightly older woman. She wasn't attractive nor was she bad looking, but her upturned nose gave her an air of snootiness that was ugly. She had shoulder length hair that was carrot red and her freckles were as plentiful as her sibling's. She was taller than Ashleigh but far from the six feet plus of her brothers.

Alma looked at her. "What do your parents think of you and Chris?"

Ashleigh looked at her. The woman hadn't spoken more than two kind words to her and now she wanted to ask about her personal business. She looked back out at the kids ignoring her.

"I guess they don't think so highly of their daughter being with white trash." The term alarmed and offended her.

Ashleigh's head spun to her. "What? Don't you call Christopher that! He's not trash!"

Alma scowled. "Christopher is poor white trash just like the rest of us. Don't think just because he works for the government that he ain't come from the same stock." Alma got up and walked in a lazy way down the porch stairs. Ashleigh followed.

"Now wait a minute-"

Alma began walking away from the house and Ashleigh knew what she was doing; she was luring them away from the rest of the family. Alma wanted to get her away from her Mother and Father so that she could finally get whatever bug she had out of her crawl. Ashleigh was all for it.

"No you wait a minute," Alma said almost casually, "because I know you think you going to run through Chris's money, use him up and when he's broke just drop him." Alma looked at her with complete dislike. "But I guarantee that won't happen. I'm going to be that little bee buzzing in his ear telling him every wrong move I see you make." And now that they were far enough away from the house that no one was likely to see them, Alma turned to face her, rudely pointing her finger at her.

"Coming up in here wearing your fancy clothes and your fancy shoes and talking all high-siddity, calling him Christopher when we all call him Chris. You might got them fooled but I know your type. Pretty girls like you always trying to get their hands on an officer's money-"

Ashleigh covered her mouth. Did Alma just call her pretty? "God, I thought you were just prejudiced. But you think I'm with Christopher for his money…?"

Alma scowled. "I never said I wasn't prejudiced…well truth is I don't give a damn if you're black. You high class, I can see that. You ain't never had to get down on your hands and knees and pull weeds out the garden because if you didn't and the weeds took over then you wouldn't have no vegetables to eat at dinner."

"Alma!" Ashleigh said. "I make damn near hundred thousand a year. I don't need Christopher's money! And I call him Christopher because that's the way he introduced himself to me. Truth is, there are nights when I'm calling him Chris and honey and baby and whatever else I want…over and over." Alma's mouth snapped closed.

"AND for your information I worked damn hard to get where I am. I graduated with two degrees and have a whopping college loan to pay back to prove it. I got turned down for jobs that white people less qualified got. I trained my own replacement once! And yeah, I never had to grow the food I had to eat, but every bit of money I make is mine to do whatever the hell I want to do with it! If I want to spend two hundred dollars at the salon every other week or buy five thousand dollar Manolo Blahniks then I will!"

Alma gave her a long look before turning and continuing to walk. She stopped after a moment when she saw that Ashleigh wasn't following. "Well we better get to the convenient store if we want to convince everybody that we just went off to buy snacks and not to scratch each other's eyes out." She waited for Ashleigh to catch up.

Ashleigh was still breathing hard. She looked at Christopher's sister, completely thrown off by the flip flop. "So you like me now that you know I don't need your brother's money?"

"I never said I liked you." Alma said. "I never said I didn't, either. I just thought…a girl like you would be a gold digger."

"Girl's like me? Black girls?"

"No," she scowled, "girls that have to look so perfect." Ashleigh saw her lip twitch as if she wanted to smile. "But I kinda liked you when I saw you carrying that cute pink Juicy Couture purse. I'll like you even more if you stay with my brother at least through Christmas so that I might get a half-way decent gift out of him." Ashleigh did intend to be with Christopher at Christmas and Alma was getting a lump of coal…but it might be sitting in a pink Juicy Couture purse. Ashleigh smiled to herself but Alma stopped walking, her face very serious.

"I might have been wrong about you. Okay…I have been wrong about you. You love him. You can't fake that look. Coming around here wasn't some attempt to ingratiate yourself into my parent's life like I thought it was." Ashleigh's brow jumped up.

"You figured all that out and you still called me out?"

"I just wanted to hear you say one thing."

"What? That I have my own money?"

"Exactly."

Ashleigh paused before they entered the little corner store. "I'm not going to take your shit. You're not going to boss me around. If you don't want to like me than fine. But I'm not going anywhere. You're going to have to deal with me for a very long time."

Doubt crossed Alma's face. She opened her mouth and closed it. "I have a four hundred and twenty-five dollar leather Louboutin purse." She twisted her fingers in distress. "I couldn't tell anybody. Nobody would understand. My family can't see why I'd pay that much for 'things'. I mean, what's wrong with wanting to get my nails and hair done?! I don't have to be a fashion model! But so what if I spend *my* money on things that *I* like?"

Ashleigh took another look at the woman. Jealous? Alma had been jealous of her? Her heart softened. "Alma, you have to do what it takes to make you feel good about yourself. You don't have to explain yourself to anyone about that."

Alma nodded. "But…I don't have anybody that I can…do those things with…" She blushed red and looked so expectant that Ashleigh further warmed up to her.

"Louboutin? For under six hundred? How?"

"QVC."

"Then it's not a knock-off…Can I see it?"

"Can I see your Manolo Blahniks?"

"Are you crazy?! I couldn't afford them." She raised her brow. "But I do have a pair of blue satin Louboutin stilettos."

"And they have the red sole?"
"Of course."

"Damn."

"Yeah."

"Can I look in your closet?"

Ashleigh grinned. "Yes. You give me time to get reacquainted with my sweetie than we'll have an all-girls night out…well one of the girls has a penis but-" She waved her hands at that.

Alma just chuckled.

When Ashleigh got home that night she called Lance and Kendra on 3-way and retracted every negative word that she'd ever said about Alma.

"Oh and don't expect me in tomorrow. I'm going to stay home and wait for my baby to get here."

"Thank god this two months is over." Kendra said. "I didn't think I'd survive your moping."

She shrugged. "Sorry if my despair annoyed you." She grinned suddenly. "Yep, gonna be busy tomorrow, and tomorrow night and the morning after-"

"TMI!" Lance said.

CHAPTER 9

Ashleigh kept watching the clock. She'd dressed in a new outfit knowing that it was ridiculous. Christopher didn't care about stuff like that. But she just wanted to look good for him. She'd gotten waxed on Friday, and her hair and nails done at the earliest possible appointment Monday morning.

She kept her eye on her cell phone hoping that he wouldn't call while she was under the dryer. She dashed back to his house and Maggie jumped down from the back of the couch to beg for a rubbing. She squatted down and rubbed the feline from the top of her head to the tip of her toes.

"Won't be much longer and you can get your rub down from your Daddy."

At three o'clock Ashleigh had kicked out of her shoes and was pacing anxiously. She called his cell phone and got the same message she always got; The number you have dialed is no longer in service…She knew that for security purposes he had to give up the government issued blackberry but still she tried anyways.

At five o'clock Mrs. Jameson called.

"Is he home?"

"No Ma'am." Ashleigh's brow was creased. "Does he sometime get home this late?"

"Well…not normally but maybe because he's on a different mission…"

Ashleigh felt her throat getting tight. It was a repeat of how she'd felt being trapped in the elevators all of those long months ago. She felt suddenly sick.

"I'll call you when I hear something." She said distantly.

"I'll do the same." They said their goodbyes and Ashleigh rushed to the bathroom and threw up.

That night Ashleigh lay in Christopher's big bed staring at the ceiling. It was almost one am. Christopher hadn't come home and he hadn't called.

~***~

Ashleigh prepared for work with a purpose the next morning. She didn't bother with her morning smoothie and didn't dress for her normal work-out or pack a bag containing her change of clothing. She drove to work and once she had entered the doors she flashed her access badge which allowed her to bypass being scanned.

"I need to speak to someone with The Department of Homeland Security." It was still too early for the average person to show up as it was barely seven am. The only people in the lobby manning the doors were security people. The security guards looked unsure but Ashleigh noted that one man stepped forward. He was dressed in a nice dark suit and seemed in his late forties or early fifties.

"Yes Ma'am? Is there a problem?"

"You're with Homeland Security?"

"Yes, Ma'am."

"I need to speak to Commander Bruce Koepke."

The man's brow went up slightly, almost suspiciously. "Follow me, please. He led her to a secured room. It was set up like a doctor's office with a receptionist area enclosed behind glass--but no receptionist. He offered her a seat.

"Your name, please?" Ashleigh gave her name and he politely told her that he would be just a few moments.

A few moments turned into ten but she was patient because as soon as she spoke to Christopher's commander she would know if he was okay.

The man returned to the room. "Miss Dalton, you were involved in an incident in the subbasement gym?" Ashleigh's brow gathered again but before she could answer he answered for her. "It wasn't really a question. There is an incident report. You collapsed during a workout. You were taken to the nurse's station and then released to two of your co-workers. Is that correct?"

"Well, yes, but I wasn't here due to that incident. You see I'm dating one of the Commander's men. His name is Lt. Christopher Jameson. They went out on a mission and were due back yesterday but he didn't come back. I'm worried and I needed someone to tell me if...if there's been a problem."

The man watched her a while longer before answering. "I'll see what I can find out for you Miss Dalton. Is there a number where I can reach you?"

She felt as if she was being given the heave-ho. Reluctantly she gave him her cell number. "You'll call me the moment you find out something?"

"Yes. I promise you'll be contacted by an ombudsman as soon as possible."

"Om...what?"

"Ombudsman. A military intermediary. They will work with you until we get this resolved." He led her out of the room and handed her a card that had his name and number on it. Well that was something. She accepted it feeling marginally better.

The rest of the day was horrible. Luckily for her their management team was in another state. Kendra and Lance picked up the work that she left lacking and didn't even think twice about it. Ashleigh just couldn't keep her head together. On top of everything else, her stomach felt like a big empty cavern.

She'd been so good with her diet, eating only the healthiest foods. Not since that first three weeks had she allowed one bit of junk food cross her lips. After a few moments of debate she finally just jumped up and went to the vending machine where she got two bags of chips, a candy bar and a bottle of soda. She ate the junk food and then quickly hurried down to the first floor bathrooms where she purged.

She called Mrs. Jameson that night when she got home, frantic for some information. She told her about the ombudsman. She could tell that Christopher's mother was trying to hold it together...or maybe she was trying to be optimistic for her benefit. She thanked her for the information and told her to stay in contact; to call her even if she just wanted to talk.

Ashleigh resisted the urge to talk to her own family. She wished that she had the type of relationship with them where she could turn to her mother for comfort, or chit chat with her sisters. Oh, she had tried it but quickly conversations about things that caused her anguish were just pushed aside as her sister's turned the conversation around to something more interesting to them; like themselves.

Her parents knew that she was no longer dating DeAngelo and the only thing her mother cared about was how good looking he had been and how it was such a pity that they were no longer together. It was no wonder that she had never talked to them about Christopher. She couldn't bear the negative energy that she knew the revelation would bring. It wasn't out of shame, she just knew her family. Besides, now was not the time to tackle those issues. For now she would just have to agonize without their support.

Lance and Kendra called but understood when she explained that she didn't want company. They each told her that they loved her and after she hung up she finished the entire pizza that she had ordered. She intended to purge but didn't have to. Her system, unaccustomed to the deluge of junk food made her sick on it's on.

Afterwards Ashleigh climbed on the treadmill. She stared forward, not seeing the mounted television or the wall, only picturing the man that she had grown to love so much. She began to run and to think about Christopher.

As soon as the alarm clock sounded on Wednesday morning, the first thing she did was to check her cell phone for messages. Nothing. She buried her head into her hands knowing that at some point soon an officer would go to Mrs. Jameson's house and inform her that her son had died in the line of duty. They would give her a letter signed by the President of the United States and then at his military funeral they would offer her a folded American flag...

Ashleigh staggered out of the bedroom and threw open the refrigerator. She found a jar of jam and ate it with her fingers, and then she saw a block of aged cheddar and she stuffed her mouth with it. She barely recognized the tears on her cheeks as she threw open the pantry searching for food to eat; crackers, NESTLE'S milk chocolate powder, a can of black olives, pickle relish...

After she purged she lay on the bathroom floor. The ache that had developed in her head began to recede. Maggie meowed loudly and nestled against her panting body.

~***~

The next morning was Thursday and Ashleigh dressed for her workout and then headed for the gym that felt so much like her and Christopher. Ashleigh slipped Pink Floyd's The Darkside of the Moon into the boombox and then she climbed onto the treadmill and began to run.

Christopher's crooked smile. Christopher's smoky gray eyes. Christopher's muscles and the way they moved beneath his skin. Christopher's big, calloused hands and the way they moved gently over her body...

This is what she pictured as her feet went pounding away on the treadmill; pounding as if she was running into his arms.

The music abruptly stopped and it was like cold water had been thrown on her. She stumbled as her pace changed and then she pulled the safety line to stop the treadmill's movement. She turned expectantly, hopefully only to see the grinning face of the man from the other day.

"Hi. Tom Kardel. So sorry to interrupt you." He said in an almost mocking tone. "But again…you seemed very focused." Ashleigh knew that she must have had a ridiculous look of confusion on her face as she tried to understand why this man was even talking to her. He could not possibly be trying to pick up on her while she was in the middle of run!

"It occurred to me that I've introduced myself to you, but you didn't introduce yourself to me."

Ashleigh stared at him coldly. He came forward and held out his hand. His eyes held a certain look…there was something there that wasn't quite nice.

"I don't see any reason why I should stop my workout to meet someone. I'm not here for that. I'm here to exercise." She moved past his hand to the boombox and pressed play again. Tom Kardel stepped right into her path when she moved back to the treadmill and Ashleigh remembered something that knowing Christopher had caused her to forget. This was a subbasement.

She was alone in a room with a man she didn't know…the operative word being MAN, and not all men were nice like Christopher Jameson…all she had to do was look at the scar on her friend's forehead to know that.

"Mr. Kardel," Ashleigh said in a tight voice that defied her anxiety, "let me make this clear; I don't want to introduce myself to you and I don't want to talk to you and I would appreciate if you wouldn't turn off my music-"

"See," He flexed his swollen muscles and the not-so-pleasant smile disappeared. "Its women like you that make men like me jump through hoops."

Ashleigh decided her workout was over. She turned to leave, deciding that she would leave her towel and the music—Tom Kardel moved swiftly to block her exit, standing once more, directly in her path.

"I thought that story you mentioned about The Marines stationed down here was pretty funny. Egg on my face. Then I realized that it was just another way that a bitch will try to make you feel foolish."

Ashleigh figured she could move fast enough to grab one of the free weights. He would catch her, but if she was lucky she would get her hand on the weight and swing it at his head. It was the only way she would get out of this.

But before Tom Kardel could give in to his desire to lash out at the pretty girl that had rejected him like so many before her, and before Ashleigh actually turned to make a run for the weights where his steroid-induced rage would come to life, the door swung opened slamming against the far wall with a crash.

Ashleigh's heart leaped in her chest and Tom Kardel spun in surprise. If this was a John Hughes movie than a Psychedelic Furs tune would begin playing and Christopher would be standing in the doorway with a dark angry scowl on his face.

But this was not a John Hughes film, and Christopher did not appear in the doorway...but it was the next best thing; sixteen Marines crowded into the room wearing their meanest expressions and fatigues that stretched across toned bodies.

"Are you harassing this woman?" Spoke a black man wearing sunglasses even though it was barely seven am.

"I-no. I was just—"

Tom Kardel turned to Ashleigh as if she would corroborate his story but she just moved away from him.

A Hispanic man took a step forward. "You need to leave, buddy." He was nearly as tall as Christopher and just as cut. He cracked his knuckles and it sounded like twigs breaking "And never come back."

Tom Kardel moved past the bodies of the military men. They did nothing to move out of his way, forcing him to go around them as if he was walking through a maze. Two of the men followed him and the others focused on Ashleigh. The angry expressions immediately changed to looks of concern.

"Are you okay, little trooper?"

"Uh…yes." Little trooper? "Where is Christopher?"

They all looked around. "We thought you knew." The guy wearing the sunglasses said.

Her breath froze in her chest and tears welled up in her eyes. "Knew what? Is he okay?"

A different man scowled. "Dude, you're scaring her!"

"I'm not trying to!" The black man said looking suddenly horrified. "We thought you knew where he was."

"We were going to come down to ask you and then we saw that ass…um the man harassing you."

"He switched missions-" Someone said.

"Yes! He switched missions." Ashleigh was nodding her head frantically. "The Commander...he knows where Christopher is-"

"Nobody switches missions!" The black man spat. "You risk everyone. You risk yourself!"

"TK, shut up." The big tall man said. "The Commander took Beast's place. You don't switch missions, Ma'am, because it leaves your team short and it means that your new team will have to learn a new team member."

"Beast risked us all-" The Hispanic man responded angrily.

"Yeah but if he got a bad feeling…then he did the right thing." The men all got thoughtful looks on their faces.

"I need to talk to the Commander." Ashleigh said.

Everyone suddenly avoided her eyes. Finally TK spoke. "Chief Warrant Officer Bruce Koepke was hurt in the line of duty." Ashleigh's hands moved to her lips.

"Oh my god…Is he…?"

"He's going to live but he's in intensive care. The thing is-"

"Don't tell her!"

"I gotta tell her now, idiot!" She was overwhelmed and their bickering was making her a nervous wreck.

"What?! Tell me!"

The man with the sunglasses placed a calming hand on her shoulder. "Maybe it was a good thing that he did change his mission because what happened to the Commander would have happened to Beast. It was just dumb fate and being in the wrong place at the wrong time. But the Commander was doing what Beast would have normally been doing-"

"We might not know where Christopher is but he sure as hell ain't lying up in an ICU ward." Someone spoke bitterly.

"Don't worry Little Trooper. We're going to find him."

Ashleigh was trembling but was so much more relieved. Now she had people working on it from the inside….even though some of them looked like they wanted to find him for a different reason then she did.

It was Thursday and Christopher was missing for four days now.

~***~

Two of The Marines stood outside of the lockers as Ashleigh got dressed, just in case Tom Kardel should return. She hadn't asked them to do it but was very happy because that man had been totally unhinged. Ashleigh saw that she had a message from the guard from The Homeland Security Office and she got dressed and quickly thanked the men standing guard for her. She went upstairs to the lobby and knocked anxiously on the door to the security office there. She got the official notification.

Christopher Henry Jameson was officially missing.

Ashleigh sat down in a chair and shook like a leaf until the kind man explained that it wasn't the same as being missing in action. The reason Christopher was missing is because he was taken off all active duty rosters. In layman terms; Christopher wasn't on a mission. Then she remembered his long sent message. It said something about him not being active…

Ashleigh was put into contact with her ombudsman through the Department of Homeland Security and then she called Christopher's family and tried to explain but they asked questions that no one had answers for. If he wasn't on a mission then why didn't he call? Why didn't he come home Monday?

Mrs. Jameson received a call later that evening promising that her son would be located within 72 hours. Ashleigh got out of bed in the middle of the night and hurried to the grocery store where she bought a gallon of Graeter's Chocolate Chip Raspberry ice cream and a plastic spoon. She sat in her car and ate half of it.

For three days she'd been binging on anything she could get her hands on, it didn't even matter if it was food or a condiment. She suddenly threw the other half of the ice cream out the window and laid her head on her steering wheel feeling too defeated to even stick her finger down her throat to throw up.

~***~

Christopher distantly remembered the familiar pain. He'd experienced it before hadn't he? But when? He tried to move but forgot why he should. The pain stopped dancing around as long as he lay very still. Christopher fell asleep…or something that felt like sleep. All he knew for certain is that it was another day filled with pain and dreams of Ashleigh.

"Lt. Jameson? Can you open your eyes?"

Christopher winced and grumbled. "What?" He managed though he was still groggy.

"It's time for your lunch."

"What?" He reached up and found that his hands were strapped down. His brain began to clear and the nurse undid the straps.

"You keep trying to take off the bandages."

"Freaking hurts…" He managed.

"Well you were warned. You're the one that wanted to squeeze six surgeries into two months."

When his hands were free Christopher reached up and tentatively touched his face. It was completely wrapped in bandages. There was a slit for his eyes and another for his mouth and then a slash for his nose. Even his hair was covered. He felt like he had a soccer ball for a head!

"Careful. The incisions are held together by tape and glue, no stitches."

"I feel like crap."

The male nurse chuckled. "You don't say. Reconstructive surgery like yours is no joke. It's like that Makeover show where they change a person completely in a matter of weeks, except they never had to harvest bone from other parts of your body in order to build up your facial structure. Add to that creating a bridge for your nose where there never was one before. Pulled out all of your teeth and bonded you a brand new pair. Repaired the fissure, redid the prior surgery to fix your lip and scar reduction. I can't say that I've ever seen anyone take six facial surgeries in nine weeks."

Christopher didn't want a re-cap of all of his surgeries — WHAT? Did he just say nine weeks?! He sat up in the hospital bed that had been customized to accommodate someone of his size.

"What day is it?!"

"Uh...it's Friday the 25th."

"Shit! I was supposed to be home on the 20th!"

"That's impossible." The nurse was watching a monitor intently. "You just had your final surgery Sunday. You need two full weeks for recovery."

Christopher was already climbing out of the bed. "Ow! What the-?"

"Catheter. Lieutenant you need to lay back down-"

He gave the man a serious look. "One of us is going to pull this thing out. You or me?"

The nurse removed the catheter while he stood and then Christopher yanked off his hospital gown and walked naked around the room, opening drawers to locate his clothing.

"Lieutenant!"

"Where are my damned clothes?!" He finally found them hanging in the closet; just a pair of fatigues and a camo shirt. He glared at the nurse who was staring on in disbelief that he was actually making attempts to leave.

"Lieutenant, you don't understand. Your face is being held together by tape and glue! You are not even allowed to smile! We've been keeping you asleep so that you don't move. You just can't get up and leave!"

Christopher already had his pants and shirt on and had plopped down into a chair in order to pull on socks and shoes. "Y'all told me you can do it in two months."

"Yeah! The surgeries! That didn't include the time it would take to heal afterwards."

"Look! I have a girlfriend and family expecting me. They are probably worried sick! Get me a phone!"

"You can't call from here. This is a military hospital for Special Forces. Nobody can know the location! Protocol-"

Christopher stood and stalked toward the smaller man who quickly retreated back a step. "I'll get you that phone."

Dr. Weitz came in a few minutes later, looking concerned. Christopher was pacing back and forth, waiting for someone to bring him a phone.

"Lieutenant, I'm sorry to hear that you want to be discharged before the recommended time."

"I need to get home."

"You'll have to sign a statement saying that you refuse treatment."

"Certainly."

"You know that it's against the rules to make a phone call to civilians while in action."

"I would laugh but that guy has me afraid that my face might crack. You and I both know that this isn't a mission. And if it was a mission it would have ended five days ago. If it was a mission than I'd say that you're not following protocol right now because my family has no idea where the hell I am and that's your fault for keeping me asleep!"

The doctor reached into his pocket and pulled out a phone which he handed to Christopher in light of his escalating anger.

"Thank you." He said, though he didn't think he should have had to waste even a minute explaining why he should be allowed to call his family. He quickly dialed Ashleigh's cell phone. He didn't know if it was night or day because there were no windows where he was. The phone rang and rang. Next he dialed his Mom and Dad.

"Mom!"

"CHRISTOPHER???!"

"Mom I'm so sorry-"

"Are you okay?!"

"I am. I'm okay-"

"Christopher you need to come home immediately."

His heart began to drum rapidly in his chest.

"Where's Ashleigh?!"

"Chris, Ashleigh got very sick. Honey, she went to sleep the other night and didn't wake up. They got her in the hospital…"

The blood seemed to drain from his body. He turned to the doctor who had already heard enough of the conversation to determine that something very bad had happened. He told Chris that he would get him on the first available flight home.

"Mama," Christopher asked when the Doctor left the room. "Is it her diabetes?"

"That…and, well…," He heard his mother take a deep breath. "You just get home. How long will it take?"

"I don't know Mama. They are making arrangements for a flight out as we speak."

"Christopher, your voice sounds so different. Are you sure you're alright?"

Christopher touched his stiff bandaged face. "Yes. And I'll explain when I get there. I love you and I'll call you when I get my own cell phone back. I love you Mom. Tell Ashleigh I love her and that I'm alright, okay? Tell her I'll be there soon!"

"I'll tell 'em son."

He hung up and began pacing, barely feeling the throbbing of his healing facial surgery. All he could think about was how he'd left things. He should have gone on the mission. At least then he would have been back by now. But for the first time ever, he'd been plagued with bad feelings about a mission. Whether it was because he didn't want to leave Ashleigh or if it was because he had bought into the superstition he wasn't sure. But he saw things in a totally different light now that he'd given his life up to Ashleigh.

There was a layover in Atlanta and Christopher immediately headed for a payphone, cursing the fact that he didn't have his cell phone. He wouldn't be allowed access to personal property until he had gone through 'debriefing'. He wasn't sure how his Commander intended to handle that since he hadn't actually gone on a mission.

He dialed Ashleigh's number and he listened intently to her sweet voice as it went to voicemail. "Hi Baby. I miss you. I have a layover in Atlanta. I love you…" He sighed in misery. "I hope you're alright, Sweetheart. I should be at the Greater Cincinnati airport by 5 am and then I'll see you as quickly as I can. Bye, Sweetheart." He hung up and contemplated calling his mother but decided against it due to the late hour. He wouldn't want to cause his father to wake up and make more work for his mother to get him back down. He was worried sick about Ashleigh, and desperate for news.

Was she in a diabetic coma still? He paced half scaring people in the terminal. Yeah, if it wasn't one thing than it was another; scars or bandages…

When he boarded the next flight, he wished he'd taken the painkillers that Dr. Weitz had tried to give him. His face felt like someone had taken him by the back of his head and slammed him against a brick wall repeatedly. He'd eaten chicken soup as his in flight dinner since it didn't require him to move his sore jaw by chewing. He finally drifted off to sleep filled with guilt that something had happened to the woman he loved and he hadn't been there…again.

Christopher called his mother as soon as he got to The Greater Cincinnati Airport terminal.

"How's Ashleigh?"

"Son, she's awake and alert and waiting anxiously for you to get to her. The hospital has already released her. Her blood sugar level was good and her parents have taken her back to her house. You wait there and I'll send Butch over to get you-"

"No, I'm going to catch a cab. It'll be quicker. I'll be over later Mom, but I need to check on Ashleigh first."

"You do that son. Just call me. You need to be with your family."

He tilted his head at her silly words. "You are my family. Look, I'll talk to you later in the evening. Love you Mom."

"Love you, too."

Christopher hung up and went out to hail a taxicab. He reached Ashleigh's condo an impossibly long time later even though it was still early morning due to the rush hour traffic. He hurried up to her apartment and rang the bell anxiously. He didn't have a key since they always spent time at his place.

A moment later the door opened and a pretty black woman looked at him in surprise. She had very light skin and blonde hair with hazel eyes and he knew immediately that it was Ashley's mom. Her hands flew to her mouth and she looked like she was about to scream.

"I'm Christopher." He said quickly. He'd scared her just as badly with the bandages on as he would have with his scars. It saddened him and this is precisely why he needed the surgery.

"Christopher? Ashleigh's Christopher?" The woman said in disbelief. "But you're..." white? Is that what she was going to say? The woman quickly recovered. "Ashleigh never said you were so...big."

"Yes, Ma'am." It seemed a stupid response and even stupider that he'd rushed all this way only to be standing right outside of her door blocked by a mother he'd never met and that knew pitifully little about him. He held out his hand and she gave it a tentative shake.

"Come in," she finally said, realizing that he was waiting for her to allow him in. "I'm so sorry. Ashleigh never mentioned that you were so...big." What Ashleigh had actually told her mother, only upon learning that Christopher was alright and coming home, was that he had a cleft palate and not to be alarmed. But maybe she should have mentioned that he was a giant. "Ashleigh's father had to leave and Ashleigh is in bed resting. Go in, she's exhausted but keeps fighting sleep waiting for you."

Christopher nodded and hurried into Ashleigh's bedroom. The shades were drawn and the room was dim. Ashleigh was curled up under her blankets with just her golden brown hair showing. He could see that she was sleeping and he lingered in the doorway a moment, not able to move, just drinking in the sight of her. God but he'd missed her.

He eased forward so that he wouldn't wake her, and worried how she would react to the sight of his bandaged face. But as soon as he stepped forward Ashleigh's eyes opened and she turned sleepily in his direction.

She scrambled up in bed and gasped. He held up his hands.

"Don't worry. I'm okay, Sweetheart." He said quickly. "I just got reconstructive surgery."

She climbed out of bed and hurried to him throwing her arms around his large body. "Where were you? Why didn't you come home? I was so scared!"

He allowed his hands to roam her body as he held her, but not in a sexual way. He was alarmed by her weight loss.

"Ashleigh...what happened?"

"Your face..." She stared up at him in disbelief. His entire head was completely wrapped!

"Honey, you've lost so much weight..."

Ashleigh ran her hands over his chest and arms. "You have too." Then she hugged him again and he held on to her, wanting to kiss her but not able to because despite the fact that his face didn't have stitches, his lips did. He had peeked and they were nasty looking with black threads poking out.

He gripped her shoulders and gently pulled her back so that he could look at her. He'd seen her when she had first come into the gym. She was a pretty girl that was overweight. Now it was nine months later and she wasn't overweight at all. She was wearing sweatpants and a t-shirt that hugged her curvy body.

He couldn't stop staring. She looked fantastic but he didn't like seeing her like this if it was at the risk of her health.

"What did you do to your face? Why? Christopher you didn't do it for me, did you? Because I love you just as you are—"

"I know you do, Sweetheart." He pulled her into his arms. He had to hold her. He gently rubbed his hands down her back feeling her shiver. His body tensed and began to react but he pushed down his desire for her.

"I couldn't go on that mission. I couldn't risk it. I kept thinking…what if I get hurt? What if I can't come back to you?" Ashleigh held her breath as she thought about Christopher's Commander. Did he know?

"You didn't go on a mission?" She looked up at him, clinging to him possessively.

"Sweetheart, I told you all of this in the message-"

"Baby! I couldn't make out a damn thing you were saying! I had no idea…"

He blanched. "What? You didn't know that…Oh Ashley. I'm so sorry! And when I didn't come home…" He had no idea that they didn't understand that he had never been in combat. Yeah, he knew that they would worry as he hadn't come home Monday as planned but he had never considered that they didn't know that he was never in any danger of not returning home to them. The worry that they must have faced when he didn't return Monday would have been unimaginable. They would have truly thought he was dead.

He immediately explained about approaching his commander with his request for the surgery. Bruce had told him about the possible surgeries that he could get, all paid for by the military, when he'd first set eyes on the severely scarred man. He'd done the research for him and when Christopher declined he told him that he would make it happen for him if he ever changed his mind.

When Christopher came to him with the request he knew that his medical needs would take precedence. He'd made the calls and told Christopher that the surgical crew was very interested in his case and could assemble a surgical team immediately.

Everything had happened fast after that. He wouldn't be allowed back on the active duty roster for six months and by that time he figured he would have another position.

"Had Bruce not been such an all-around good guy, I would have never been able to pull that off. I would have been made to put in my request for surgery after my mission. But he knew that I'd put in my request to be taken off active duty well before the mission even came up."

Ashleigh looked away at the mention of Bruce. She met his eyes. "Baby, I don't know how to tell you this but Bruce Kopeke got hurt during the mission. He's in ICU and he's expected to survive. I talked to your friend TK earlier to tell him that you were okay. He said that the Commander was in Ft Campbell. The guys are going down to see him and TK told me to tell you that they were all going to be waiting for you."

Though he wasn't supposed to, Christopher's found himself frowning beneath his bandages. The Commander had been hurt doing his job...and now the guys were waiting for him...He blinked back his guilt. He needed to call down to Ft. Campbell later, but for now Ashleigh was all that he could think about.

"What happened to you, Sweetheart? Was it your diabetes?"

Her face transformed immediately. He'd never seen her with such a look. She took his hands and held them. "I had too much insulin in my system. The doctor has taken me off of it. I've lost enough weight to be able to take just one pill once a day." She smiled softly. "I do have to check my blood sugar levels more often now. The doctor said I'm at high risk because of the baby. But after the pregnancy I might not even need medication at all."

"Because of the baby?"

She nodded with a smile. "Sorry that everyone else knows before you." Christopher was frozen and she had no idea what his expression was. "When I was brought into the hospital I was out of it. Your Mom was there, my mom and Dad, Kendra and Lance. And the doctors just assumed that they all knew. So...they knew even before I did." She smiled nervously. "So...I'm two months...I guess our going away celebration was-"

Christopher's eyes blinked and his mouth had grown dry and his legs weak. He was a man that had brought other men to their knees with nothing more than a few well placed blows of his fist. He was a man that had endured the physical torture of having his face basically peeled back and his skull rebuilt. He'd seen his brother buried, felt loneliness so vivid that he swore it had a taste.

And this man went to his knees before the woman he loved, gently pushed up her shirt exposing her brown belly, flat now, yet still a sanctuary for his child. He placed his head against her warm flesh. He wasn't supposed to smile but he did.

Ashleigh's hands moved to his shoulders. And he lifted his head and looked at her.

"Marry me Ashleigh. Marry me and I'll never disappoint you. I'll never give you a moment to worry or to wonder. I'll devote my life to making you happy; you and our baby." He looked at her in complete devotion. "We made a little baby…"

She smiled and giggled. "It wasn't that hard either, was it?"

"I don't know about you but I was working pretty hard."

She stared into his bandaged face. "I'm all yours, Christopher Jameson. I'll be yours for as long as you want me. I want to be your wife more than anything in the world, and the mother to your children." He stood slowly.

"Your…Mom is still out there?"

"Well, she's probably listening at the door." He took her hand and led her to the bed.

"Get back in bed, Sweetheart. I want you to rest." Ashleigh pouted. Her body was already slick and ready for him.

"By myself?" She asked.

"Get some rest," was his answer as he tucked the covers around her, "because I intend to wear you out as soon as you wake up." Her lips tugged upward at the corners in pleasure.

"Okay."

His hand lingered on her shoulder. "I wish I could kiss you." He allowed his hand to stroke her cheek. Her skin was so soft. "I have to call and find out when I can get these bandages removed!" And he needed to call his family…ah; his family. That is what his mother had been alluding to. He had a much bigger family now; including the woman that had given birth to the love of his life — his soon to be mother-in-law, who was out there either listening at the door or cooling her heels waiting for him to come out.

He stroked the stray strands of Ashleigh's hair. "I'll be back in a bit. Get some sleep, okay?"

Now that Christopher was here, Ashleigh allowed her body to relax and she nodded as her eyes closed.

~***~

When Ashleigh awoke, it was to find herself snuggled against Christopher's large sleeping form. She burrowed against him deeper being careful not to awaken him and reveling in the 'Christopher' smell that she had missed. She had also missed having her favorite 'pillow' to snuggle up to.

Her poor baby must have been exhausted. He was sleeping soundly on his back with his arm around her. She could see the steady rise and fall of his chest and hear his soft snores. As some point he had showered because he was no longer wearing fatigues but had changed into work-out pants and a t-shirt that he had left behind.

Without moving she studied his bandaged face. She absolutely couldn't see a thing. He was wrapped like a mummy, not even his hair was visible. She was tempted to tug a bandage aside as she was intensely curious about the changes he had undergone. Two months of reconstructive surgery would have surely changed him completely.

There was something slightly scary about that. She had more than grown accustomed to his facial features...she had grown to love them. Ashleigh's eyes scanned the rest of his body. Mmmm. Now this hadn't changed much. He was a bit leaner but even with clothes she could see the lines of his tight muscles.

Though she knew that she should allow him to sleep, she couldn't help but to allow her hands to lightly roam his body. His arm around her suddenly tightened at the same time that his breathing changed.

"Missed waking up to that..." He murmured.

"Sorry I woke you. I think you needed the sleep." He stroked her arm and muffled a yawn before glancing at the clock. It was just after 1 pm. He'd gotten a couple hours of sleep which is all he needed in order to rejuvenate. He looked at Ashleigh and tried not to smile, though it was tough. This little lady had definitely broken down every one of his barriers.

"Did you sleep well?"

She snuggled against him. "Mhm. Best sleep I've had in weeks. Is my mom still here?"

He shook his head. "No, she said she'd call you. She had to drive back to Tennessee." Truth of the matter is that she seemed skittish around him not that he blamed her. Who wouldn't be nervous around a 6'5" behemoth wearing a mummy mask?

Ashleigh didn't seem to care. She touched his chin gently. "When can these come off?"

"When I talked to the doc before I left he said they had to be removed by a surgeon."

She frowned. "Are you in pain?"

He shrugged. "Tolerable."

"Well I have Motrin in the-"

"Yeah, found them and already took some before lying down. They helped." He was watching her. "They don't freak you out, do they, Sweetheart? My bandages?" She said nothing for a few moments.

"A little." She admitted softly. "I don't want you to look different."

He pulled himself up on his elbow and watched her. "I'm sorry. I never…dreamed that you wouldn't want…" Ashleigh quickly kissed his neck which remained uncovered. He sighed.

"Baby, I love you. I'll love you no matter what you look like. Okay? I'm just used to you the other way." Christopher's hands moved to cup her face.

"I can't kiss you. God, I wish I could kiss you." She lifted her head to kiss his bandage covered lips and he moved back. "You don't want to do that. My lips are swollen. I look like a freaking trout."

"Oh?" Her brow quirked up. "You're going to have full lips?"

"By the looks of things I'll have freaking Mick Jagger lips."

"Mmm…" she wiggled her brow and he chuckled.

"Oh…not supposed to do that either. I can't move my face at all. I'm not supposed to smile."

"Jeez…how long?"

He shrugged. "Not until the bandages come off."

"Oh…Christopher…" She scooted away from him with a frown.

"What?"

Ashleigh sat up in bed and looked down at him with a frown. "We can't have sex."

He did the same. "Babe, what are you talking about?"

"Christopher…" She blushed. "You should see the faces you make when we're…you know…doing it."

"Ahhh…*what*?"

"And when you…cum," She whispered. "your face gets all like…" she made a growling face.

Christopher couldn't help it, he laughed.

"Baby! Don't laugh. You're going to hurt your face!"

He climbed out of bed still chuckling. "We're going to get to the bottom of this." He rooted in his wallet until he came up with a card. Ashleigh jumped out of bed and followed him into the living room where he picked up the phone and began dialing. After being transferred a few times he was speaking to Dr. Weitz. He put the phone on speaker.

"Doctor, I'm here with my girlfriend."

"Ahh the lady that you left the hospital to be with. Are you okay, Ma'am?"

Ashleigh nodded. "I'm fine. Thank you. I'm more concerned with Christopher's face. He said he's not allowed to move it and…well he's been laughing and smiling and I even suspect that he's frowned a few times." Christopher lifted his brow and looked at her. She pointed at him quickly. "And I bet you just lifted one eyebrow!"

Dr. Weitz spoke. "I'm sure he'll be fine. There is an elastic face mask beneath the bandaging holding everything in place. I'm going to give you the name and phone number of a colleague in Ft Campbell." Ashleigh looked at Christopher quickly. That's where his Commander was. "I want the stitches removed from your lips Monday and I want the bandages removed 1 week later. That will have allowed 2 weeks for healing. Now, barring any facial trauma, minor facial movements shouldn't cause any harm."

Christopher got the necessary information for the Doctor in Ft Campbell and Dr. Weitz said he'd call him personally to get the appointment made.

After hanging up Christopher crooked his finger at Ashleigh. "Come here baby." Now he didn't have to stop himself from grinning. She squealed and hurried into the bedroom. Christopher stopped her before she could get into bed. He slowly stripped off her clothes and when she was nude he allowed his eyes to scan her body.

She felt her face warm but it wasn't the only part of her body beginning to get hot…

"I can tell you're pregnant."

"What?" She placed her hands over her flat belly.

He was shaking his head. "No, not there." He used his fingers to lift her breast. "Your nipples are so big…your aureolas." His breath shuddered when he exhaled. "God, I wish I could…" He stroked them lightly and she sucked in a deep breath and groaned.

"Too hard?" He asked.

"Just so sensitive."

Christopher made a sound like a whimpered moan before quickly shedding his own clothes.

Dayum…she thought as she scanned his nude body. She had been surviving on memories for over two months. She thought she had memorized every inch of him. But the sight of his perfect body took her breath away. Since he couldn't use his mouth on her, Ashleigh sank to her knees and used hers on him.

"Ahhh!" He exclaimed when she sucked him, dragging him deep into the hot wet cavern of her mouth. His knees almost gave out. Christopher touched the sides of her face and watched her as she sucked him. As good as her mouth felt, there was one place that he wanted to be even more. He pulled her to her feet and led her to the bed.

When she made to lie on her back, he had her get on her knees on the end of the bed. He loved the missionary position with her but not while he was covered in bandages. She looked over her shoulder at him anxiously, ready. But she'd teased him and now it was time for him to tease her some.

He rubbed his finger along her slit and saw her back arch. She groaned and lowered her head. Christopher's wet fingers parted the swollen folds and it was his turn to groan at the sight of her glistening, pulsing flesh, so ready for him. He placed the head of his penis against her opening. It seemed too small and tight. He pushed in gently, not pausing until he was fully inside of her.

"Oh god…" She groaned, "so big…"

He held onto her hips, pushing in and out of her with as much control as he could muster. The sensations were overwhelming. She was so hot and tight, tighter than he remembered. He was careful, not sure how sex would affect the baby.

Thinking about that suddenly caused him to feel even more turned on. He had planted his seed in this woman and now it was growing…Christopher reached forward and cupped her full breast in his palm. It overflowed his grip but he held it carefully, feeling it swing as the thrusting of his hips intensified.

Christopher's low groans and then the careful way he held her breast was Ashleigh's undoing. She cried out loudly, her legs shaking and she pushed back against him.

Christopher quickly replaced his grip on her hips and he quickened his speed even more. Before he knew it, his own cries of release mingled with hers. He kept pounding, not hard but rapidly, until he had emptied the contents of his testicles into her womb.

~***~

Christopher was anxious to get home. Besides, Ashleigh had no food in her house. He learned that she had pretty much moved into his place, a fact that he planned to make official just as soon as possible. Later they could decide about a bigger place in a nice neighborhood. He smiled at the thought of that. Seven months ago he had been sitting in his lonely home with not even the slightest inclination that he could know so much joy.

Christopher unlocked the door and Maggie came rushing across the room. He laughed when she walked figure eights around his feet.

"You missed me, girl?" He picked her up, not sure if she would be alarmed with his bandages. Evidently she recognized him by scent and sound and not by sight. He loved on her for a few minutes while Ashleigh watched. She knew that he was going to be the best Dad.

"I'm going to feed her." He announced. "Get changed and we'll go out for something to eat."

"Alright, babe." She headed for the bedroom and quickly made the bed. She didn't want him to think she was a slob, even though it wasn't exactly her fault that the bed had gone unmade. After all, she had been unconscious.

Then she went through the closet for something nice to wear for her man. She heard him come into the bedroom but he didn't say anything. She decided on a summer dress and when she turned from the closet it was to the sight of Christopher standing in the doorway holding the trashcan. Bandaged face or not, she could see the questioning look on his face.

"Ashleigh…there are empty packages of cookies, pizza boxes, donut boxes." She suddenly moved from one leg to the next. "Ashleigh, have you been purging?"

"I…"

"Is that what put you in the hospital? You said your insulin was too high. Is it because you've been throwing up your food? Binging and throwing up?"

Ashleigh had a stricken look on her face.

"Don't lie to me."

"I…" she twisted her fingers. "Yes."

"Jesus. Do you understand that you could have killed the baby? You could have killed yourself. What were you thinking?" He turned and stormed out of the room.
Ashleigh followed him, his words stung; hurting her down to her soul.

"Chris, I didn't know that I was pregnant. I swear. I didn't know that until I woke up in the hospital—"

He had dragged the plastic liner out of the trash bin. "But you know that it was dangerous for you to do something like that!"

God, he was yelling at her. She nodded slowly, her face twisting in sorrow and guilt. He slammed the trash bin to the floor and carried the half filled liner out to the garage through the kitchen door. Ashleigh just stood there feeling sick and unsure.

When he didn't return she went out the kitchen door and saw that he was sitting on the back porch stairs. He didn't look at her as she approached. She sat down next to him and he gave her room, but she took it as if he didn't want to touch her.

"Sorry." She whispered.

He turned to her. "How long have you been doing this?"

"Since I was a kid." She looked at her folded hands. "Off and on. Nobody knows, not even my parents." She stared at her hands and cleared her throat. "I was the fat kid in the family. My sisters were really pretty. And my mother...well she was always trying to make me look like them. My parents divorced when I was young. It's very Freudian, but I replaced my Dad with food. Sometimes I would feel sick...like an addict, if I didn't have something I wanted to eat. I'd dream about food. Then when I ate my head would clear and my heart would stop racing. But then I'd feel guilty."

"Is...that why I never met anyone in your family until we had this emergency? Were you ashamed of me?"

"Oh god, no! Christopher no!" She looked at him openly, alarmed that he could ever think that. "Christopher, I was afraid for them to judge you. I was happy. I just didn't want them to rain on my parade. But baby, you have to believe me when I tell you that I've never ever been ashamed of you or the way you look. I've been angry at the way people stare, I've been curious at your shyness, but never ever ashamed."

He studied her eyes and it occurred to her that he didn't instantly believe her. She slipped her hands into his. "Christopher..."

"Because your mother knew nothing about me when I showed up today. I don't think she even knew that I was white."

"You're right. I only told her to expect a man with a cleft palate. I didn't even think about your color. Plus she doesn't care about you being white. She's half white herself. I don't care either. When it comes to you I don't care about anything but you!" She searched his face, wishing the bandages were gone so that she could gage his expression. "I used to only...desire black men; dark men. Maybe because I'm light, I don't know. But I fell in love with you without ever thinking about—Wait, is that why you got the surgery? You thought I was ashamed of you? Christopher, baby, I love you. Completely. I love your looks and everything else about you."

She felt his hand enclose around hers. "I know you do. Ashleigh...I love you so much that it scares me.
Everything I do, I have you in mind. Even when I changed my mission, I was thinking about you. You have to take care of yourself AND our baby. Because I don't know what I'd do without either of you. I only just found out about the baby and already...I..." He took a deep breath. "Don't ever lie to me again." She gave him a surprised look.

"I—"

"A few months ago your blood sugar level was high. I asked you what you'd eaten. You lied to me Ashleigh, and you didn't tell me about the two candy bars that you'd gotten out of the vending machine."

Her face turned red. "How--?"

"I saw. Don't ever lie to me."

Her eyes glistened. "I wasn't trying to be sneaky. I mean--I just didn't want you to think you had a girlfriend that was such a pig that she couldn't even control herself-"

He pulled her into his arms. He was angry, and he was scared and unsure but he was also sorry that he'd made her cry. He felt her wipe away her tears and then she held him. "I don't care if you're big...I fell in love with that big girl, okay?" She nodded her head. "And you have an eating disorder. It's not going to go away on its own. You don't have to do it by yourself, Sweetheart. There's medicine for the anxiety, or whatever you want to do. But I'm going to stand by you, okay?"

She nodded. "I won't lie to you about anything." She looked up, still holding him. "That was our first fight."

He nodded. "Yeah. Can we make that our last?"

She nodded earnestly. "Yes."

"Ashleigh, don't get mad but your mother has blonde hair and light colored eyes and...well are you trying to look like her?" Ashleigh didn't speak. "I mean, you don't have to, not for me, not unless you just want to. But honestly, I'd rather see your brown eyes and...um...I have no idea what your real hair is like since you...you know...wax."

Her mouth parted and her cheeks reddened. "Okay. You want me to...grow out my hair...in both places."

He nodded slowly.

She smiled. "Yeah. Okay, I'll do that."

~***~

Sunday at his folks was a celebration; of his return, of their pregnancy and of their engagement. He was pleasantly surprised when he learned that Ashleigh had been coming to visit each Sunday, even without him. He was equally surprised when she stayed in the kitchen with the ladies and he walked in for another soda and saw Ashleigh and Alma whispering and giggling at the sink.

He couldn't have been more pleased. The only drawback is that he wasn't able to rough house with the kids.

At dinner his father stared at him while chewing on roast beef. He leaned into his mother. "Am I supposed to know who that is with the bandages, mother?"

His mother placed a patient hand on his arm. "That's Christopher. He's gone and gotten reconstruction surgery."

His father's eyes grew sad. He blinked back tears and looked away. "I never forgave myself for not having the money to get you the surgery you needed, Christopher. I've always wished that I could have traded places with you, son. Watching you in pain..." The older man swallowed.

"Daddy..." Christopher's voice was deep with emotion. "I never once blamed you or anybody else. I...I guess I think like you and I feel that I would have gladly taken the burden on myself before I'd see any of you carrying it. God just gave me my wish."

Alma sighed and looked away, swallowing back her tears. But she reached out and clutched Christopher's hand in hers while Ashleigh gave his other hand a brief squeeze.

On the drive home she noted that he was very quiet and thoughtful.

"What's wrong, baby?"

He glanced at her as he drove. "I just…"

"What?" She touched his hand and he moved it from the steering wheel and held her smaller one.

"I wonder if I'll have the guilt that my Dad has if our child…" He couldn't even say the words.

"If our baby has a cleft palate we'll have the money and knowledge to get it corrected." She said softly.

He nodded. "Even…even when it's fixed there is still so much stigma. The scars are sometimes very visible. What if we have a little girl and—"

Ashleigh squeezed his hand firmly. "We're going to teach our children that beauty is on the inside."

He paused at the word children. "You…want to have more with me?"

When Ashleigh didn't answer he glanced at her. She was staring at him in anger. "If you don't know the answer to that then you really don't know how much I love you." She made to withdraw her hand from his but he captured it quickly. He brought it to his lips and kissed her through his bandages.

"I'm learning, sweetheart. Just...please be patient with me. It's hard to undo a lifetime of insecurities."

She gave him a solemn look. "I know."

Later that night he held Ashleigh's sleeping form in his arms. He was having a much harder time sleeping. Tomorrow neither he nor Ashleigh would go into work. They were going to drive down to Ft. Campbell Kentucky in order to arrive for his noontime appointment to have the stitches removed from his lips and his bandages changed. Then after that he wanted to face Bruce.

He'd called earlier and found that his Commander had been moved from ICU. There had been an explosion; the details were sensitive but Christopher thought he could figure it out pretty easily. When you gave arms to people that had never received formal training, you really had no idea of the outcome. Sometimes a frightened civilian didn't want to tell you that he didn't understand...friendly fire was the risk of helping to develop another country's military force.

He tried to pretend to be upbeat for the drive down. He and Ashleigh talked about the type of wedding they'd have and they made plans to sale her condo and what pieces she would store and what items she'd bring to his house. She desperately wanted to move into his welcoming home.

They made good time and met with the doctor who would be in charge of taking care of his surgical issues from now on. Dr. Singh was young, pleasant and very knowledgeable. Christopher and Ashleigh took to him immediately.

When he began unwrapping the bandages Ashleigh sat on the end of her chair, hoping to get a peek of his face. But no such luck. Christopher wore a mask beneath the gauze that resembled a ski mask and all she could see were his eyes, his lips and a shock of messy red hair poking up from the top.

His lips were angry and swollen and he did look a lot like someone had gone crazy with the silicone injection needle. Black threads poked through his flesh and when the doctor began tugging at them Ashleigh had to leave the room in order to be sick.

When she was able to return she gave Christopher an apologetic grin. He was already re-wrapped in gauze but this time there wasn't quite so much. The doctor left his hair at the top uncovered and Ashleigh couldn't stop staring at Christopher's unruly locks. He had curly hair! She would have never guessed since he'd always worn it shorn to almost non-existence. The doctor put salve on his bruised lips and then the final layers of gauze covered that as well.

Dr. Singh informed them that they could return next week for the big reveal. Then the two of them made their way to the Commander's room. Christopher grew quiet and Ashleigh gripped his hand.

"Babe, I'm going to wait in the waiting area while you visit with him." Christopher nodded and leaned forward to brush his bandaged lips against her cheek.

"I won't be long."

"No, take your time. I'll be right here."

He nodded and headed down the short corridor to his Commander's room. He knocked once and received a gruff response.

"Come in."

Christopher opened the door and looked at his Commander and friend.

"Beast." The older man said. "Come in."

"How'd you know it was me?"

Bruce scowled. "Who the hell else would it be? Nearly seven feet tall with a bandaged face…"

Christopher entered and closed the door. He was having a hard time breathing as he took in Bruce's injuries. He had a bandage similar to Christopher's covering half of his face. He was banged up pretty good; black and blue. But that wasn't the worst of it.

His friend had lost his arm.

Bruce watched where Christopher was staring and then he looked at the stump that ended below his left elbow.

"It was my left, thank god." The older man extended his elbow curiously. "Still feels like it's there." He met Christopher's eyes. "The kid was just holding the grenade. He fucking froze. I yanked it from him but I knew I wouldn't have time to get rid of it. I watched it leave my hands and I thought, 'just a little bit further…' then I saw my fingers disappear." Bruce sighed. "Not sure why they had to take half my arm. I still had my hand…" He shrugged and looked at Christopher. "I lost my hearing on my left side. Got it back on the right-"

"Commander, I'm so sorry-" Christopher choked.

"I'm not your Commander anymore. Just Bruce."

Christopher looked down and swallowed past the lump in his throat. "This is my fault."

Bruce scowled. "No."

"You were doing the job that I should have been doing-"

"Yeah. And? You're twenty-five years old. You got your life before you." Bruce sighed and looked away. He finally turned back to the younger man. "Listen to what I'm saying to you and then I never want to talk about this again."

Christopher met his eyes curiously.

"I fucked up, okay? I fucked up. I handed that kid live ammo without making sure he knew what the hell I was telling him. I treated him like I treated you men; as if he knew what the hell he was doing. My attitude...it was my own fault, okay? I know you wouldn't have made the same mistake. I watch you with people. So I know you wouldn't have made this mistake!"

Christopher straightened his posture. "Commander-"

"I'm not your Commander-"

"Sir, with all due respect, you will *always* be my Commander. You trained us in order to train others how to protect themselves. You did a damn good job at it sir. Without your training none of us would have been able to do this job for as long as we have. And sir, THAT was your job!" And had Christopher been there to do his job than he wouldn't have had someone get injured doing it for him...and that was something that he would never forgive himself for.

Bruce was quiet for a very long time. And when he spoke again it was to ask about the 'little trooper'. The two friends talked for a while longer, and each knew that they would never speak of what had caused Bruce's injury to the other again.

Christopher would not be allowed to return to work for months but he planned to go in Tuesday. He had to face his team...his ex-team the way that he had faced Bruce.

~***~

"I don't want you to go to the gym today." Christopher said as he prepared Ashleigh's protein drink early Tuesday morning.

She frowned. "Why? The doctor said that running on the treadmill won't hurt the baby and the exercise is going to be good for me."

He felt himself smile at the mention of the baby. He wondered if he would do that for the next seven months. He already felt like a proud father. He grew serious as he poured the drink into a glass instead of a thermos.

"I'm not going to lie to you. The guys aren't going to be too happy with me. And I need to go and talk to them."

She frowned in confusion. "Why? They were worried about you. They were going to help me find you." She accepted the offered beverage and relished its frothy goodness. Kiwi, strawberries…spinach? She wasn't quite sure. All she knew is that she missed his special concoctions.

He began cleaning up. Yeah, they wanted to find him alright. They knew he'd come to them. If there was any doubt than they would have already shown up at his door. He didn't know how bad things would escalate and he wasn't taking any chance of Ashleigh getting in the middle of things.

"Those are your friend's, Christopher. They care about you. They won't do anything to hurt you." She frowned when he remained quiet. "They wouldn't…hit you in your face would they? Christopher?"

He gathered her in his arms. "No. They are not going to hit me in my face." He pressed his cheek to her forehead. "Now, I don't want you to worry. If you want we can meet for lunch, how about that? Invite Kendra and Lance and we'll all go out; my treat."

She grinned. "Yeah?"

"Yeah. I'll meet you guys in the lobby like before."

She stood up on her tiptoes and kissed his bandaged lips. "Okay."

Christopher dropped Ashleigh off at the front door of The Federal Building and then drove to the main office where he had to collect his personal items and fill out paperwork. He was done within the hour and then drove into the underground garage and parked in his normal spot. He still hadn't decided on a new job, but he wasn't allowed back to 'work' so he supposed that this would no longer be his parking spot. They would be hiring some other guy to replace him and this would be his spot.

He frowned.

He scanned in and wasn't surprised when sixteen guys were waiting for him on the other side of the door. Security cameras…they worked both ways.

"Shit." TK said. "What happened to you?"

Ashleigh hadn't told them. Great. Maybe the bandages would bide him some time so that he could actually get a few words in before he got jumped by sixteen angry Marines…no sixteen angry *Special Ops* Marines.

"I had six surgeries to fix the problems with my face."

There was prolonged quiet. "Oh." Carlos said. "Wanted to be pretty for the girl-"

"Don't go there." Christopher said tightly. "I did it because I was sick and tired of not having a face."

"Well we think you just wanted to cop out of the mission because you didn't want to leave your girlfriend." Lem said stepping forward.

So they'd chosen Lem to face him. They were the same height, roughly the same build and evenly matched…well except for the fact that Christopher couldn't take a punch to the face.

He held up his hand. "Look. I came to talk to you guys, not to fight."

"The Commander got hurt filling in for you!" Someone said.

"I know! I was down in Ft Campbell visiting him yesterday, so I know!"

"Then you know that he lost his arm," TK said evenly, "and his career."

"I know," he said, calming down some. "We talked about it. That's why I'm here." He looked at each of the men. "The Commander told me that it wasn't my fault-"

"Bull-!"

"I KNOW IT'S MY FAULT!" Christopher began to pace. "Bruce Koepke is my Commander, my friend, the father I lost to dementia…" He stopped pacing and faced the men. "And he's the person that I owe my life to." The Military had given Christopher's life direction. But Bruce had given him a chance to be someone truly special. "I apologized to Bruce…and that's between us. I didn't come to talk about Bruce with any of you. I came here because I owe each and every one of you an apology and an explanation. And I mean to give it." No one spoke and he continued.

"I met a girl and I fell in love. No different than any of you all have done; met a girl, got married, had kids. But there is one difference. Each of you made the decision to stay in Special Ops. I made a different decision. I made the decision to get out. I'll deploy again and when I do I'll go and serve my time. But I want off the roster for special assignments. I went to Bruce and told him that. I'm a Marine for life but not with the special forces; not anymore. He tried to talk me out of it but I told him, just like I'm telling you, I choose my life with Ashleigh over the missions. Period. End of story.

"Bruce okay'd it and told me to start putting in for other jobs." Some of the guys looked at each other. "I hadn't found any," Truth is, every time he'd think about not being able to look at the cameras to monitor his sweetheart, or not being able to personally protect the building that she worked in, he'd find an excuse to keep looking. He'd passed up many jobs that he would have surely qualified for and gotten but...

He focused his attention back to the men glaring at him. "Then we got called down. I wasn't supposed to be on any more missions. I'd requested off and he'd okay'd it weeks before this mission came up! I should have been taken off the roster once my Commander okay'd it. But it didn't work like that. My name wouldn't come off the roster until I BQ'd for a new position." He stared at them, waiting.

"But you still got out of it. You used your face as a way to get out of it!"

Christopher sighed and looked at the ceiling. "The Commander okay'd my surgery." He looked at them again. "He didn't have to. Don't think for a second that he didn't know that he was getting me out of a mission." Christopher glared at them angrily. "And while each of you dickheads have been finding girlfriends and knocking up women and getting married, I have been alone. Okay? I could have had surgery and...maybe found the confidence to find someone too. But then it would have taken me away from the team for upwards of six months. I wasn't willing to do that! This team...this was my life. And I happen to know what facial surgery feels like; it ain't pleasant. And guess what? I'll still be ugly, okay? I fucking know that!

"But for Ashleigh..." he nodded his head. "I'd do it in a

heartbeat if my face will just look a little bit better for her. If people will stop staring and…"He shook his head before saying, 'if it means that her ex can't talk his way back into her life'.

No one said anything.

"Look. I know I was still wrong. But I put in a request to be taken off the roster long before the mission came up."

Carlos rubbed his cheeks eyeing Christopher. "Sounds like you stalling, son. Anybody would have pick you up with your training."

Christopher was shaking his head. "I just need to find the perfect job for me."

"Yeah." TK said. "One where you can shoot a gun and throw some grenades while in the field and then come home and perv your girlfriend at work all day. Yeah…that's a hard job to top."

Lem turned away with a look of disgust. "Don't worry dude. We'll watch her for you, even though that's supposed to be YOUR job to keep juiceheads off her in the gym. But…I'm pretty sure she would have hit that guy in the head with a free weight had we not gotten down to the gym in time."

"He was pretty big, though." TK added. "Good thing we were watching."

Christopher felt like he was going to black out. Stars moved in front of his eyes. "What the hell are you saying?" He managed to growl past the fury that was overtaking his thoughts. Were they saying that someone had accosted Ashleigh in the gym?

TK and Lem exchanged looks. "She didn't tell you?" TK spoke.

Though no one could see Christopher's face, the change to his posture spoke volumes.

"Tell me what?" He asked.

Lem gave him a smug look. "Couple days ago there was an incident in the gym. We had to go down and prevent a highly volatile man from…"

"From?!" Christopher said.

"Some guy was hitting on your girl." TK finished. "And he wouldn't take no for an answer-" Lem scowled at TK for stealing his thunder.

Christopher swore. If they could have seen his face they would have seen that it was now beet red with fury. "Did he put his hands on her?"

"Not exactly," Lem continued. "But he wouldn't let her pass-"

Christopher swore again. His hands had formed fists. "Who is he?"

"Beast, calm down. We handled it." Lem said. His attitude was completely different now that it was obvious that Christopher was being pushed over the edge. It was his job to push the big man but not to cause him to lose it.

"I want to know who this guy is!"

"He doesn't even work in this building." Someone spoke, attempting to diffuse the situation.

"I want to see the report!" Christopher charged to the file cabinet where the incident reports were kept. He had been the one to file the last one on Ashleigh, when she had collapsed in the gym.

"Beast! There is no report!" Carlos yelled stopping him in his tracks. Christopher stared at Carlos. The young Hispanic man looked around at the other members of the team.

"We...took care of it."

Christopher's body tensed instead of relaxing. He understood what it meant that there was no trail. But it was very bad that someone else had had to take care of this problem for him. He stood there, breathing like a bull in helpless frustration.

One of the members of his team explained. "Two of us followed him out and...secured his identify...and then..." there was a brief cough. "We gave him a very painful warning not to ever return. He won't be back."

Someone chuckled and it sounded purely evil. "It'll be six weeks before he'll be able to use his fingers again."

The information should have made him feel better, but it didn't. Yes, he was grateful that his team had been there to protect Ashleigh. But his woman had needed protecting and he hadn't been there and there was nothing that made him feel more useless. Not to mention that he had this pent up rage and no one to pound.

Christopher turned and headed out the room. Why hadn't Ashleigh told him about this? He needed to talk to her. He wanted a word by word replay of the incident and then he would decide if a few broken fingers was all the asshole would end up with. What if he had touched her? What if he had hurt her? What if someone else did?

"Beast!" Someone called after him. "You know you don't want to leave us. And you damn sure don't want to leave her here where any old fool is going to be walking in watching her on that treadmill!"

Christopher's steps faltered and he looked over his shoulder but didn't turn. Lem chuckled in satisfaction. "We'll do what you ain't willing to do."

His chest felt constricted with barely contained rage. "I know what you're trying to do." He said after another pause. "But it ain't going to work. I made up my mind. I'm thinking about her and I'm thinking about our baby."

"Baby?!" Someone yelled.

"Yeah. She's having a baby." He left the room and headed for the elevators that would take him to the Federal building. He didn't even hear TK until he spoke just behind him, having followed him out. Christopher almost swung on him, he was so wired with frustration.

"Christopher."
He frowned at the name. No one called him Christopher. He studied the big black man that had been much like a brother to him, just as much as he had been a friend and highly trusted cohort.

"You want to keep egging me on? This ain't nothing but a game to you, to all of you; something to keep you from being bored now that the mission is over!" Christopher spat. "But this ain't a game to me. This is my life, TK; my woman, my baby, my life! Nothing comes before that!"

TK held up his hand. "I know. Okay? I'm not...I just wanted to tell you that no one would ever disrespect the little trooper. We watch her back as much for you as we do out of respect for her. If you leave here we're going to continue to watch her. But, none of us want to see you leave."

Christopher sighed feeling conflicted. "I can't be in special ops and not go on missions-"

"Maybe they can make this a fulltime position."

"What do you mean?"

"Only a fool would want to stay in the subbasement year in and year out and miss out on all the fun of a mission—a fool or someone like you. You actually...like being down here." TK sighed. "The guys want to keep you, even if you don't go on special ops missions. But don't think you're getting full pay!" He growled.

Christopher's brow quirked up. "You...want to continue working with me? Even after what I did?"

TK turned and headed back to the security room but Christopher heard him speak. "I'm acting Commander until they find a replacement for Bruce. I'll tell command central that we need a man stationed down here permanently." He stopped and looked at the bandaged man. "Consider that your punishment for trying to get away from us. Do it again..." TK's expression was suddenly severe, "and we really will break your face." The door closed behind him and Christopher stood there for a few moments just smiling.

Damn; those guys; his brothers; his family. He shook his head and quickly stabbed the button to take him to Ashleigh.

~***~

When Kendra and Lance had asked about her weekend Ashleigh hid a smile. "Christopher came home with a big surprise."

"Bigger than the one you're carrying in your belly?" Kendra asked.

"Wait…is this going to be TMI?"

"No!" Ashleigh laughed. "Although that was pretty damn big—"

"Ugh, Ashleigh!" Lance said. "Nasty!"

Ashleigh laughed before growing serious. "Christopher had never gone on a mission. It was a big misunderstanding. He'd gone and had facial reconstructive surgery."

Her friend's were in total disbelief and kept asking questions even though she had very few answers. All she could really tell them is that she hadn't seen any of his face with the exception of his lips which looked like giant balloons.

She grinned knowing that she still had another big revelation. "Oh guys. Christopher wants to take us out to lunch today is that cool? It's not our regular day but-"

"Oh yeah! I want to see him wrapped up like a mummy!" Kendra said.

"Cool," Ashleigh tried not to beam. "We can talk about the wedding-"

Lance screamed. He fanned himself and then covered his mouth and screamed again. Kendra slapped his arm and the both of them hugged her tightly. The other people in the office ignored them, used to Lance's extreme excitability.

"You guys are going to be my bridesmaids okay?"

"Oooo! Can I wear a kilt?" Lance asked.

"Of course, Diva!" Ashleigh said seriously.

Kendra rubbed her swollen belly. "Crap. I'm going to look like a hot air balloon. No chance of you two postponing it until after I have the baby and loose my baby weight?"

Ashleigh cocked her eye at her. "No. I want to get married while my stomach is still flat. God knows that it might never be this flat again."

"Yes it will." Lance said while giving her tummy a brief pat. She gave them both serious looks.

"No…it probably won't." she took a deep breath. "I…hid something from you guys." Her friend's expressions grew serious. "I'm telling you now because I'm going to need your help."

"Oh my god," Lance clutched her hand. "What is it?"

"I'm...bulimic."

Lance held her hand tightly and then Kendra placed hers over it. "How long?" She asked.

Ashleigh swallowed, feeling her eyes mist. "Almost all of my life."

"God, Ash." Lance said. "I didn't know."

"Does Christopher know?" Kendra asked, her brow furrowed in concern.

Ashleigh nodded. "We talked about it. He wants me to get help and I think I want to get professional help."

"We love you." Lance said while hugging her. "We'll be your support system. Just tell us what you need." His eyes closed momentarily as if he was coming to a decision, then he pulled back with a pained look on his face as he glanced away.

"I have something to tell you also."

Ashleigh thought she was going to black out. She heard the words, 'I'm HIV positive' come out of his mouth even before his mouth opened.

"Rick and I broke up."

Ashleigh stared, blinking. "No...Oh Lance. Oh sweetheart, what happened?"

He gave them a shaky smile. "I broke up with him because, I think I deserve more. You two are going to have babies. I want to have a baby, too." Kendra frowned and Lance turned to her before she even opened her mouth.

"Figuratively…not literally. I can't have that with Rick. He is so deeply in the closet, and I understand why, but there is no way that he can come out without risking his career. You don't play pro football as a gay man. Period.

"I want…the happily ever after." Lance's eyes were glistening with unshed tears. "I want to be someone's partner and not their dirty secret."

Kendra placed her hands on the man's cheeks. "You are no one's dirty secret!"

"That's right." Ashleigh said. "You deserve everything that your heart desires, my friend."

Lance lowered his head and sobbed into his hands. "I know. But why does it have to hurt so bad?"

Ashleigh pulled him into her arms and kissed the top of his blond head. "I know it hurts but it won't last forever. I promise." And Ashleigh believed with all of her heart that she was speaking the truth. She had known this pain and how desperate it made you feel. But given time the pain healed and became nothing more than a bad memory.

~***~

Christopher surprised everyone when he entered the room a few hours later, totally unannounced. There were several offices in one room and when one of the ladies saw the giant bandaged man she shrieked and dropped the file that she was carrying and sent papers scattering along the floor.

Christopher bent to help her pick them up and she gave him an embarrassed chuckle and apology. "Not a problem, Ma'am." He said politely while handing her the papers. "Can you tell me where Miss Dalton's office is?"

The woman pointed down a short corridor. He nodded and headed for Ashleigh's office. He passed Lance's first. He was leaned back in his chair and talking on the phone. He gasped when he saw Christopher and a big smile spread across his face.

"Let me call you back, Gloria. Yeah, promise." He hung up the phone and hurried to greet Christopher who held up his finger to indicate he not mention his presence. Lance nodded and followed him to Ashleigh's office. They passed Kendra's office. She was absorbed in working on something on the computer. She swiveled her head at Christopher and Lance and then took a double take. They held up their fingers to their lips to indicate that she should be quiet and she joined them as they all headed to Ashleigh's office.

Ashleigh was staring out the window with a slight smile on her face. She was obviously daydreaming and when she saw Christopher suddenly appear in the doorway she squealed in delight and leaped to her feet.

"Baby! You're early!" She dashed to him, throwing herself into his arms. Christopher caught her, wanting to kiss her so badly. He hated the bandages and his sore lips and the shooting pains in his head and face. But somehow, holding Ashleigh in his arms made it all bearable. It was all for her.

She had been daydreaming about him and how wonderful it had been to wake up in his arms, not to mention all of the things that they had done before falling asleep. Her body was humming in anticipation of tonight. She could barely wait to get home and had even contemplated leaving with him after lunch today. But that was just too pitiful…wasn't it?

"Hi Sweetheart. I think I might have some good news for you." He looked around to include all of them. "I'm sure Ashleigh told you that I've been looking for a new job within The Marine Corps."

"Right, so that you won't have to go on anymore missions." Kendra said.

"Right. So that I can leave Special Ops."

Ashleigh grinned in excitement. "Christopher, you found a new job!"

"Uh…well, not exactly." Ashleigh grinned at him expectantly. "There's a chance that I might not be going anywhere. TK is acting Commander. He wants me stationed in the subbasement permanently; no missions."

"Oh my god. You won't have to leave?!" Ashleigh hugged him and Christopher laughed and swung her around once before setting her on her feet.

"It's not set in stone, Babe. TK has got to put in a request for me to work the subbasement on a permanent basis." He shrugged. "But truthfully, it's something that would be a win win situation. They need someone with my experience," Christopher chuckled and Ashleigh thought it was the most beautiful sound in the world, "but no one but me would want to work down there permanently." He lifted her hand and placed it against his lips.

"I want to make sure that no one ever bothers you again when you're working out." Her eyes got big and then she smiled. Yes, he would surely keep an eye on her every move and that made her feel safe and secure. Chris would always know when she needed him.

~***~

Later in the evening, Ashleigh walked out of the Federal building and Christopher was parked right out front waiting for her. She hurried to the car and kissed his neck lightly. Lunch had been wonderful and Ashleigh was so proud of the way her friends had warmed up to her man and how easily he acted around them.

At the house Maggie hurried to her and meowed for some loving. Christopher shook his head as Ashleigh reached own to scratch the feline's neck.

"Not sure how you won her over. She's always been skittish around others."

"Mags took care of me when you were gone."

Christopher took her hand and pulled her up and pulled her close where he wrapped his arms around her body. "I'm going to take care of you now."

He leaned down and lightly rubbed his bandaged lips against her cheeks.

"I want to kiss you so bad."

"You are kissing me." She murmured, her eyes closing.

"I want to taste you…" He whispered.

Ashleigh sighed. She slipped her hand beneath his shirt and felt him shudder. She loved that he reacted to just her touch. She unbuttoned it and he pulled it off and tossed it onto the couch. Ashleigh kissed his chest as her hands ran slowly down his back and over the swell of his ass.

"Mmm." Christopher moaned when her lips found his little nipple. She circled it with her wet tongue while Christopher's hands moved along the front of her blouse, cupping her breasts. Moving quickly he tugged at her clothes until she was down to her bra and this he quickly unsnapped until her breasts had spilled from the cups.

"God…" he moaned. "So beautiful…" Christopher brought his head down to her golden brown breasts and its dark brown nipple, already hard in anticipation. Christopher opened his mouth and brought it down on the nub and Ashleigh's body began to tremble.

His mouth on her felt so amazing. And then his tongue swept over the sensitive flesh repeatedly and Ashleigh's back arched. She clutched at his arms, digging her fingers deep into his skin.

"Chris!" He grunted and moved back from her nipple. She worried that she might have hurt him, but he immediately lifted her into his arms and stalked to the bedroom. He placed her on her feet and quickly finished undressing her. When he slipped off her panties he inhaled the scent of her lust and groaned.

"Oh, Ashleigh…lay down, baby." She climbed back onto the bed and watched him standing above her, still in his pants and she writhed on the bed in anticipation for what she knew was coming. He wanted to taste her and she wanted so badly to be tasted…

Christopher dropped to his knees and hooked his hands around her thighs and pulled her until her bottom was hanging off the end of the bed. Ashleigh's feet went to his shoulders and she spread her thighs wide and began to shake, no, her body quaked with need.

"Please, baby..." She moaned. Christopher pushed his bandages from his lips, his eyes glued to the sight of her wet crease. He didn't care if his bandages became saturated with her juices, he would carry her scent around with him gladly. He spread her lips and moaned at the sight of her swollen, silky folds. Christopher leaned forward and lapped at her opening. Ashleigh's body jerked and she cried out in pleasure. His tongue travelled along each fold, languishing in the exquisite taste of her, a taste that he'd yearned for over the last few months.

It didn't take long, when his mouth closed over her clit, Ashleigh's body bucked and she pealed out a loud cry seconds before her body exploded in orgasm. Immediately, Christopher pulled down his pants and he entered her slick opening, slick but still so tight. How could she still grip him so tightly after the number of times they'd made love? He groaned as he sank into her and rapidly pumping his hips against her.

"I love you, Ashleigh! I love you!" He cried as her legs closed around his hips and gripped him tight. "I love you so much!"

He felt her body begin to tremble and shake again. He couldn't believe that he'd brought her again so quickly, but she was clutching him and her hot canal spasamed around his shaft.

"Don't stop, don't stop, don't ever—" She suddenly pulled his head down and Ashleigh kissed her man's lips for the first time in months. She was careful but she needed his kiss. Christopher cupped her face and gently kissed her lips as he pushed deep into her and deposited the last of his seed deep into her body.

"God, Chris…when these bandages come off…" He sat up on one elbow and began unwrapping them.

"Stop! What are you doing?" She yelled.

"These bandages gotta go. They aren't necessary and I have the elastic mask on. Help me take this shit off."

She reached up tentatively and began unwrapping the bandages. When they finally got down to the elastic mask Ashleigh blinked in surprise. His facial structure was so different. She couldn't tell what his nose would look like but he actually appeared to have one. It was covered with a protective shield. She reached up and touched his messy curls and grinned.

"I love your hair."

"I can't wait to wash it and shave." He bent down and kissed her nipple. She gasped and then giggled.

"Your lips are really swollen and bruised. We didn't hurt them did we?"

"I don't care." He moved to kiss the other nipple.

"Christopher." She spoke seriously. "I care."

He rolled over onto his back. "Okay, Sweetheart. I'll take it easy with the lips.

She came up on her elbow and gently traced along his face.

"Does that hurt?"

"Mmm, feels good. My face itches. I can't wait to get this off." She watched him intently. He looked differently already. His teeth were straight, he had a nose.

"I'm not going to be some male model when it's all said and done." He whispered. "You do understand that, don't you? I'm not going to ever be the handsomest guy in the room-"

"Do I care about that?" She gave him a severe look.

"I just want you to be prepared."

"I am and I don't care."

CHAPTER 10

Several days later, as they drove down to Ft Campbell Kentucky to have the last of the bandages removed, Ashleigh intertwined her fingers with his. She was scared, she didn't know what to expect. All she knew is that no matter what she would love him.

They held hands as they headed for Dr. Singh's office and Ashleigh felt his grip tighten a bit. She knew that Chris was nervous and she gave his hand a reassuring squeeze. Dr. Singh didn't make them wait and they were surprised that a webcam was set up directly to Dr. Weitz's office. There were also several other doctors in attendance and Christopher was informed that he would be the subject of an article on severe cleft palates in adults.

His response was an embarrassed shrug. "I never liked getting my picture taken but if it'll help others." Ashleigh noted that his country drawl was more pronounced and she had to fight not to run up to him and throw herself into his arms. Maybe she was a perv but she had grown accustomed to seeing her over-sized fiancé wearing a mask. It was kind of sexy and she joked that he should take up wrestling and then they sat around making up funny names for his pro wrestling career. The winner was *El Bestia!*

She tried to stand back out of the way as Christopher sat on a stool with a light shining in his face but Dr. Singh wouldn't have that and wanted her to stand right next to him so that she could see every move that was made.

Using surgical scissors, Dr. Singh made a cut upward from Christopher's jaw near his ear to his hairline. He did the same on the other side and removed the material from the back of Christopher's hair. Dark red curls sprung up and Ashleigh grinned. She couldn't wait to run her fingers through his silky curls, maybe he'd let it grow out for a while before going back to the military cut.

Christopher watched Ashleigh's anxious expression. The only thing he cared about is that she would like the results. He felt the mask loosen and Dr. Singh removed it from his hair. He wanted to reach up and run his nails through his scalp and scratch like an old hound dog, but resisted. He held a mirror in his lap but closed his eyes when the Doctor had him tilt his head back so that he could remove the rest of the mask from his face.

He used some sort of probe to loosen it from his chin and Christopher knew that he would have a fairly thick beard as a barrier between his skin and the mask. It's where the mask touched skin that it pulled some. The pain was negligible, though, after the torture of having his skull rebuilt and his face peeled back, not to mention having a brand new nose forced into place. He held his breath as the mask was loosened around his lips and nose. The doctor tediously ran the probe around the circumference of the mask, still allowing it to stay in place. The room was so quiet that the only sound heard was the breathing of the occupants of the room.

"Are you ready Lieutenant?"

"I been ready." Everyone chuckled at his response.

He opened his eyes and looked at Ashleigh who gave him an encouraging smile. Dr. Singh lifted the cotton and cloth adhesive mask from his face and his skin began to tingle as the cool air met his freshly uncovered skin.

No one said a thing. Dr. Singh used the probe and lifted the bandage over his nose and that did pull and sting a bit. When that was removed Dr. Singh moved back on his stool and just stared. Christopher looked at Ashleigh and was only met with a look of confusion. His brow furrowed at the way they were looking at him, so quiet. He suddenly remembered the mirror and quickly lifted it to see what they were seeing.

Christopher's eyes widened. He brought the mirror closer and squinted and then pulled it back trying to take in everything at once. He couldn't remove his eyes from the sight before him.

His face was perfect.

He looked at Ashleigh again and she had tears in her eyes. She smiled and quickly wiped them away.

"Hi Christopher."

He smiled. "Hi Ashleigh." And then he reached out and pulled her into his arms. She kissed his lips and then burst out into tears.

"Them happy tears, babe?" He asked a bit worried.

She nodded enthusiastically. She pulled back and laughed and placed the palms of her hands on his bearded cheeks.

Ashleigh was in a state of utter disbelief. Not only had they corrected his cleft palate but they had given him the nose that his deformation had taken, they had repaired the concaved look that had caused him to have a gorilla appearance and they had given him a beautiful set of full lips. And Ashleigh was hard pressed to see any scars, only something that looked like faint creases which were easy to overlook.

His perfectly chiseled face was covered in a thick, rich auburn moustache and beard and with the frame of his dark red hair he looked like a rugged lumber jack. Ashleigh's heart began to thump rapidly in her chest. To her, he was the most perfectly beautiful man that she'd ever seen. Even with his unruly hair and unkempt beard, Christopher looked like a movie star.

Dr. Weitz could be heard from the video feed. "Perfect."

Dr. Singh lifted his curls and examined his hairline and he and Dr. Weitz conferred back in forth using technical terms that Ashleigh and Christopher quickly lost interest in. She held his hands and stared at him in amazement. He chuckled at the sheer surprise on her face and then he lifted the mirror and studied his features again.

The face was familiar to him though he'd never seen it before. It was the face of his family; the similarities that each person in his bloodline had. He could see his dead brother Walt and he could see his Daddy and Butch and his other siblings and aunts and cousins. He smiled to think that this face might even look a bit like the baby that was growing in Ashleigh. He was thankful that Dr. Weitz had not tried to make him look like some stranger but just what he had always meant to be…well maybe with a few improvements. And that was fine by him.

"This…feels like a dream." He said while staring at his reflection. His eyes moved to Ashleigh, his mouth standing slightly ajar. "Is this real?" He felt an emotional well of tears in his eyes and alarmed he quickly blinked them away. "It looks good. I can't believe how good it looks."

Ashleigh squeezed his hands. "Christopher, YOU look good. That's you, baby, all you."

He looked into the mirror again and let out a deep breath filled with pent up emotion. His; his nose, his lips, his almost invisible
scars. This was…him.

Dr. Singh and the other attendants discreetly moved away to allow him to become acquainted with his new looks. They continued to confer with each other in quiet tones.

He looked at Ashleigh again and saw that she was equally emotional. "This is not freaking you out, is it Sweetheart? I know I look like a different person-"

She could no longer resist the urge to run her hands through his silky curls. She hugged him against her and sighed. "I'm far from freaked out." He was different but she could still see her Christopher there, familiar and comforting. His eyes were still the warm dark and light that mesmerized her, and when he smiled up at her his lip twisted in that familiar crooked smile of his.

No. She hadn't needed him to change. But he had needed it.

They spent more time than either of them wanted taking pictures of his new face and receiving instructions on care. But Christopher couldn't even think about heading back home until he had visited with his commander.

"Ashleigh, do you care? I don't know when I'll see him again." Soon he'd be released and Christopher wanted to tell him about his meeting with the team. He also wanted to show off his face. The Commander was a pivotal part of him looking brand new and he wanted to share it.

"Not at all." She actually wanted to see the Commander again. He had been nice to her. Christopher had forgotten that he hadn't explained about the Commander's injuries and when they were invited into the room, her face dropped at the sight of what remained of his arm.

Bruce Kopke looked from Ashleigh to Christopher. "You got to be shittin' me..." His mouth was hanging open in complete surprise.

Ashleigh perched herself on the side of his bed and Christopher was surprised that she talked to him like he was an old friend. And he could have hit the floor when the old S.O.B smiled and blushed when Ashleigh leaned forward to kiss his cheek goodbye.

"I'm not surprised that the team doesn't want to lose you, Beast." The Commander spoke as they headed out the door.

Christopher grinned. "I'm not Beast anymore."

Bruce cocked his head in surprise. "You do know that we called you Beast because of how you are out on the field, right? The way you went through Crucible and everything else you tackle is what makes you a beast."

Christopher shrugged. "I guess I didn't know that. But it didn't bother me. I don't mind being called Beast by you guys..." He left the rest unsaid and headed out of the room.

Ashleigh slipped her hand in his as they walked out of the medical facility. She glanced at him and considered how wrong it was that she so desperately wanted to make love. Why did it feel a little bit like she was cheating on him? Would he be jealous if she…liked his face?

Two women walked past them as they walked hand and hand to the car and both began squealing and giggling. They looked behind them and Ashleigh saw that the two grown women were almost tripping over their feet craning their necks to look at Christopher.

"He is so hot!" They were whispering and giggling. Ashleigh
rolled her eyes and Christopher looked at her in surprise.

"Did you hear that? They said I was hot?"

"Baby," She heard herself whine. "Didn't I always make you feel like you were hot?" Crap, she hated the sound of insecurity in her voice. This was not a repeat of DeAngelo. Christopher wasn't waiting to bang every good looking girl that passed him by. Christopher didn't want her to be his fluffy girl and she would never ever be a fluffy girl again.

Christopher reached over, tilted her chin up and studied her eyes. "Ash, I love you. I'll never want another woman, do you understand? You are all I've ever wanted." She nodded and tried to smile. "What's wrong sweetheart? Are you sure that my face doesn't bother you?"

"It's not that. Christopher I love your face so much!" She said in a rush. "Oh baby, but I don't love the old you any less. I swear it-"

He threw his head back and began to laugh. "Oh Ashleigh, honey, I want you to totally accept my new looks! I did it for you, for us!" He leaned forward and gently kissed her. "You're the one that reminded me that this face is all me." Ashleigh's eyes closed as she eagerly returned his kiss. Oh god, she wanted him so badly. He gave her one last peck before withdrawing. She noticed that his grey eyes had darkened.

"We have to go visit Mom and Dad. They are going to be anxious." He said, either trying to convince her or to convince himself.

"Oh…yeah. Of course." Damnit, she wanted to jump into the next available dark corner and bang the hell out of him!

"We won't stay long," he promised.

"No. We should. They're just as anxious about the surgery as we are."

He gripped her hand and led her to the car. While they drove he touched his lips and nose and she would catch him smiling to himself. When he realized that he was being watched he blushed.

"I'm not being vain, but I just can't believe this face is mine." He chuckled.

She was watching him and hiding her smile. "You sorta look like that guy who played Thor, except with red hair."

He scowled. "No. You think?"

"A little. But better."

Now it was his turn to roll his eyes. He glanced at her and gave her a crooked grin and she saw him, her old Christopher, so clearly in the new angles of his face.

"God, I love you." She whispered.

The smile slid from his face. "Mom and Dad can wait…" He changed lanes and drove towards the next exit. "I need you now."

"What are you doing?"

"I'm finding a hotel. You need to eat, I need to shower and shave, but first," he gave her a smoky look. "You need to cum. I know when my baby needs to cum."

Her eyes got big and she squirmed in her seat. Wow, he was talking dirty. Yum.

They quickly located a Highway Inn which didn't look appropriate for more than what they wanted it for. Christopher checked them into a small dingy room. Ashleigh pulled the comforter from the bed, allowing it to land on the floor where it surely belonged. When she turned Christopher was standing right there. He lifted her easily and sat her on the blankets.

Christopher came out of his shirt and Ashleigh resisted the urge to run her hands along his muscular chest. He kicked out of his shoes and pulled off his jeans and boxers. She gasped. He was already so hard that his big thick shaft was nearly purple.

Moving quickly she squirmed out of her clothes while he watched her. She was aware of exactly where his eyes landed on every part of her body.

His eyes rested on hers. "I want to do this right..." he went down on his knees before the bed and she shuddered in anticipation, spreading her legs wide for him. The sight of her soft, wet flesh swelling from her brown lips caused Christopher's salivary glands to go into overdrive. He loved Ashleigh's pussy; the way it smelled, the way it looked the way it tasted. He quickly lowered his lips to her mound and he licked and sucked until she was whimpering and gyrating uncontrollably.

Her hands slipped into his hair, but instead of gripping it she rubbed him gently holding him in place while she gyrated against his face. He rubbed his beard against her flesh and she arched to meet it. The friction was incredible! She suddenly bucked.

"No! Don't make me cum. In me baby, inside of me, please!"

Christopher quickly moved up the bed until he was covering her body. She ran her hands over his taut body while he guided himself into her wet and ready opening. Ashleigh's eyes closed and her lips parted.

"Ohh..." She cried. "Oh, Chris..."

Christopher squeezed his eyes closed fighting to control his strokes; steady, not too hard, not to slow. His baby liked it fast. He dipped his head and sought her plump brown nipple. He sucked her into his mouth and it was the move that brought her over the edge. Ashleigh gripped his back, her fingers dug in while her legs closed tightly around him.

Christopher gasped as her hot satiny walls clenched around him, squeezing him and pulling him inside of her further.

"Yes! Ashleigh, cum, baby!" He growled as he drove into her faster. He could feel her body shaking. He didn't know if all women did that but his Ashleigh did. Her shaking intensified until she let loose one last shriek of pleasure. With that sound and the intense pulsing that gripped him, Chris allowed his own cry of pleasure to mix with hers.

Christopher clutched the blankets in his fists and grunted his release into Ashleigh's still pulsing body. "Oh my god…" He said as he allowed his body to collapse partially over hers. "So good…" he murmured.

All she could do was lay there and stroke his curls and his shoulders and his back. He rolled onto his side and stared down at her. She reached up and silently ran her finger over the bridge of his nose, and then allowing it to dip down into the cleft of his lip before she traced his upper lip. Christopher closed his eyes, relishing the feel of her fingers on his face.

"I love when you do that." He whispered. He grasped her wrist lightly and returned her fingers to his lips where he kissed each fingertip. "I never thought I'd have this."

She inhaled a shaky breathe. "Me either."

~***~

Sharing his face with his family was like watching each of them open a valued present at Christmas. Christopher never realized how much his scars had so profoundly affected everyone until every single person that had come to his Mom and Dad's house cried tears of joy for him. His mother was shaking and she kept touching his face. His father shed tears as well, but mostly because he thought Chris was Walt. And he kept saying that he knew Walt wasn't dead, that his boy had come back. Christopher just buried his head against his father's chest and let him think that he was Walt.

By the time they got home later in the evening, Christopher was emotionally drained. He dragged himself into bed but Ashleigh wasn't ready for sleep. She changed into shorts and a sports bra and then went into the workout room. Maggie yawned and hopped up on the weight bench and watched as Ashleigh got on the treadmill. It had been days since she had run but once the endorphins released into her system, she got lost in the joy of her muscles working; tightening and loosening with each pound of her feet against the treadmill. It became a song for her, this sound of her running. Ashleigh didn't even remember that once upon a time she had thought women who ran the treadmill like she now did were peculiar. Once upon a time, Ashleigh had thought a lot of things.

The next day Christopher made Ashleigh's protein shake and dropped her off at work promising to pick her up in the evening so that they could go wedding ring shopping. Ashleigh gave him a lingering kiss and hurried down into the subbasement for her workout. This was her gym, hers and Christopher's. It's how she would forever think of this place. She didn't even worry about that creepy guy showing up because she knew that Christopher's team would be watching her and making sure she stayed safe.

She entered the room, turned on the lights and then slipped a cd into the disc player; George Clinton and Parliament Funkadelics. She loved Christopher's music but it was nice to mix some good funk into the workout. She turned to the treadmill and paused. Resting on the handles was an army fatigue hat and folded shirt. On top of the neat bundle was a folded piece of paper. She reached for the paper, looking around curiously. Written across it were two words; LITTLE TROOPER.

Ashleigh grinned. She placed the hat on her head and unfolded the shirt. It had USMC written across the front just like Christopher's shirts, only this one was a whole lot smaller. Ashleigh looked up at the little camera nestled in the ceiling and tilted her head at it in thanks.

Lance and Ashleigh couldn't wait until the end of the day so that they could walk out to Christopher's truck to get a look at his new face. He wasn't in his truck but standing out front talking to TK. Ashleigh immediately recognized the black man decked out in sunglasses even though she had never officially been introduced to him.

While Kendra and Lance gushed over Christopher, Ashleigh gave her attention to the man.

"Hello…?"

"Lieutenant Kennedy, Ma'am." He tilted his head at her and looked like he was ready to salute then he relaxed. "But everybody calls me TK."

"TK." She smiled. "Thanks for helping me when that idiot wouldn't leave me alone."

"Not a problem. Did you like the shirt and hat? The guys…well they wanted to give that to you." He looked suddenly embarrassed.

"I like it a lot." She showed Christopher her gifts when he looked at her curiously. "Can you tell the guys thanks for me?"

"I will. See you tomorrow."

"Uh…?"

TK chuckled as he went into the building. "I know, you won't see me, but I'll see you."

"Ok, that was creepy." She mumbled with a chuckle when he was gone. But it was also sweet. After a few more minutes of gushing over Christopher, Kendra and Lance headed to the parking lot. Christopher looked after them thoughtfully.

"I can't wait until your belly is big like Kendra's."

Ashleigh grimaced before it switched automatically to a smile. "That part is going to be hard but…it'll be worth it."

Christopher stooped down to kiss her. "Yes it will. Ready to go do some engagement ring shopping? There are some nice jewelry stores right on this street."

"I am more than ready!" She decided not to say that she was born ready.

Jewelry stores lined Main St. and it was a beautiful evening. The two walked hand in hand, staring into windows and discussing the finer points of diamond rings.

Ashleigh wasn't picky; she would have chosen the first ring that
made her go 'oooh' except Christopher insisted they continue to look. They finally ended up at Tiffany's. She wasn't sure why he suddenly looked so nervous. He was the one that kept urging her towards this store.

"Welcome back sir."

Ashleigh gave Christopher a quick look and he just smiled. He'd already checked out all of the rings then. Hmmm, interesting. She focused on the cases and went ooooh several times. And then she saw the ring of her dreams. Ashleigh's eyes lit up and she looked at Christopher excitedly. He glanced down at the display that had excited her and gave her an amazed look.

Ashleigh cringed. It was too expensive. She could find a different one to love. But the salesman was already there unlocking the case and slipping out the gorgeous ring.

"This is our platinum, three stone Lucida. Would you like to try it on Ma'am?" Ashleigh could just nod. The salesman handed the ring to Christopher who took her hand and looked deeply into her eyes.

"Will you marry me, Ashleigh?"

She giggled. "I already told you that I'd marry you, silly."

"Yeah but it wasn't official since I didn't have a ring to put on your finger. Now I got the ring."

She smiled. "You have to buy it first. I believe that's how it works, baby."

"I already did. This ring is yours."

Her brown face paled and Christopher slipped the beautiful ring on her finger. Ashleigh looked at it in surprise. She looked from
Christopher to her ring, unable to find her words.

"Thank god you picked the right one. But Lance and Kendra seemed to know that this is the one you'd want."

Ashleigh made a strangled sound and then she threw her arms around his shoulders. He chuckled and lifted her off the floor as she stared over his shoulder at the ring on her finger.

"You had me worried the first time your eyes lit up at a wayyyy cheaper ring." But it didn't compare to the look she had when she had seen this one. To him, that look was priceless.

Everyone in the store was looking at them and smiling. The clerk handed her a blue Tiffany's bag with care instructions and thanked them.

She looked at Christopher in amazement. "I can wear it out?"

"I hope you don't take it off, but yes. It's bought and paid for."

"I won't ever take it off!" She promised.

Christopher's hand rested her on soft hip as they walked out of the store.

She was smiling brightly. "I can't believe Kendra and Lance! They didn't let on once!"

"Ashleigh?"

Christopher looked over at the tall black man that was heading for them. The smiled slipped from his face. DeAngelo. Shit, why did he have to show up to mar this perfect moment? He could have replayed this in his head over and over but not anymore. Now all he'd do is get pissed off.

The man had hurried from across the street. Christopher studied his athletic form and knew that he was the type of man most women went for. He was a tall, good-looking, dark skinned guy with a well-kept build.

"Ashleigh!" He said while coming to a stop right in front of them. "I can't…believe it. You look wonderful!"

Christopher looked down at Ashleigh who had a forced smile on her face. His arm around her waist tightened and it might have been a bit on the possessive side but…hell! How dare this old boyfriend come out of the blue and look at her like that!

DeAngelo was staring at her with a wide happy smile on his face. It was a look as if he didn't know that this was no longer his woman; as if he had every right in the world to look at her like that. Christopher had to clench his teeth because he wanted to punch him right in the center of his face!

"Hi DeAngelo." She said and the slightly older black man finally looked at Christopher. It wasn't impolite but it was curious. "DeAngelo, this is my fiancé Lt. Christopher Jameson-"

"Fiancé??? You're getting married?" His eyes almost bugged out of his head.

Ashleigh narrowed her eyes. No he didn't!!! He did not just go there…

DeAngelo looked down at Ashleigh's hand and the big gleaming rock on it. His face fell and he met Ashleigh's eyes once again.

"Oh." He said softly. "I know that you always wanted to get married."

Christopher shifted positions. This guy was really pissing him
 off. "I'm just lucky that no one snatched her up before me." He
 said stiffly.

DeAngelo looked at him and took in the way his hand rested comfortably around her waist, and not just that, but also the way that she leaned in to him. Ashleigh looked up at Christopher.

"Honey, this is DeAngelo Murray, my ex-boyfriend."

Christopher tilted his head in a brief greeting. "Well if you'll excuse us, DeAngelo, I need to feed both of my babies."

DeAngelo's eyes bugged even further before he masked the look. "You're pregnant. Congratulations I..." He sighed. "Are you happy?"

Christopher glared at him and all he could think was *kill kill kill kill…*

Ashleigh placed her hand over her belly. "I am. I'm finally happy." Ashleigh led Christopher away without another word; without a goodbye. Christopher smiled to himself.

~***~

The family reunion had been pushed back to allow Christopher's bandages time to be removed. But Uncle Ray was anxious to get it underway while all of the school age children were off for summer break, so the weekend after next was designated family reunion time. But before Ashleigh could even think about joining Christopher at his family gathering she knew that it she had to rectify her own wrong in not formally introducing Christopher to her family.

So on Saturday Ashleigh made plans for her own mini-family gathering. Her father wasn't able to fly back up so soon after returning to Florida but invited them down to spend a few days, an invitation that they readily accepted. Ashleigh's Mom, having just made the trip was unable to come back up but promised to return at Christmas, which just left her two sisters and their families. Ashleigh decided on Buca di Beppos for a family style dinner. Christopher didn't understand why she didn't want to have dinner at the house. He was willing to put together a nice barbecue and pull out the lawn furniture and put up a gazebo.

Ashleigh just shook her head explaining that it was too much trouble when they'd be heading down to Cobb Hill a week later. The truth is that she wanted the ability to leave if they got on her nerves. Ashleigh loved her sisters, she just didn't always like them.

Christopher noticed that Ashleigh spent an extra long time selecting her outfit, looking at herself in the mirror, running her hands over her stomach and poking at her butt. She was…uh… callipygian; a fact that he hoped would never change.

He moved behind her and kissed her neck. "You look beautiful."

"You think I look okay?" She had a worried expression on her face.

"I've never seen you look more beautiful." Which wasn't the exact truth. When she was beneath him and her mouth was opened in a silent scream of pleasure, her eyes rolled to the top of her head and a pink flush flowed beneath her brown skin, it was a look that he found most pleasing.

She seemed satisfied with his answer and they headed to the restaurant. Both sisters were so late that Christopher wondered if they would show. The two sat at the bar anxiously and Ashleigh kept checking her cell phone.

"Why don't you call them?"

She shook her head adamantly. "It's CP time. You don't call. They'll get here."

Half an hour late, the first sister showed up. Christopher and Ashleigh left the bar to greet her and the sister was still craning her neck, searching the room even though Ashleigh was standing right in front of her.

"That heffa left..." She said. Christopher stiffened a bit at the use of the word 'heffa' but couldn't help the smile when she finally looked at Ashleigh in confusion and then shocked recognition. Her expression was priceless, she almost recoiled. The woman squealed and grabbed Ashleigh in a hug.

"Oh my god! Oh my god..." She pulled back and examined Ashleigh at arm's length. "You are so thin..."

Ashleigh giggled happily.

Ashleigh quickly grabbed Christopher's arm. "

"This is my sister Darlene and her husband Luther and this is my fiancé Christopher."

Darlene stared in shock. But…Mom said…uh, hello." She offered her hand and Christopher shook it. Darlene was a little thing and maybe a little more made up then to his liking. But he couldn't deny that she was beautiful, yet a little uncouth. He shook her husband's hand. He was dark skinned, handsome, very fit but still dwarfed by Christopher's height and weight.

"Well maybe we should head back to the bar and wait for Venita."

Darlene made a face. "Girl, please, that heffa is going to make up some excuse not to come." Ashleigh looked alarmed.

"She wouldn't do that-"

"Honey, Venita is trifling. I invited her to a party a few weeks ago and the bitch didn't even show up and it was RSVP…" Her words trailed at the look that crossed Ashleigh's face. "Oh…I would have invited you but I know how you don't like that sort of thing…"

Venita showed up then, thankfully, saving Ashleigh from having to decide how to address her sister's snub. Venita came in looking like a model. She was the tallest sister at approx 5'10" without heels. With them she was impressive. Christopher noted that the sisters were all very pretty but they had a penchant for lots of makeup and glam. Ashleigh was now a woman that went for comfort over glam though she still dressed up for work. But at home she had taken to shorts and a t-shirt.

Venita's husband was white and Christopher was just beginning to understand that his race had never been an issue. He was beginning to form an idea but pushed it back for now. The couple was accompanied by two kids; a boy and a girl.

Venita eyed him before acknowledging any of her sisters.

"Sorry I'm late. Is this…your fiancée?"

Ashleigh made the introductions again and Christopher greeted everyone. "I think we better get our seats. They're holding our reservations." He resisted the urge to look at his watch. He was military and it was unheard of to be forty-five minutes late for anything and then just give an off-handed apology. It was more than unheard of, it was plain rude.

Venita never mentioned how good Ashleigh looked but Christopher caught her eyeing her younger sister up and down when Ashleigh wasn't watching. Darlene grabbed Ashleigh's hand and blinked at her ring.

"Jesus…that's a rock!"

Ashleigh blushed and stared down at it. "Yes, I've named him Lamar and I kiss him every morning and say, hello there, lovely."

The kids laughed and Christopher smiled at them wondering if he and Ashleigh's kids would look something like them. Venita's husband Keith was just as friendly as Darlene's husband Luther but there was definite tension between the two. After being seated at a large table the conversation centered on Christopher.

"Well how and the hell do you keep finding these handsome men?" Venita asked.

"Lucky I guess." Ashleigh said while looking at Christopher.

"Well I need to go where you go." Venita said, not realizing or caring that she'd just insulted her husband who shot her a look. Yeah, things were definitely not great with them.

"You look so good." Darlene said for about the millionth time.

"Remember when you were little and how you used to hide food?" Venita chuckled. "We would find cookies and donuts and candy sometimes years old; shoved behind the VCR or behind the hutch-"

"Remember the time she hid a candy bar in the drop ceiling and it attracted mice? The exterminator showed it to Mom where the mice had gotten at it." Darlene said while laughing. "Mom tanned your behind."

Ashleigh smiled good-naturedly though she didn't remember anything particularly funny about it.

"And she was so cute and fat." Venita said. "But Mom had to buy her clothes in the old lady section."

Darlene laughed. "Remember those polyester pants that used to squeak when she walked? She was twelve wearing a seersucker suit!" Venita and Darlene cracked up and Ashleigh's stomach grumbled. She sipped some water and nibbled on a breadstick.

"I bet she was adorable." Christopher said while looking at her with nothing but love. She met his eyes and smiled.

"Adam! Put down that roll!" Venita shouted. The little boy replaced the roll shamefaced. "That is your third roll. Don't think I haven't been watching you. Why do you have to be the greediest person at the table, huh?"

"Honey," Keith interjected.

"Look, he knows he's on a diet." She rolled her eyes at her husband. Ashleigh looked at the chubby little boy. Oh my god, he was just seven or eight years old!

Venita had already turned her attention back to Christopher. "So you have to keep yourself in shape when you're in The Marines, huh?"

Ashleigh excused herself to go to the restroom. She wanted a breather, but soon her sisters accosted her at the sink.

"Okay, where the hell did you find the cute Marine?" Venita asked.

"Huh? I...what? Venita, you are married!"

Venita rolled her eyes. "I'm not staying with that fool forever." Ashleigh's eyes grew big. Darlene didn't even seem surprised by their older sister's revelation.

"Mama told us your dude had something wrong with his face." Darlene said. "There is nothing wrong with that man's face. He's fucking gorgeous."

"Well you know Mama is a liar and a crazy bitch." Venita said bitterly.

"Thank god she moved to Tennessee, girl she was getting on my last nerves."

"You telling me," Venita checked her make-up in the mirror.

Ashleigh stared at her sisters in disbelief. She rarely hung with them since leaving home, but she didn't remember their out and out disrespect of their mother.

"Wow, all this time I thought you two and Mom were tight." Where did the hostility come from? They were the chosen two.

Venita made a face. "Girl, I don't talk to her unless I have to."

"Please," Darlene rolled her eyes. "When Mom came up to take care of you she told me I needed braces." Darlene flashed her perfect teeth. "I sat my dumbass in the mirror for half an hour looking at my teeth before Luther told me that there wasn't anything wrong with them."

Ashleigh frowned. "We should go back out. The food should be here." Ashleigh didn't care if the food was there or not, she just didn't want to be alone with them any longer than she had to be.

The meal was delicious and the conversation easy, mostly because her sister's kept asking about Christopher who became the center of attention. At one point Venita asked if he had any single brothers and Keith turned red. Christopher wisely ignored the question—both times she asked it.

They were both ready to leave when Venita took her son Adam's plate away from him because she said that he had already eaten more than his share.

Ashleigh leaned in towards Christopher. "Please get me the fuck out of here."

"Gladly."

Christopher stood and reached in his back pocket for his wallet while everyone stopped eating and talking to look at him. "Please excuse us but Ashleigh's not feeling well. The food just isn't sitting well with her." He tossed two hundred dollars on the table. "Please have desert on us." Ashleigh stood up and waved because she didn't trust herself to open her mouth. Everyone rushed to tell her goodbye and to make false promises to call and to get together soon.

"Pleasure meeting you." Christopher lied, and then they left. He put his arm around her when they were outside and felt her relax.

"I understand. I understand everything completely. Do we have to invite them to our wedding?" He asked, half joking.

She shook her head. "Hell no. I don't owe them anything. She thought about how her sister, Darlene hadn't even thought to invite her to her party. "Besides, they are probably sitting in there already talking about me like a dog." And they were.

They were halfway home when Ashleigh let out a tense breath. "Christopher."

"What, Sweetheart?"

"I think I need some ice cream."

"Okay."

"I just really feel…like if I don't get some ice cream then…"

"It's fine." He turned the car. "Graeters?"

"Yes." Ashleigh could feel her heart pounding in her chest.

"I want you to test your blood sugar. Did you bring your kit?"

"Yes." By the time they pulled in front of Graeters ice cream shop she had the results of her test and it showed that her blood sugar level was good.

He opened the door for her and held her hand. "You okay?"

She nodded. "Yeah but I just need some ice cream."

"Okay, its fine." At the counter she ordered a triple scoop of raspberry chocolate chip but Christopher changed it to a single scoop. "We'll come back and get more if you want it."

She nodded her consent. They sat at one of the tables and she began eating her ice cream quickly.

"Slow down, baby. It's not going anywhere." She looked at her cone in surprise and then she smiled and ate it slowly. They ate their ice cream in silence and when she was done he asked her if she wanted another. She nodded and said she wanted a scoop of chocolate. He bought it for her and after she ate half of it she gave him the rest.

"I'm good."

"You sure?"

"Yeah, thank you."

"Was that the baby or seeing your sister?"

"I'm not sure. I think a little of both."

"I'm pretty sure that I have a good picture of how it was like for you as a kid."

She looked thoughtful. "The way Venita treated Adam is the way my Mom treated me. I just took it all and buried it." She knew that Adam would more than likely grow up with low self-esteem, or become shallow or both.

CHAPTER 11

Where do you go if you are on a mountain for three days with a bunch of people that you don't know and you happen to be the only black person…well except for the colored people that live down at the bottom of the hill? There is no place to run and hide. You have to pull up your big girl pants and face it head on. And that is what Ashleigh knew she had to do. But after confronting her family she was more nervous than ever about another family confrontation. She couldn't stop thinking about how hard things had been with Alma. In the end it had all turned out okay but she couldn't stop imagining twenty Almas and having to try to win them all over.

Christopher loaded a cooler into the truck and turned to Ashleigh. She was wringing her hands and watching him doubtfully. He pulled her into his arms and kissed her nose. "Sweetheart, you're going to have fun. They'll be all kinds of stuff to do and I'll make sure that you won't be left alone.

"I know. I just want everyone to like me."

He smiled. "I'll tell you a secret."

"A secret? Oooo skeletons in the closet?"

"Not exactly. The secret is that your reputation precedes you. Everyone already knows all about you, Ashleigh. And everyone in my family has nothing but good things to say about you. Not sure what you did to win Alma over but my Mom told me that she's your biggest cheerleader. So you have absolutely nothing to worry about."

She relaxed. "Okay."

"Are you ready? One last bathroom break?"

"No, I'm all set."

Christopher picked up his guitar and placed it in the backseat, and then he helped Ashleigh in. The ride down to Corbin Kentucky was long but Christopher tried to make it interesting by telling her stories about the mountains. He made it seem like a wonderful place to grow up. When he wasn't telling her stories he was singing and about half way down she fell asleep. It seemed that she hadn't been asleep but a few minutes before Christopher was pulling up into a field of parked cars. She yawned and looked around.

"Aww. I missed the drive up through the mountains."

"Don't worry. We'll make enough beer runs so that you'll know it backwards and forward. It's dry."

She gave him a surprised look. "You mean there are still places that are dry?"

He nodded. "Yeah no liquor sold here. You have to go down to Corbin."

Several kids were running around and playing but they only looked at Christopher curiously not recognizing him. He didn't worry about it; there would be time for reintroductions later. They headed for Uncle Ray's house and as they got close Ashleigh fell in love with the large A-frame house. She was even more impressed when Christopher told her that Uncle Ray had built it himself many years ago and as he and Aunt Lonnie had more and more children he had just added on. Now it was a big gorgeous house.

They headed up the porch steps.

"Hi everyone." He greeted the people they passed. Everyone responded in a friendly way but once they were in the house Ashleigh heard someone ask who that was. She glanced at Christopher who seemed to enjoy being the mystery man.

As they walked through the crowded house Christopher greeted everyone in a friendly manner and they all responded in a friendly manner. It was obvious that no one knew exactly who he was but no one wanted to be the one to ask. Ashleigh thought Christopher was so bad not to tell these poor people who he was but she kept her smile to herself.

They finally reached the kitchen where a few people were preparing enough food to feed an army. Christopher walked up to an older man that was nearly as tall as him.

"Hi Uncle Ray." He smiled.

Uncle Ray looked up and beamed. "Christopher!"

Christopher raised his brow in surprise. "How did you know it was me?"

"Son...you're 6'5". There's not too many of us quite that tall." He gave Christopher a hug and then the other people in the room exclaimed as they realized that Christopher was the mystery man. Ashleigh got slightly lost in the crowd as thirty people crowded the kitchen to get a look at Christopher, ask him about the surgery, touch him, and hug him. It was like being around a movie star!

Christopher gently grasped her hand and pulled her forward. "Hey everyone, I want to introduce you to my fiancée Ashleigh. We're also…um, about to be parents."

That announcement caused some good-natured comments and everyone hugged her and welcomed her to the family. She relaxed. Not all family reunions were filled with dysfunctional people.

Ashleigh met Christopher's other two siblings who lived out of state; a brother Gregory and his wife and children and another sister. She was nothing like Alma and she immediately hugged Ashleigh and exclaimed that Mom and Dad loved her. Her name was Beverly, she was single, spirited and had more freckles on her face than anybody she'd ever seen.

Mr. and Mrs. Jameson arrived later that evening. Butch had driven and he gave her a hug that made her feel more welcomed than anything else. Mr. Jameson was tired from the trip so they got him fed and he lay down to rest in one of the bedrooms designated for him and Mrs. Jameson.

They had a fish fry with corn on the cob from a neighboring farm. There was corn pudding and corn fritters. Christopher explained that corn and potatoes would play a huge part in their meals since Uncle Ray could get them free. But in addition there would be all kinds of farm fresh vegetables. Everything was delicious and Christopher didn't bat an eye when she piled her plate high.

After dinner, Ashleigh could tell that Christopher was anxious to play football with some of the older boys and young men so she told him she was going to join some of the ladies on the porch. He walked with her and sat with her a while until Beverly shooed him away, promising to take care of her. Ashleigh nodded her approval and then he hurried away like a big kid.

"I can't believe how changed he is." Beverly commented.

"He's transformed," Mrs. Jameson said, "and I'm not referring
 to the surgery." She gave Ashleigh's hand an affectionate pat.

She enjoyed talking to the ladies. Their slow country accents made her feel right at home. As it grew dark they began to tell ghost stories. Mr. Jameson found his way to the porch and seemed very alert. He gave her a hug and actually remembered to call her Ashleigh.

"You be sure to stay with someone and don't go off in the woods by yourself. There are wildcats around here."

"Okay." What the hell was a wildcat? Was it like a cougar? She didn't ask, she would just stay out of the woods.

She decided to go inside and lay down. The long drive, her pregnancy, meeting new people and good food all worked to exhaust her. Uncle Ray had given them the den and someone had blown up a huge air mattress for their use. She supposed that they had to have a huge one due to Christopher's size. She placed the sheets on it and then kicked off her shoes and lay down fully dressed, just planning to doze for a bit.

She felt the mattress dip down and her eyes popped open. Christopher sat propped up on his side, watching her with a smile. "Sorry I woke you. I checked on you a few times. You were sound asleep."

"What time is it?"

"Two am."

"Wow, sorry I left you for so long. I was just exhausted."

"It's okay. But if you want to shower now is a great time."

"Great idea and I need to brush my teeth." Christopher quickly gathered their towels, toiletries and things to sleep in then led them to one of the bathrooms. He turned on the shower and got the temperature correct as she undressed. He slipped off his clothes with a sigh.

"What?" She asked as she stepped into the shower.

"I'm horny."

"Oh." Not that she was surprised but just that there was no way she was going to have sex with a house full of in-laws that she'd just met only feet away. That was just not going to happen. He stepped into the shower.

"How quietly can we have sex?" He was actually asking her how quietly SHE could be. He didn't have to yell in scream the way she did.

She shook her head with a wry smile. "You are just too good for me to be quiet. I'll either forget or won't care. Then I won't be able to face anyone in the morning." He grabbed their soap and sponge and quickly created a sudsy lather. He gently washed her front, taking special care with her nipples that had grown bigger since pregnancy. He swallowed past the lump in his throat.

Ashleigh glanced down to where he was rapidly becoming erect.

"You are such a glutton for punishment. Now what are you going to do with that thing?"

"Well…I was planning to place it in one of your orifices but…I guess that's a no go."

"I'm afraid not." He continued to wash her body, watching the suds flow down her curvy brown legs.

"I hadn't really considered this part of the deal. I guess I just thought we'd do it…" He had knelt down on his knees and was now concentrating on her V and the way the dark peach fuzz was just now growing out. He urged her to spread her legs so that he could wash her there. He 'accidentally' allowed his finger to graze her clit and her response was a quick jolt.

"Christopher!" She hissed and grabbed the sponge. He came to his feet with a mischievous grin. "I'm going to wash you and I'm going to do it right!"

She rinsed the sponge and got it soapy again and then concentrated on washing his muscled body. He playfully flexed them for her and she hid her smile, trying to be serious. Since he'd returned, there hadn't been one day in which they had not made love, and most times it was more than once.

His erection had deflated some. She gave him a warning look and he smiled innocently while she lifted him carefully in her hand and gently applied the sponge.

"Oh my god." He moaned. "If you just do that a couple more times…"

"Christopher you are not getting off…unless I get off too."

He smirked. "I was hoping you'd say that. I have an idea." They finished washing quickly, brushed their teeth and got dressed. After depositing their items back to their designated room, Christopher led her out the back door where they wouldn't disturb the girls that had set up sleeping bags in the living room.

The yard was dotted with many tents. Several families had opted to set up tents or had driven RVs. A few had stayed as guests in neighboring homes. No one had been forced to get a hotel and Ray took a lot of pride that he'd been able to accommodate everyone. Ashleigh followed Christopher. He was wearing athletic shorts and the bulge between his legs had her mouth watering.

They headed toward the parked cars and she wondered if they were going to do it in the truck. Not the most comfortable place to do it; they'd already done that back before he'd gone. Christopher led her past the cars and into the woods.

"Uh…" She said anxiously. "You want to have sex in the woods? With the bugs and wildcats?"

He chuckled. "I know the woods and wildcats aren't going to bother us if we don't bother them. As far as bugs…your pretty little body will never touch the ground. I promise."

"Okay…" She said.

He was breathing hard when he finally turned to her, having found a location deep enough into the woods but not too deep. He pulled Ashleigh into his arms and kissed her insistently, as if he'd gone days instead of hours without her. He quickly pushed his hands down into her shorts. She had gone panty-less and his fingers found her wet core. He wiggled them back and forth against her and she bucked.

"Christopher!" She tilted her pelvis against his hand and then sought his erect penis through his pants. How could he get so hard? Christopher groaned and quickly pushed her shorts down. She kicked one leg out; too afraid of taking them off completely less a bug find its way into them. Christopher scooped her up and Ashleigh's legs went around his waist, shorts dangling off one ankle.

He planted his hands against her ample bottom and Ashleigh knew just what to do. She gripped him by his swollen base and guided him into her slick opening.

"Oh god!" He cried as he thrust upwards and buried himself deep into her. She was so wet. Ha! So she had wanted it just as badly as he had. He pumped rapidly in and out of her listening for the familiar mewling sound that she made that told him he was hitting it just right.

Ashleigh clung to Christopher, her arms going around his neck. It felt so good that her groans sounded like she was in pain. She buried her head into his neck and sucked on it, desperate not to scream and yell. His long dick hit her spot and dragged repeatedly over it as he pumped in and out of her. She clenched him tight when she felt that he was too controlled. His legs buckled and he almost went down to his knees.

"Ash...you're going to make me cum!" He began thrusting harder and faster. It was too good, she lost the last of her control and cried out loudly, clutching and digging her fingers into his back. Christopher grunted and then showered her insides with cum. His fingers buried into the flesh of her buttocks and held her flush against him as the last spurt of semen dribbled from the head of the penis that was deeply buried against her cervix.

He waited until his dick was soft enough to slip out of her on its own before lowering her down to her feet. Ashleigh grimaced as she stepped back into her shorts and dragged them up over her dripping wet inner thighs.

"Ugh, Christopher that was a lot."

"Sorry, I should have thought to bring something."

She smirked. "Well, just remember tomorrow night."

His brow quirked up happily.

~***~

The next morning Ashleigh was up well before Christopher, her grumbling belly sending her into the kitchen for something to snack on before breakfast.

Several ladies were already awake, including Mrs. Jameson. They were slicing potatoes and onions for home fries. Uncle Ray gave her a quick good morning before heading out to supervise the whole pig that was going into the ground to roast. Yum, a pig roast.

"What can I help with?"

"Good morning dear." Mrs. Jameson gave her a broad smile. "Here have a danish." She said while passing her a fresh baked danish still warm from the oven. She accepted it gratefully. Aww, why couldn't Mrs. Jameson be her Mom? Well...then Christopher would have been her brother. She decided that having her as a mother-in-law was the next best thing.

"Thank you Mrs. Jameson."

"Honey, you are going to have to call me Edith if you don't want to call me Mom."

She blushed and bit into her delicious pastry. "This is good Mom. Did you bake it?"

"No Barbara Annette did." Barbara Annette inclined her head in Ashleigh's direction. "Barbara Annette has her own bakery shop and is a real pastry chef."

Another woman scowled playfully. "I still make the best berry cobbler."

Barbara Annette bristled. "That is not an authentic cobbler." The women bickered back and forth while Ashleigh watched and ate her pastry. She drank a glass of milk and then helped to crack about a hundred eggs.

Christopher woke a while later, his hair an unruly mess of curls. His eyes searched the room until they rested on Ashleigh and then he visibly relaxed. He came over and kissed her neck before giving his Mom a kiss on the cheek. Edith shooed him away and told him to return in an hour.

Uncle Ray rang the breakfast bell and everyone came running to the outdoor picnic area. There was biscuits, toast, fresh butter, homemade jam, thick cuts of bacon, homemade sausage and goetta, eggs and home fried potatoes.

She whispered to Christopher that you couldn't pay for a breakfast more perfect. Mr. Jameson concentrated on buttering a biscuit with shaky hands.

"Damned wildcats kept me up half the night with all that loud screaming. They sound like women, I tell you!"

Ashleigh's eyes got big and she felt her cheeks redden. She glanced at Christopher who pretended that he hadn't heard him.

"Wildcats are around humans too much. Almost sound like they're screaming oh my god..." Ashleigh damn near choked on her eggs. She noted that the ladies were grinning and Edith nudged her husband.

"You hush now Pawpaw, you were young once, too." Ashleigh was alarmed when she saw Mr. Jameson chuckling. This time when she looked at Christopher his face was flaming, but he kept eating his eggs without once looking up. When she looked around the table there were several couples with embarrassed, red faces.

Mr. Jameson was a hoot. She decided that she more than liked him.

"When are we going to the furnace?" He asked once breakfast was finished.

Ahh the furnace. She had forgotten to ask about that.

"It's too hot to go to the furnace until later in the evening." Butch replied to his father.

Ashleigh turned to Christopher. "What is the furnace?" And are there goats in it? And are they cooked goats. And more importantly...is there a reason to want to get into one?

Christopher gave her hand a brief squeeze. "It's...something you should just see."

"O...kay." Now she was excited to see this damned furnace.

They made a beer run a while later and Ashleigh finally had a chance to see the beauty of Cobb Hill. She decided that it was not technically a mountain but it was steep but beautiful. Butch had come along to help load the liquor and it was he that pointed out the blind bend in the road where Walt had met his death.

Christopher drove them around to where their old house was located. Someone else lived there now and it seemed such a small place to try to raise five kids. Next they pointed out an old shack where their grandmother lived up until the day she died. It looked like a slave cabin and she wasn't surprised to find that it had been handmade.

Once they got back the men unloaded the truck and Ashleigh saw Uncle Ray sitting on the porch with some of the kids so she made her way over there. She saw Alma's daughter Rachel who climbed into her lap happily.

"I hope you're having a good time. I know you don't know the people here but we're enjoying your company."

"I am having a good time." She said honestly. "You have a beautiful home and a friendly family." She talked with him for a while and then saw Christopher searching for her so she went to meet him.

"Hey, I was going to ask you if you wanted to walk down to the spring." He said. "It's a pretty good hike but the payoff is some of the sweetest, coldest water you've ever had.

"Sure," She said while nibbling on a wedge of apple.

He frowned. "Were you just talking to Uncle Ray?"

"Yeah."

"Did he…cut that apple with his pocket knife?"

Ashleigh stopped chewing. "Yeah…why?"

He grabbed the apple piece from her and threw it to the ground. "Baby, spit that apple out!"

She did quickly and even wiped her tongue. "What?!"

He was grimacing. "Baby, don't EVER eat anything that Uncle Ray has cut with that knife. That's the same damned knife that he uses for everything, from cleaning his nails to scraping dog shit off the bottom of his boots."

Ashleigh began to gag. "Oh, I'm going to be sick…"

~***~

The trip to the furnace happened after Ashleigh lay down to get rid of her nausea. They loaded up in Butch's van and included all of the Jameson siblings and their kids.

Christopher wouldn't tell her exactly what the furnace was until they got there. "Is it a real furnace?"

"It's a real furnace." He replied.

"And there are goats in it?"

"Sometimes." Christopher answered vaguely.

After parking, Christopher took his father's arm and led him up to a strange large building with a crumbling, whitewashed stone front. There was a signpost and Ashleigh took a moment to read it. The Fitchburg Furnace. Well hells bells, it was a real furnace.

Built in 1868 it was the only double steam-stack coal burning furnace in the entire world. Christopher returned to her and they read the signposts together.

"This is where they produced iron ore? Did your Dad work here?"

Christopher put an arm around her and led her into the strangely shaped building. The walkway crumbled in places and he was afraid that she might lose her footing.

"No," He chuckled. Fitchburg was only operational for 4 years." He explained. They couldn't get the iron ore back down for distribution. And it was a pain bringing up the coal. As magnificent as this place is, it only operated four years."

"Damn." She looked around. "It's impressive. Why does your Dad like it so much?"

He thought about it for a while. "I guess because here in Estill County we didn't have that much. This place is a part of the National Historical Registry and it's the only one of its kind in the world. I guess it's just something for us to be proud of."

Mr. Jameson was sitting on a big boulder while the young kids checked out all of the nooks and crannies for a stray piece of coal or iron. Ashleigh sat down next to him.

"Where are the goats?" He asked.

She looked around. It looked to her as if they had been refurbishing the place. They may have run the goats and stray animals away.

"It must be too hot." She decided to answer.

He nodded. "Yeah." He sighed in contentment. "This is home. Covington was never home. I remember my pappi bringing us here to picnic. Back then it was a mess of broken stones and stray bits of coal. We used to hunt for pieces and come up with some ore. Once we even found some machinery but it was too rusted and big to do anything with. The goats had set up inside away from the heat. They tolerated us in their home and we were respectful that we were just visitors. I never seen anything like it. Daddy goats, mommy goats, baby goats just relaxing in the same area that humans came traipsing through."

Ashleigh listened to him intently. It was the longest that she'd ever heard him talk. This trip was really doing him good. "I always thought...I kinda thought I'd live here and die here."

"Do you want to move back?"

"It'd be hard. Make more work for Edith." He said softly. "I didn't think it would be like this." He watched the kids running about with a forlorn look on his face. "I thought

I'd be bringing my grandkids here…" Ashleigh gave him a serious look.

"You just did."

He turned to her and smiled. "I guess I did."

When they returned they had dinner of roast pig and then Christopher pulled out his guitar along with his brother Butch and several other people and they sat around an open fire and had a mini jam session. They were amazingly talented!

"Play that song, Christopher." Mr. Jameson said in a tired voice. He had forced himself to stay up just to listen to the jam session.

Christopher sat on the stairs at his father's feet. Most seemed to know which song Christopher was going to sing or else they were curious. Even the kids grew quiet.

As he began to sing the familiar song, Mr. Jameson looked out into the night with a peaceful expression on his face.

"Blackbird singing in the dead of night. Take these broken wings and learn to fly. All your life, you were only waiting for this moment to arise…"

~EPILOGUE~

"Black bird singing in the dead of night. Take these sunken eyes and learn to see. All your life, you were only waiting for this moment to be free-"

"Daddy daddy daddy!" Yelled the little girl as she dashed on tiny legs through the cemetery. Christopher Jameson looked up from where he was playing his guitar. A smile fell across his face, replacing the look of sadness that had been there a moment before. He carefully moved the guitar behind his back just in time to catch his little girl as she flung herself into his arms.

"Hey Princess. Where's Mommy?"

The three year old pointed behind her. "Mommy's there!" She said in the highest pitched voice imaginable. Christopher grinned wider. One day his little girl might be an opera singer and break wine glasses with that voice.

Ashleigh waddled toward them. Her stomach was swollen and so were her ankles. She was ready to pop. The baby was due in less than two weeks but if she managed two more days it would be a miracle. Still, she had the biggest grin on her face as she ambled towards them.

Christopher stood and sat the little girl on her feet. "Go say hi to everybody and then we gotta go," he said gently.

"Okay Daddy. Hi Papaw." She said to Mr. Butch Jameson's gravestone. She blew it a wet kiss and went scampering from gravestone to gravestone. "Hi Uncle Ray. Hi Aunt Lonnie. Hi Uncle Walt."

He met Ashleigh half way and pulled her into his arms, kissing the tip of her nose. "Why did you walk all the way up here? You should have called me-" She held up her hand containing his cell phone.

"Oh." He said sheepishly.

"Besides, I took your Mom's car." She and Butch Sr. had moved back on Cobb Hill two years ago. He'd spent the last year of his life here and for that Christopher was thankful. "If you want to beat the traffic we should leave now...unless you want to skip the birthday party and stay another night." Ashleigh said hopefully. She enjoyed their monthly weekend stay on Cobb Hill.

Christopher wouldn't mind staying one more night, either. A birthday party with a bunch of three, four and a five year old would surely be tiresome. But he knew his baby girl was looking forward to it. "No, Lance and Kendra will be disappointed if we don't come." He yelled for his daughter. "Brianna, baby, it's time to go." She came running towards them holding a bundle of flowers. Ashleigh's eyes got big.

"I picked these for Pawpaw!"

Christopher swooped her up into his huge arms as if she was just a little toy. "We can't pick flowers from other people's graves, honey. Show me where you got 'em and we'll put 'em back."

After returning the flowers to their rightful place, the family drove back to the large house that Edith had built on one of the acres that Ray had left for them in his will.

Poor Ray hadn't lived a year after his Lonnie had passed and Butch Sr. had wanted to end his days the way Ray had, surrounded by family up on the mountain. He'd gotten his wish.

They said their goodbyes and Edith promised to come up as soon as the baby was born to help with Brianna. Ashleigh and Brianna were both sound asleep no sooner had they had gotten on the highway. Christopher smiled proudly as he looked in the backseat at his little girl. She had a peaches and cream complexion with skin that turned 'toasty' during the summer months. The thin scar that ran beneath her nose to her perfectly formed upper lip was barely noticeable. She'd been born with a unilateral cleft palate which had been corrected with one surgery 90 days after her birth. Still, when he had looked down at the tiny pink thing in his arms he had thought her to be the most beautiful thing on the face of the earth.

She had grey eyes set in a round face with a pointy chin that his mother had proclaimed 'The Jameson' chin. Her auburn hair was long and wavy and not much different than his. She did, however, have her mother's beauty and small stature.

They drove to their large house at the end of a cul de sac. There were four bedrooms besides the master suite and Christopher meant to fill each of them with children. If they thought they were going to have time to relax before the party then no such luck. Lance saw them pull up from his window and was calling five minutes after they'd unloaded the car.

"Help! The clown cancelled and they want to send a cowboy. I think it's too violent with the guns, what do you think?!"

Christopher chuckled. "Uh, I guess you're asking the wrong person. I handle a gun daily."

"Oh, true. Can you put Ashleigh on the phone?"

"Sure." He called Ashleigh who had rushed to the bathroom.
"Ash, phone, Lance." Those were the only words needed to be spoken.

While the two strategized he got Brianna changed and fed and then he went out back. He checked over the privacy fence. Rick was blowing up balloons. He and Lance had bought the house next to theirs right before adopting their son Chad who was turning five today.

Rick dropped the balloon he was holding and smiled happily. He and Christopher were the best of friends now. "I swear, I never want to see another balloon as long as I live."

Christopher opened the gate and went next door. The backyard was a five year olds fantasy. There were balloons, a play tent with little plastic balls, a piñata and…

Christopher squinted his eyes. "Is that an obstacle course?"

Rick grinned and smiled sheepishly. "Yeah just in case any of the kids are interested in football training."

Christopher nodded and rocked on his heels. "Yeah, but they're all just four and five, right?"

"You can't start too soon."

"True. So I guess we better start with the balloons." After about the fifth balloon Christopher frowned. "You know they make machines for this."

"I'll keep that in mind next year." Rick was the assistant coach at a local college. He was gay and he loved football. He also loved Lance and this was the only way to keep everything that he valued.

Kendra's husband, Jackson arrived outback just as the last balloon was finished and the two men guessed that it had been planned. No matter. Payback was a bitch and he had two little girls; two and four and Kendra had a penchant for princess parties with tiaras and makeup and the whole nine yards. Hell if they would be makeup dummies again. He was on his own.

Lance arrived outside carrying an armful of streamers. "Okay, anyone who is over six feet tall and not pregnant will need to hang the streamers."

Rick scowled as Lance and the ladies smiled. "Why is it always the guys?"

"Well," Lance conceded, "You can watch the three, four and five year olds if you prefer."

Christopher and Jackson quickly accepted the streamers.

~***~

That night Christopher placed his palm on his wife's belly. "Do you ever regret...me going back to Special Ops?"

"No." She turned on her side to face him. "Not one bit. You love watching me and Brianna." Their child went to the daycare in the Federal building and now he had not only Ashleigh to watch on the cameras but also Brianna, Lance, Kendra, Chad, Lacey and Amber. Soon there would be little Chris Jr. "But I know you need more than that."

He had missed the missions. He had gone two years with his team returning each time all hyped up, and enticing him with tales of rescues and captures. Bruce was now a civilian consultant for the Department of Homeland Security and during one of his dinner visits the two had spent the evening longing for the 'good old days'. That night Ashleigh had told him to place himself back on the roster.

He resisted for a while but it was fruitless. The first mission that he'd taken after his two year hiatus had resulted in the conception of Chris Jr. Ashleigh wondered if they would conceive each time he announced that he was going away. Of course his return was filled with double the joy.

They both knew that another mission was due and only hoped that it would be after the baby was born. But even if it wasn't she had a network of friends and family to help her through.

"No regrets?" He asked.

"I can't imagine my life any differently."

"Me either." His eyes began to drift shut and he yawned. "No," he muttered. "I remember a different life, a different face, and never dreaming that I'd have a day like today." He smiled as he felt Ashleigh's fingers gently tracing the familiar path down his nose and over his lips...

THE END

Preview:
Miscegenist Sabishii

TONY

I guess you could say my mom is prejudiced, although she just sees it as preserving her culture. But I'm Japanese American. That is *both* Japanese *and* American.

Bringing home non-Asian friends would cause her to refer to them as Big-American-Oxen. So during High School I didn't even think about having a girlfriend. The reason is like that song says; "*I like big butts and I cannot lie.*" Translation; I like black females. But me bringing home a black girlfriend was just never going to happen.

I grew up in a predominately black neighborhood and went to an all black school and as a result I was attracted to the girls that I saw everyday; black girls. My preference was dark skinned, big bootie girls, the more bodacious the better. Does that sound prejudiced? As if it is a fetish? It just means that you don't yet understand that just because I am Asian on the outside doesn't mean that culturally I am not every bit African American.

Oh, and by the way, if we are speaking of stereotypes let me clarify; I am Japanese *not* Korean. Not all Asians that live or work in all black neighborhoods are Korean. And NO, my parents do not own a hair care store or run a Chinese restaurant! When I speak about my own miscegenistic desires it is not in an attempt to be racist. I like dark skin. I like big butts. Unfortunately, growing up in an urban black neighborhood and going to an all back school meant people saw me as the stereotypical Asian with an identity crisis. But, what do you do, when you feel black and look Asian?

Growing up I talked like my friends, listened to hip hop and rap, and liked the same sistas that my boys in high school did. But I never got any play. The sistas were not trying to bring a little Asian boy home to meet moms and pops. Even when I wrestled and bulked up, the girls would give me the up and down, but every time I'd try to rap to them it would always end up the same way; I'd hit a brick wall and fall flat on my face. And for the record, you have no concept of being dissed until you are dissed by a sixteen year old black girl!

I did date some in high school. I dated this little blonde white girl for a while, but she dumped me for a black kid that still sucked his thumb in the 10th grade.

In college I finally got mine. Jackie Chan and Jet Li movies were real popular and so was I. I made up for lost time in college, but two years later...guess what? It got old for me. Yes, sex with random beautiful girls gets old when you want it to go somewhere but you discover that they don't. I am now the fetish and the experiment and the secret.

I discovered that I desired romance much more then sex with big bootie black girls. So while I was hoping for a long term relationship, my girlfriends were still not trying to take a rap music-listening-to Asian home to meet the parents. For them it was just the curiosity of sleeping with someone outside of their race. I did not see black women as being outside of my race. In my mind I'm every bit as black as my friends.

Now I'm a thirty-three year old mortgage broker that lives alone-- except for my dog, Wu-Tang.

I work in a semi-conservative office, so when *SHE* walked in through the door she had every bit of my attention. Unfortunately trying to step to her wouldn't be easy. But on the plus side none of the other males that work with me would be stepping to her, either.

The obstacle for me being that she would be working under me. But for them; well, they are all blue-eyed, Armani suit wearing types and she walked in looking like Queen Latifah.

Discreetly I checked her out despite the fact that she was twice my size. But from that weaved pony tail that sat at the top of her head to the silver painted nail polish that her open-toed shoes revealed I was hooked.

Julia from personnel introduced us. "Toi," don't laugh, that is my name, "I want to introduce you to the new assistant broker. Toi Yakamoto, this is Nikita Mason."

I shook her hand. Her nails were manicured and the same shade of silver as her toes. She was wearing a grey skirt that hugged her fuller figure cut right above the knee, a pearl pink blouse that accentuated her ample cleavage, and a grey matching suit jacket. I appraised everything from corporate sexy clothing to the silver polish that spoke of a need to be daring. Also, her make-up was flawless. Yes, I appreciate a woman that pampers herself and I could tell that Miss Mason did. And not just because she had shown up on her first day at the office looking on point.

"Miss Mason." I asked innocently. "Is it Miss?"

"Yes. Nikki is fine."

I cut my eyes at Julia before returning my attention to Nikki. "Not many people call me Toi or Mr. Yakamoto. Just call me Tony."

Back in my younger days everyone called me T-Baby. Back then everybody had a nickname. Julian was Jay-Dog. Dean was Big Daddy-D. There was Budda, and well...we were young. People at my office wouldn't know anything about having a nickname like T-Baby, but Nikki might.

Julia left me in charge of showing Nikki the ropes since I would be her team leader. We don't like using the word 'supervisor' here. We are all a team, haha. Anyways, there was pretty much a lull in the day so I decided to drag it out. First stop, the canteen.

"So this is where we keep the vending machines, refrigerator and microwave if you like to bring your lunch. But there are plenty of fast food restaurants in the general vicinity." I led her out of the small room. "Have you done this type of work before?"

"A little" she said in a naturally husky voice, "I've been a real estate agent for 3 years."

"A real estate license will take you far in this business." I lead her to an empty office. "I guess this is where you'll be hanging your shingle." Nikki's mouth opened in surprise.

"I get my own office?"

"It looks more professional to the clients than sending them to a cubicle."

"Wow," she said, looking around. Since she was in a good mood I decided to make my move.

"Lunch is in about 10 minutes. If you'd like to join me over a burger, I'll fill you in on the ropes." Her eyes met mine and I gave her an innocent smile.

"Thanks. That would be great. I've been filling out paperwork all morning and haven't had time for even a cup of coffee."

I took Nikki to a popular cafe within walking distance of the office. She was wearing heels, but knew how to work them. During the walk I told her about the company, hoping that we could focus on more personal conversation during the meal. Unfortunately she enthusiastically asked question after question about her new position which kept everything professional.

"...but you know those companies that hold the closing fees are skyrocketing. How do you guys feel about completely absorbing those fees, even from the back end?"

I raised my brow. "It would cut out some commission but it could make us more competitive."

Nikki dabbed her lips with her napkin. "People are savvier, Tony. They know about all the tricks we use to inflate the fees." I liked the way she said my name so easily. I even liked the point she was making. But the executive board wasn't going to be that forward thinking. The Board was creative in finding more ways to hide fees — not trying to be up front about them.

"Nikki, this company has found a comfy little niche with customers well off enough to disregard our extra fees but not so rich as to hire a slew of tax attorneys to loophole their way through them." Nikki smiled at me like there were a million things she wanted to throw at me, but professional courtesy stopped her from it.

"We're bottom feeders, okay?" I'm not sure why I admitted that to her. "But I don't have to look into the eyes of some poor old lady dipping into here widow's pension. Our customers are the Baby Mama's of some professional ball player or the bank president's ex-wife."

"Not the bank president or the pro ball player?" She interjected.

"Generally, no." Good god, I was hoping that she was not the Baby's Mama to some ball player. And why in the hell had I admitted all of that to her? Maybe because once upon a time I had been something other than that evil corporate figure head that the rest of the world warns against.

On the short walk back to the office, I was finally able to get my wish and find out some personal info about her. "Is Cincinnati your home town?" I asked.

"Born and raised. I grew up in Lincoln Heights, graduated from Walnut Hills."

"Me; Bond Hill, I graduated from the School of Creative and Performing Arts-"

"Bond Hill?!" She asked, head swiveling, unable to hide her shock. Bond Hill is considered a "nice hood", nice houses, tree-lined streets--but still the hood; and virtually all black.

"You don't know Julian Beatty, do you?"

"Jay-Dog? Yeah we used to get-" I almost said high. "…into a lot of mischief Friday nights." Julian was one of my very best friends but we'd lost touch after I went off to college.

"That's my cousin!" She yelled happily and a few passer-bys turned to look at her curiously, but she didn't even notice.

"No!" I laughed. "What's my boy been up to?" I started sliding easily into familiar vernacular.

"Married, two kids and still D.J.'ing on the weekends."

"God, are you serious?"

"He's still the best D.J. in the city...well in my humble opinion. You know he has a regular gig playing clubs."

"No, I didn't know that. Where is he playing?"

"Club Ritz on Old School Sundays."

I laughed in genuine pleasure. "I gotta check him out." Club Ritz used to be my spot!

Nikki gave me a long look. "I can't believe you grew up in Bond Hill." She seemed to see me for the first time. "What was it like growing up in the hood with a name like Toi?"

I smirked. "I wouldn't know. No one knows that's my real name." I remembered agonizing at the beginning of each year when the teacher called out roll, hoping that the forged note I sent to school would take care of making sure my name was listed as Tony. "Honestly, when I did take my friends home they thought my mom was calling me Tony--you know, with the accent and all."

Nikki burst out laughing and we walked into the building having to stifle the sound. "I like you Tony." She said while going into her office.

I straightened my tie. Half way there.

Nikki

I've made one friend at work; Tony Yakamoto. Other than that, the people are the same cold, corporate types that worked at the real estate agency I quit. I made good money there but I needed more. More job fulfillment I guess, I don't know. But I started looking for something different and the salary was right. So here I am.

Although I've never done refinancing, this work is familiar. Anybody can do it--but it takes a person with a real estate license to legally sign or quote numbers. Tony has made the training very easy but this place is a world away from my prior job downtown in the city. Then, my customers were mostly black, as were my co-workers.

The ladies I now work with invite me to eat lunch with them but I would much rather NOT. It's not that I don't like them, but all they talk about is shit I'm not even trying to be interested in; like sorority sisters, forty dollar t-shirts at the GAP, vacations in the mountains and boyfriends named Todd and Beau. Hell, I'm not struggling financially, but there is no way that I would shell out forty dollars for a t-shirt! You see in my circle you are bragging about how much cute shit you can get for a hundred bucks.

And the last vacation I took was a shopping spree at the outlet shops in Tennessee--and believe me, we didn't stay in a chalet, but a seventy dollar a night motel off the strip where my friends and me pushed the beds together and slept in a pile. As for Todd and Beau...let's just say that all men seem to be thinking about these days is hittin' it and quittin' it.

Most times I end up having lunch with Tony. At first I thought it might come off as peculiar to others but no. Tony is just that down to earth that he is easy to hang out with. He's a young Asian dude who I at first thought was trying to act too familiar with my race. You know how people do (white people)? They think they are showing how comfortable they are with your culture by testing out their slang-knowledge. But it just comes off making them look stupid and leaving you feeling awkward. *'Hey, I told him. I'm just not down with that...'* *'Oh my god I saw this purse that was so phat! It was sick!'* Please white people...don't do that.

But Tony is not like that. He actually is black! I know it's strange because he is a short Asian but he grew up in Bond Hill and happens to be best friends with my all time favorite cousin, Julian who I call Jay.
In some ways work is like being in school and trying to make new friends. Tony is probably the only one I could really consider a friend. And that's because he never switches hats on me. He can give me direction as my supervisor then ask me if I want to take a break with him and one of the Board of Directors. That's what's so cool about him. He can hang at the top and schmooze with the tax attorneys just as comfortably as he can sit across from me at a burger joint.

And listen to this--his nickname used to be T-Baby. This I learned from Jay. You can't get blacker than that! Jay told me to watch out because Tony liked black women with big asses and big titties which I happen to have an ample amount of both. I told Jay he should be happy that we were talking over the phone and I couldn't pop him in the head. Tony is at least a foot shorter than me and I have about 50 pounds on him, so there was nothing happening there even if he wasn't my team leader.

I can say that I've warmed up to the job a lot. I especially love Fridays--not only for being the end of the work week, but because it is dress down day and I can be more myself. This Friday I decided to wear a sheer cream blouse; billowy and ethereal, then a spaghetti string tea length dress that hugged me in just the right spots. The cover-all made me appear demure and though beneath it I was rocking a skintight skirt I thoroughly pulled off the 'corporate sexy' look. I realize that I'm a bit flamboyant. But I am still tasteful.

First thing Fridays we have meetings for like two hours. People bring things to snack on. Tony doesn't drink coffee, so he always brings a good Asian tea and almond cookies. I don't even eat the donuts and danishes anymore, the cookies and tea are *that* good.

After two months I just finally had to know and so I asked. "Where do you get these?" I was on my third cookie.

"I make them."

"Are you serious?" He shrugged. "They're not hard to make."

"I bet your girlfriend loves and hates you for this." He gave me a quick look then laid out more cookies on a tray.

"It's just me and Wu-Tang."

"Wu-Tang?"

"My dog; my boxer."

I chuckled. "Wu-Tang. That's a cool name."

"Did you get some of the tea?"

"Did you make that too?" I said, half joking.

"Yes, I actually did. I blend the leaves myself."

"Jeez Tony..." I gave him an impressed stare. Then Mr. Milton called the meeting to order.

AVAILABLE ON AMAZON AND BARNES AND NOBLE

Awards
~~***~~

Pepper Pace is a popular author on Literotica.com. She is the winner of the 11th Annual Literotica Awards for 2009 for Best Reluctance story, as well as best Novels/Novella. She is also recipient of Literotica's August 2009 People's Choice Award, and was awarded second place in the January 2010 People's Choice Award. In the 12th Annual Literotica Awards for 2010, Pepper Pace won number one writer in the category of Novels/Novella as well as best Interracial story.

PEPPER PACE BOOKS
~~***~~

STRANDED!
Love Intertwined Vol. 1
Love Intertwined Vol. 2
Urban Vampire; The Turning
Urban Vampire; Creature of the Night
Wheels of Steel Book 1
Wheels of Steel Book 2
Wheels of Steel Book 3
Angel Over My Shoulder
CRASH
THEY SAY LOVE IS BLIND

~SHORT STORIES
~~***~~

Someone to Love
Blair and the Emoboy

About the Author

Pepper Pace is the pin name used by the author. Born and raised in Cincinnati, she has always enjoyed creativity. At a very young age, Pepper had a gift for art and would spend most of her spare time drawing images that she later began adding stories behind. Soon writing became more important than the illustrations and took a back seat to her real love.

Pepper wrote her first novel when she was 12 years old and had written 2 more by the age of 18. Too shy to share her work with anyone, Pepper stock piled her many stories into notebooks until she came upon Literotica.com and was compelled to share her craft.

Pepper became instantly popular and won several awards each year in which she submitted a story to the site. After receiving popular feedback, she grew in confidence and created a popular blog entitled Writing Feedback where she encourages her readers to interact with her on topics concerning, music, writing, art and pop culture. She can be reached at her blog: **pepperpacefeedback.blogspot.com/**